My Cat Burglar

Middlemarch Shifters 8

Shelley Munro

My Cat Burglar

Print ISBN: 978-1-99-106309-0
Digital ISBN: 978-0-473-35750-4

Editor: Mary Moran

Cover: Kim Killion, Killion Group, Inc.

Munro Press, New Zealand.

First Munro Press electronic publication August 2016

First Munro Press print publication December 2022

For Paul.

Introduction

Laura Adams is a cop with ambition, and a job in Middlemarch isn't what she wants for her future. Hooking up with the wrong man is responsible for the inappropriate turning, and she refuses to repeat the mistake, especially with a sexy thief.

Leopard shifter Jonno Campbell takes one look at Laura and desires her as his mate. He's enthralled with the fiery cop, and when she arrests him, he's ready for a strip search. Convincing Laura he's innocent and that they should work together to capture the thieves stealing from Middlemarch residents isn't easy. A kiss laced with his easy charm does the trick and sparks fly. Passion escalates into primitive hunger. A night of hot loving convinces Jonno.

He wants forever with the gorgeous Laura, but her ambition, his feline heritage and a gang of thieves stand in the way of his progress. Then there's the ex-boyfriend who wants Laura back. This time charisma and erotic promises mightn't be enough to win the lady.

Chapter 1

Under Arrest

"Hold it right there. You're under arrest."

The man froze in the bright stream of moonlight, his muscular bulk rigid as a marble statue. Police officer Laura Adams scanned him, alert for the slightest sign of trouble. A head taller than her with tawny hair, he appeared more than capable of causing a disruption.

She'd spied him as he'd prowled past the wooden display case in the Millers' formal lounge, each studied move laced with leashed power and grace. She was positive she hadn't seen him during her two weeks of working at the Middlemarch police station.

Him, she'd remember.

Her gaze skimmed his broad T-shirt-clad back and drifted over his tight arse, showcased in black jeans. What she wouldn't give to strip away the cloth and stroke the firm, rounded globes of his butt. She'd bet his cock—

3

Her breath hissed out in horror and her head jerked in a sharp shake of denial. What the hell? Since when did her fantasies include ripping clothes off men in the middle of a bust? A criminal, caught red-handed, dammit.

"Put your hands in the air where I can see them." Thankfully, her voice emerged on a steady note, hiding every sign of her disorientating sexual awareness. Laura grabbed the handcuffs off her belt and stalked closer, her boots a whisper on the thick carpet.

"Are you gonna cuff me?" the man drawled, his rough intonation raising a series of goose bumps across her arms and legs. Not a shred of concern tinged his voice.

How had he known she'd shifted position? She hadn't made a sound. Perplexed, she dragged in a deep breath, cursing seconds later. How had criminals obtained these sneaky secret weapons? A sexy body *and* he smelled good. Crime number two.

Laura stretched, standing on tiptoes to cuff one thick wrist. He was a tall sucker, topping her by six inches and she wasn't a shrimp. She jerked his arm behind his back and reached for the other, trying to ignore his seductive scent of something vaguely Oriental. It sure made a change from vomit-scented Friday-night drunks.

"There's a bed in the other room," he said. "Just sayin', 'cause that sounds more fun. For both of us." His smoky voice throbbed with innuendo and an underlying teasing.

Immediately her body softened in reaction, her mind agreeing horizontal would work well with this man.

"So what about it? You. Me. A flat surface."

Laura gasped, a swarm of heat engulfing her face at the man's words and her inappropriate thoughts.

Charlie, her partner, snickered behind her and the mortification intensified, her heartbeat thundering in her ears. "Have you checked the rest of the house?"

"Yeah." Charlie's mien shifted to professional. "All clear. No one else here."

"Good." Charlie was okay, or he would be once he understood there were boundaries in their partnership and they included nothing sexual. He probably resented the fact she had seniority and charge of the station.

"The bed?" her prisoner reminded her in his sexy voice.

Laura barely suppressed her shudder of awareness. Hot damn, this was ridiculous. She took care of her reputation—well, apart from one major snafu. Jumping men on the first date—no. And fantasizing about doing it with a prisoner never happened. *Never*. She preferred to get to know a man before thoughts of sex clouded issues and made a relationship complicated.

Like every woman her age, she experienced sexual needs—a normal and healthy thing. But despite swearing off sex only two months ago, she obviously needed to score on her next day off—a hookup with one of her old boyfriends back in Dunedin. That might soothe away her edginess.

"There is a bed for you in the holding cell," she snapped. "What are you doing in the Millers' house?"

"A holding cell, huh? That could be kinky. Yeah, we could make that work."

Laura ignored the husky remarks with difficulty, just as she disregarded the urge to run her hands through his thick tawny hair and over those wide shoulders displayed to perfection by the tight T-shirt.

What did he want? Why was he in the Miller house? And was he responsible for the recent jewelry thefts throughout the surrounding district of Middlemarch?

They'd caught him trespassing. It was enough to take him in for questioning. He looked the part, dressed in black to blend with the night.

Damn, she'd have to search him. Her hands tingled at the thought, images taking wing before she jammed on the brakes with a soft curse. Charlie could do the search. She scowled and shoved away the jealousy springing into her mind to concentrate on practical thoughts. If he'd stolen the jewelry, why had they captured him so easily? Laura knew she did a good job, but in her experience, thieves didn't make solving crimes this simple. It made no sense. "What's your name?"

"Jonathan Campbell." His voice lowered to intimate. "You can call me Jonno."

It wasn't the name that popped into Laura's head first. *Lover* beat Jonathan and Jonno by a wide mile. She shook herself and urged her prisoner from the room, alert for trouble. Her heart pounded faster than normal and Laura cursed again.

The application of chocolate...ah...the eating of chocolate might help soothe her peculiar mood and the plain weird sexual urges. Yeah, a good, old chocolate splurge to hold her until the weekend when she could let loose and get laid in multiple positions and places. She mentally paged through her address book, considering her past boyfriends and current male friends while she narrowed the field of fuck buddies.

Hell, listen to her.

Concentrate, Laura.

Her gaze swept the man's shoulders again, drifted over his butt, and her friends-with-benefits plan flew right out the door. Damn and blast.

"Move it." Laura gave him a shove in the middle of the back to get him moving. A charge of electricity shot from her fingertips and up her arm. She jerked away in astonishment, squeezing her hand into a fist and shaking it.

"Where are we going?" Jonno asked.

"The police station." Laura read him his rights, rattling off the requisite words while she directed him from the luxurious and formal lounge of the Miller property into the passage and toward the front door.

Damn, she hated this situation.

Jonno Campbell prowled rather than walked, restrained power emanating from him. If he attempted an escape, she suspected the cuffs wouldn't hinder his determination. To her relief, he didn't offer resistance, playing the model prisoner.

She let out a thankful sigh when the rear door of the police car slammed shut, trapping Jonno Campbell inside. Unfortunately, she could still see him, and the front view looked even better than the rear. Big, yet he moved without a hint of clumsiness. His hazel eyes twinkled—bright, wide and full of mischief whenever they lit on her. The impish quality echoed in his generous mouth while his nose appeared a trifle on the big side yet fit with the rest of his body. His face begged a second glance, and Laura bet he never had a shortage of girlfriends.

"Fuck," she whispered, knowing she'd landed in a mess of trouble. One thing was certain. Her dreams would turn X-rated tonight.

Charlie walked around to the driver's side and climbed inside the vehicle. She opened the passenger door and perched on the edge of the seat. The man watched her. She could feel his scrutiny on her back. To her consternation, her breasts prickled, arousal letting out signals in the form of tight nipples. She resisted the urge to cross her arms to conceal the evidence. *Just.*

The engine of the vehicle hummed to life, seeming to echo through her sensitized body. Only a short trip to the police station. She'd book him, finish her shift and head back to the house she shared with Charlie as part of her wage package. She'd forget Mr. Sexy. *Forget him.*

"Remember your seat belt, sweetheart," came a husky reminder from the rear. "I don't want that pretty face scraped."

"Shut up," Laura snapped.

"Has anyone told you that you curse too much?" the prisoner asked, amusement tingeing his voice this time. "Didn't anyone ever wash that sexy mouth out with soap?"

"Nah, they gave her prunes instead," Charlie quipped with a sideward glance.

"Drive," Laura snarled at Charlie.

Men. She fumed all the way back to the police station.

Jonno cooperated, walking into the police station even though he could have escaped in an instant, or told them Saber Mitchell, one of the Feline council, had arranged for him to enter the Miller house. Heck, he should have moved the instant he'd recognized the cops' presence, but her scent had shocked him, robbing every ounce of good sense. One whiff of her, and he'd become rooted to the spot. Hell, instead of evading capture he'd hesitated. The cuffs rubbed his wrists as he leaned to counteract a corner in the road, reminding him of his willing captivity. A mature feline shifter, such as himself, needed stronger restraints than the piddly handcuffs the female police officer had secured around his wrists.

He scowled, thinking back to the scene inside the house. Someone had lifted the Miller heirloom diamond necklace before he'd arrived, not that he'd bothered enlightening the police. Not yet. Besides, he was enjoying the attentions of the female officer. Her hands had developed a faint tremor when she cuffed him, letting him know she experienced the same power shimmering between them, even though she didn't understand what it meant.

A mate.

Jonno hadn't expected to find one so soon. Not that it mattered. He'd go with the flow. Excitement pulsed through him at the thought of a mate, his feline pushing him to touch and exert his claim. Instead, he looked his fill. Tall, she had brown hair with a decided red cast to it and a snappish temper to match. Her baby-blue eyes watched him in confusion, and she muttered under her breath, most of it pithy curses. Jonno decided he'd cut her some slack on the swearing, since if she felt anything like him, the wheels had fallen off normal with everything he knew turned askew. He couldn't see much of her figure since the police uniform wasn't formfitting.

An older woman.

The Mitchell twins would laugh if they heard, since he'd always gravitated to women older than himself. Even so, he'd expected a younger mate and accepted a wager with his best friends. Looked as if he'd lost the bet. Not that she appeared much older than him—five years maximum.

"What's your name?"

"Police Officer Adams," she said.

"Unless you want me to shout out 'babe' or 'sweet cheeks' when I fuck you, you'd better give me your Christian name. Police Officer Adams doesn't do it for me."

Thick, dark lashes swept down to block his clear visual of her emotions. "Someone should have washed your mouth out with soap," she snapped after a shocked pause. "I'm not interested in you."

"Oh, they did. It didn't stop me speaking my mind." Jonno took pleasure in her sharp inhalation and the increasingly loud pounding of her heart. Police Officer Sweet Cheeks Adams experienced the same attraction and fought, not understanding her struggle was wasted energy. "Hasn't anyone told you lies make your nose grow?"

Her hand rose halfway to her nose before she cursed under her breath and jammed it back against her side. "Why were you in the Miller house? What were you after? Jewels? Their heirloom diamond?"

"I don't know what you mean." He did, of course. He'd missed the thieves by minutes. Although he didn't recognize their scents, if he met them again, they'd never escape a second time. At least two of the thieves were shifters, which narrowed the field. Shifters joining a group of human thieves didn't make sense since any shifter must realize Saber and the council would react swiftly to stamp out a crime wave.

His mate pushed his arm to make him step farther down a passage toward the holding cell. Jonno sucked in a hasty breath, the electric surge of arousal ripping through his body at her touch. Damn, he'd heard details of feline courtships from the twins after their brother Saber hooked up with Emily. He'd

11

heard them say how powerful this mating shit was but hadn't believed a word.

He came from spotted leopard stock rather than black like the Middlemarch shifters, and since his feline line lived in pairs instead of groups, his knowledge of mating remained scanty. It didn't help that his father was an asshat and had kicked him out of their home in Australia once he'd turned sixteen. Big for his age, he'd worked several jobs and continued with his education before he'd drifted across the Tasman, met the Mitchell twins at a party and found a home of sorts.

"Are you responsible for the jewelry thefts in the area?"

"I'm not a thief." A persistent woman. Jonno couldn't wait to get her naked and push his cock into her moist pussy. One glance at her bright blue eyes told him she sensed the rightness. Despite pretending to ignore the attraction, the bloom of arousal in her face gave her away.

"In here." She indicated the holding cell with a jerk of her head.

He stepped inside, and she unlocked the handcuffs, standing back with caution. She backed from the cell and the door clanked shut behind him. He heard her small sigh of relief and grinned. He made her nervous. Good, because this thing between them scared the crap out of him. It couldn't have come at a worse time.

They had a thief, or a team of thieves in Middlemarch as he'd discovered tonight, and Saber and the Feline council had asked him to skulk around the place to help capture them. They'd wanted someone unknown, just in case the culprit or culprits were local. He came to the job with no biases. The thieves had bloody good taste because they stole jewels, the biggest hit being the Miller diamond necklace tonight. From what Jonno knew of old man Miller, he guessed there'd be hell to pay. Luckily, Saber had talked the man into replacing the necklace with a fake and giving them permission to enter the house in the hope of capturing the thieves. He wondered how long it'd take the thieves to discover they'd stolen worthless booty.

"Do I get a phone call?" Best let Saber know what was happening. Besides, he'd hate to spend any longer than necessary playing prisoner. The thieves remained on the loose, and the narrow bed looked as comfortable as a blanket harboring fleas. Not what this kitty had in mind. "I want to arrange my getaway." One eye closed in a wink, and he took pleasure in her gasp of outrage.

"We caught you trespassing," she snapped. "What were you doing there? What did you take?" Her gaze slid down his body toward his crotch.

Jonno laughed, not even trying to control his unruly body. The steal of color across her cheeks charmed him. A blusher. He wondered how big an area the flush covered. "I'm not hiding any jewels there, aside from the obvious, although you're welcome to investigate." A sly grin slid across his lips. He hadn't had so much fun with a woman in ages.

"You're trying to embarrass me."

"Is it working?"

"Yes," she hissed. "Are you satisfied? You're making me behave in an unprofessional manner."

"I'm not making you do anything, sweet cheeks."

"Don't call me that."

"Then tell me your name and I'll call you by that. Go on, sweet cheeks. You know you want to."

"Laura," she snapped, goaded by his teasing. Her chest rose and fell in heaves, a glimpse making his cock jerk against the fly of his jeans. He attempted to ignore the rush of pleasure surging through his veins, the subtle purr of his feline as it pushed against his control. Jonno wondered how this starchy human would deal with his feline nature before deciding it didn't matter. Together they'd work through any problems they encountered.

Laura was the one.

His.

"Laura," he said, rolling her name around his lips like a ripe and juicy peach. "It's such a pleasure to meet you."

"Knock it off. I'm a cop and you're a prisoner."

Jonno nodded, his brow creased in thought. "Sure. We can do role-plays. I'd have thought you'd want to try something more adventurous. How about a slave and owner? I'll be the slave if you want. I'm an equal-opportunity kind of guy." His mouth curled into a smirk and it widened at her indignant sniff. He focused on his words, creating mind pictures of them naked. Together. He'd strip naked for her any time. "My phone call?"

"Who do you want to call?"

Jonno wanted to chuckle. He wanted to do a lot of things to the starchy cop with flashes of passion slumbering deep within her baby-blue eyes. "Saber Mitchell. I'm sure the number is easy to find."

Laura whirled around and stomped away from the door of the holding cell. Jonno watched her until she disappeared from sight. With his exceptional hearing, he heard her terse curse, the slam of a phone book on a desk and the stabbing of the buttons on the keypad of the phone. Jonno heard the murmur of Laura's voice and her approaching footsteps. She passed a portable phone to him before stomping away. Again, Jonno watched the sway of her ass until he could no longer see her.

"Hi, Saber," Jonno said. "I'm in jail. Can you get me out?"

"It's Emily. Saber isn't here. Why are you in jail?" Interest rather than distress colored her voice. "And what's more, why should I get you out?"

"Emily," Jonno said, genuinely shocked. "I can't stay in jail. I'll go insane. Damn, I'll ring the twins. Joe and Sly will help me."

"No, silly." Emily's laugh stilled his sudden panic. "I'll get you out. Of course I might ring Joe and Sly myself so they can give you a hard time. Why are you in jail?"

"The cops are saying I'm the Middlemarch jewel thief."

"A cat burglar," Emily said in clear delight. "And are you?"

"No, I'm not."

"Ah, so this relates to the secret squirrel stuff you were discussing with Saber two nights ago."

"No wonder Saber mated with you. Smart and beautiful." According to his friends, Joe and Sly, Saber had wanted to marry his younger brothers off and had instead stepped into his own trap. He'd taken one look at Emily, or the *scarlet woman* as they'd dubbed her, and wanted her as his mate.

"Be there in ten minutes," Emily said. "I have to meet the new police constable. I'll invite her to dinner the next time the twins come home."

"No way! You keep those chick magnets away from Laura. She's mine," Jonno growled, hanging up to Emily's laughter. "Laura, I've finished my phone call." He raised his voice and waited for her to come running. While talking with Emily he'd come up with a plan to involve Laura. And it had better work because he needed to touch her. Badly. "Laura, are you there?"

"What do you want?"

"Someone ransacked the Miller house before me. I didn't take the diamond necklace."

Her blue eyes narrowed. "Prove it. How do you know it was a diamond necklace? I don't even know what's missing."

Jonno whipped his T-shirt over his head and took great pleasure in the way her mouth dropped open for an instant before pressing to a firm line of disapproval. Very expressive face. He couldn't wait to see the emotions rushing across her features during their lovemaking. After unlacing and toeing off his black boots and socks, he peeled his jeans down his legs. Her mouth widened to a round O. A gasp escaped, punctuated by a hoarse croak. Not a recognizable sound, so he continued, stepping out of his jeans and taking pleasure from her bemused gaze strumming across his naked body. His cock hardened and lengthened as he posed.

"See, I'm not hiding anything that shouldn't be there."

"Put your clothes back on," Laura said at a screech. "Commando. I should have guessed," she added in a fierce mutter.

"Sometimes. Don't you want to do a hands-on search?" *God, please say yes.* He couldn't wait to have her hands running over his body.

"No."

"You don't sound certain." Despite the urge to continue and push her with his teasing, Jonno reached for his jeans and donned them again. He'd heard a vehicle pull up outside, and Saber would have something to say if Emily saw him naked. He preferred his face in its present arrangement.

"Tell me why you were at the Miller house," Laura said, her attention drifting across his bare chest before darting to her clasped fingers.

"Saber Mitchell and the local council asked me to investigate the robberies. I figured the Miller house might be on the list since everyone around here has heard of the heirloom necklace with the diamond so big they call it the Miller diamond." Jonno stopped teasing and returned to business. He couldn't investigate here. Maybe he could do a deal with Laura, if she'd deviate from silly rules. And it'd give him an opportunity to pursue his mate.

17

Professional interest sparked in her eyes, and the move into cop-mode fascinated him. The way she fired orders and questions at him was plain hot. "Have you found anything? Did you see anything? You should have come to us. We can't have locals taking the law into their own hands."

Emily appeared at the end of the corridor and walked toward them. "Ah, there you are. Jonno is always misbehaving. Jail is a good place for him." She stuck out her hand. "I'm Emily Mitchell. Jonno is okay. I can vouch for him. He arrived in Middlemarch three days ago. He wasn't here at the time of the first thefts."

Good point. Laura shook Emily Mitchell's hand and considered the facts. She lived by her instincts, and her gut shouted she'd be a fool to keep this man locked up. If he was the thief, he had a cool and calm attitude. Her libido agreed. Besides, while some criminals were plain stupid, this man seemed too intelligent for an easy capture.

She sucked in a mind-cleansing breath. "Will you share information?"

"If we can talk somewhere private," Jonno said.

"Done." Laura unlocked the cell and stood back. "I'm Laura Adams, one of the new police officers," she said to Emily. "If I end up murdered in my bed, make sure you set the cops on him."

"As long as there are beds involved," Jonno said.

Emily speared a considering glance at Jonno before she turned to wink at Laura. "Somehow, I don't think that will be a problem."

Jonno tugged his T-shirt over his head and donned his footwear. "Thanks for coming, Emily. I'll ring Saber tomorrow."

"Come for dinner," Emily said. "Laura, why don't you come too? There aren't enough women in Middlemarch. We have to stick together."

"Thanks, I'd like that," Laura said, trying not to drool. She regretted the covering of the splendid real estate. Jealous of a T-shirt. Go figure.

"Good. Come around seven and we'll have drinks first. Jonno knows where we live." With a wave and an altogether too personal smile at Jonno, the woman disappeared, leaving them alone.

Jonno touched her arm, and she barely restrained her gasp of shock at the electrical current racing from his fingertips. Heck, she should have expected it by now. "My vehicle is parked at the back of the café. Storm in a Teacup. Do you know it?"

"Ah, that's where I've seen Emily." Laura clicked her fingers as the pieces slotted together. Storm in a Teacup sold excellent muffins and chocolate brownies. "Can I trust you?" She had no idea how she kept her voice even because her insides trembled with violence. What on earth was wrong with her? A strange urge to lick him pounded her resolve to keep their interaction to business. The curve of his cheek and the strong cords of his neck tempted her. A nibble of his earlobe...

"You've let the leopard out of the cage," he murmured with a wicked grin. "Isn't it a bit late to ask about trust?"

Leopard? Come to think of it, he brought to mind a big cat in the way he moved—prowled—around. "I'm off work in twenty minutes, unless something big comes up. I need to have a few words with Charlie. I'll meet you at the café."

Jonno nodded and stalked down the corridor. Laura blinked at his disappearance. None of her actions rated as professional, but her impulsive streak had her charging full ahead anyway. And the way she felt, she suspected the impulse to jump the sexy male might get the better of her. The thought made her pause for an instant, shake her head.

Crazy! Absolutely crazy, and in truth, she didn't even care about the consequences. The top brass had already harpooned her career, sending her to a country station, so she hardly thought it would matter, as long as she did her job. Yes, her fixation on the man was unwise. Too bad when her mind kept diverting to getting her hands on Jonno Campbell's delectable body...

Chapter 2

My Fated Mate

Jonno straightened, pushing away from the front of his parked vehicle as Laura hurried along the side of Storm in a Teacup café. His heart beat a little faster as he strode into the light cast by a streetlamp to intercept her, and he knew they weren't gonna do much in the way of talking for the next half an hour. Maybe he could persuade her to spend the night with him. He sure as hell hoped so. A low rumble sounded, and he took a second to realize the sound came from him. No dammit. He had to take things slow so he didn't scare her. Patience, he counseled himself. *Patience*.

Laura neared him and slowed to a halt, her shoulders stiff, as if she'd had second and third thoughts about meeting with him. A quick glance over her shoulder confirmed her nerves. Understanding throbbed through him. He appreciated the compulsion—the instinct propelling her to touch and become intimate.

A hoarse chuckle emerged, the humor aimed at himself. Damn, he knew how it felt. He understood the mating urge manifested more strongly in a feline male, yet humans weren't exempt from the sexual heat. Oh yeah. He respected the confusion and conflict she faced.

Instinctively, he sought to soothe and reassure. "Laura, I'd never hurt you. I'm not like that. I don't get kicks from terrorizing people smaller than me, people who can't fight back." Keeping his movements slow and his hands in sight, he eased closer.

"I'm not frightened of you."

"Then why are you so edgy?" He bit back his delight at the nervous way she chewed on her bottom lip and yet lifted her chin in defiance, her belligerent denial.

"Something's wrong with me. I have sex on the brain." She murmured the words under her breath, so soft she didn't mean him to hear. "I don't know why I'm here," she said in a normal-speaking voice.

"We will find the thieves." Jonno wanted to tell her about the mates thing upfront, despite her jumpy state. A feline always needed to weigh the consequences when it came to confessions of their existence. Trust came into the equation, big time. Humans didn't always understand, and learning of different species stirred fear and panic. The knowledge they weren't alone made them uneasy. A glance at Laura reassured him. She seemed so feisty and self-assured. He didn't think she'd let the existence of feline shapeshifters throw her for long. But first...first he had to kiss her, taste her.

Despite their lack of privacy, Jonno pounced, not giving her a chance to retreat. Probably faces pressed to the café window. The thought of gossip and teasing didn't stop him. He grasped her shoulders, holding her in place. Her quick intake of breath whooshed out, feathering across his neck. Her vanilla scent wound through his senses, stealing his free will.

His.

The thought crystallized yet again, and he knew he'd been fooling himself to think he could maintain a leisurely pace. Wasn't gonna happen.

Laura sighed, a mere whisper of sound, her attention on his lips even though a tremble racked her frame. Then their mouths met.

Heaven.

All thoughts floated from Jonno's head and he sank into a world of sensation, of pleasure and spicy woman. The velvet-soft contact brought a gasp. Jonno wasn't sure if it was his or hers.

More. God, he craved much more of this, of her. Slowly, he explored her mouth, learning the shape and texture before he traced across her bottom lip with his tongue. She opened to him with a quiet murmur of approval, the feminine encouragement pleasing his feline. A tremble spread the length of his body, and that was when he realized he'd landed in big trouble.

His feline purred, pushing at his control. For one horrid moment, Jonno thought he'd shifted without even picturing the cat in his head first. The subtle push of his claws as they forced under his fingernails and the surge of his canines brought alarm. He hoped his eyes hadn't taken on the eerie glow peculiar to cats slinking through the dark of night. Panic nipped at him as forcefully as his feline shoved at his restraint. Gulping, he ripped his mouth away from Laura's and hugged her tight, chest heaving while he fought the onset of his shift.

Fuck, this wasn't the time for patience and niceties. He needed her now. He prayed he could hold his feline and not let the instinct to mark her as his mate take precedence.

"Laura, I know this is weird. We don't know each other, but if I don't get you in my bed tonight, I will go crazy. Feel how much I need you." Damn, his speech sounded weird because of teeth forcing through his gums. After concentrating hard, he realigned them. A glance at his fingernails confirmed the worst. He'd need to battle his feline until things settled, and the first time with Laura would need to take place in the dark, if he didn't want to scare her. Or he could tell her the truth straight up and right from the start. Something to ponder.

"Touch me, Laura." Taking her hand, he slid it down his arm and across his hip until she touched his erection. To his relief and consternation, her fingers measured and cupped him, abrading the sensitive head against the sturdy material of his jeans. His hands fell away, and he took half a step back to give her better access. To his relief she never hesitated, teasing and coaxing until he throbbed beneath her touch. Her nimble fingers unfastened the button on his fly before he could stay her move.

"No," he said, gritting his teeth at her warm hand brushing the head of his cock. So damn good. He inhaled, aiming for better discipline of his feline, of his unruly desire to fuck her. With a determined step back, he removed her hand and refastened his jeans. Lucky for them, not a single vehicle had passed while they were groping each other. "I don't want our first time to be outside where anyone could see us. Will you come with me to my place? I'm working on a local farm and living in a house on the property. I'm the sole occupant, so no interruptions."

Laura hesitated. "I—"

"Ring your colleague and tell him where you're going, or ring Emily Mitchell or both if you prefer."

"Charlie will ask questions."

"Tell him you have a lead on the case. My house is on Seagrove Road. The farm is owned by Gareth Hunter."

"I— Okay." Laura pulled out her cell phone and rang the station, speaking briefly to Charlie.

Jonno heard both sides of the conversation. Her colleague didn't sound alarmed or even suspicious, which was good since Laura relaxed.

"I'll see you tomorrow," she said before disconnecting the call. "Thank you for understanding. A lot of guys would've made fun of my fears."

"Then you know the wrong men." Jonno worked hard not to imagine Laura with another male. Jealousy made little sense since he'd slept with other women. Hell, plenty of them. "The last thing I want you to do is worry about your safety. I'd prefer you concentrating on pleasure. Mutual pleasure." Jonno hoped she wouldn't change her mind. "Is it okay if we take my vehicle? I'll run you back in the morning and buy you breakfast."

"Crazy," she muttered before nodding in the affirmative. "I don't know what you've done, but I ache so bad I'm ready to jump you."

"Hold that thought." Jonno grasped her lower arm and led her to his vehicle. He seated her in the passenger seat, taking pleasure in the small service for his woman. Humming under his breath, he hurried around to the driver's side and climbed inside. A quick inhalation filled his lungs with her vanilla scent and anticipation heightened. He glanced across at her and found her watching him. With contentment bubbling inside, he started the engine. He couldn't wait to see if his imagination and reality matched. Yeah, naked worked best for what he had in mind.

The ten-minute trip to his quarters flew past. Neither of them talked much, instead listening to the latest OpShop album. The lyrics of the New Zealand band's hit song ramped up the tension throbbing between them. Jonno pulled up outside his house with a screech of brakes. He switched off the engine, the sudden silence a throb through his veins.

"Coming?" he asked, glancing across to Laura. She appeared as stunned and unsure as he. Not that he'd change anything about this meeting. Somehow, they'd muddle through. He grinned at the thought of being able to discuss their first meeting in fifty years. His amusement died because that wouldn't happen if he fucked this up. And with the way his nerves jangled, it was a distinct possibility.

"Yes, I'm ready." Laura climbed out of the car and he hurried to follow suit.

"Go inside. The door's open. I'm just going to take off my boots." Jonno stooped to unlace his boots and lectured himself. No touching until they reached the bedroom. Thank goodness he'd changed the sheets the day before and remembered to make his bed. His mother had told him women liked men who helped around the house. They found it sexy, she'd said. During his teens, he'd spoken out with skepticism. Showed what he knew. Now he sent a silent thanks to his mother since he needed every edge he could get. Something told him that even though Laura was here, winning her wouldn't be as easy.

"I have no idea what I'm doing here," Laura muttered, also removing her shoes. The beginnings of panic showed in the faint anxiety coloring her voice.

"Want a drink? I have beer, juice, tea and instant coffee." The normal everyday motions might quieten her unease. Jonno kept his breathing slow and even. Nope, not a help. Her vanilla scent still enveloped him, making his feline strain at the leash. He wanted to take the flesh at the juncture of neck and shoulder with his teeth. He'd rasp his tongue back and forth over the area until her flavor seeped into his senses. Then he'd sink his teeth into her flesh until her blood filled his mouth and the enzymes from his saliva mixed with her life force. Jonno's satisfaction increased as thoughts of the resulting mark flooded his mind.

His mark. He'd bet it'd look good on her upper shoulder.

"A beer sounds good," she said, shattering his thoughts of happy ever after. "Can you answer a few questions for me?"

"To you, I'm an open-source document, sweet cheeks."

A spasm of irritation marched across her face. "I thought we had a deal. I told you my name so you didn't call me that."

"What?" Jonno aimed for innocence and suspected he failed. "Sweet cheeks."

No mistaking her tone for anything except disgruntled and pissed. Jonno restrained his natural humor, so pleased with his prospective mate he wanted to cheer. "Laura, I'd be happy to answer your questions. Anything," he added, stressing the word and ratcheting up the tension in the room.

Damn, she was fun to tease. He wondered if she'd be fun in bed and decided yes, because despite the tightening of her sensual mouth, her blue eyes shone with heat and a hint of yearning.

"This way. We'll grab a beer and sit outside." Bed needed to wait while he reassured his woman. He could do this—wait for longer—since they'd have years together. Now was the time to exercise patience.

Jonno strode down the passage to the kitchen without waiting to see if she'd follow. If she turned and walked out of the house, leaving him alone...well, he didn't want to know right now because he balanced on a slender thread of control, just restraining his urge to pounce and drag her off to his bed. Knowing and admitting he had to finesse her first wasn't appeasing his feline. *Randy bastard.*

In the kitchen, he switched on the light and made his way over to the far side, near the scarred countertop. He opened the old fridge and pulled out two cans of beer, relieved at hearing her hesitant footsteps. Good. He'd hoped she'd overcome her natural instincts to run. Somehow, he didn't think his mate was a quitter. "Do you want a glass?"

"No, the can is fine."

Jonno handed her one and opened a door to step outside. The house was an old one and nothing flash, after accommodating numerous bachelors. A previous occupant had built a patio area outside the kitchen. Overlooking the valley, during the day he could see clear to the river. Jonno liked to sit outside and listen to the sounds and soak in the countryside. He enjoyed the solitude and open spaces after sharing a house with the Mitchell twins and two other students in Dunedin.

"Take a seat." Light from the kitchen spilled outside, enough to let Laura see with ease. He decided a little chitchat might relax her and again thanked his mother for the way she'd taught him social skills. The right way to treat a lady. It still beat him why she'd marry a man like his father, someone so dominant and set in his ways. He'd clashed with his father at his first shift—age thirteen—and things hadn't improved with the passing years. They didn't play well together.

Jonno snorted. An understatement. They didn't agree on anything, which was why he'd left home, that and the fact his father had wanted him gone, insisting on his departure.

He smiled at her. "Where did you live before you moved to Middlemarch?"

"Dunedin." Laura sank onto the wooden patio chair with a soft sigh.

"How long were you there?"

"Almost two years."

"What made you come to Middlemarch?"

Laura took a sip of her beer before answering. "I don't want to talk."

"Ah, a mystery." Curiosity surfaced, lingered while he observed the fleeting emotions on her face.

"There's nothing mysterious involved. Why don't you tell me what you were doing inside the Miller house? Reassure me letting you go was a good idea and that I won't find the Miller diamond or any of the other missing jewels in your possession."

"You know I don't have the diamond. It might be hard for you to believe, but I swear it's the truth."

Laura's glance speared to him. Her cop face. Tight mouth. Piercing eyes that saw everything. Her chin lifted a fraction and set in a stubborn line. "If you tell me you're the thief and possess a cat burglar calling, I'm gonna sock you in the jaw."

Jonno had to bite his lip to keep from laughing aloud. She had the cat thing right. "Why do you say cat burglar?"

"Because I do not understand how the thief obtained access to the properties. He or she needs to have a good head for heights, that's for sure."

"I'm not a thief. I told you Saber Mitchell and the local council asked me to investigate and learn what I could of the thefts. They're concerned it might stop people attending the functions they've organized to draw tourists to the town."

"And I told you they can't take the law into their own hands," Laura snapped. "I should arrest the lot of you."

"A hint, sweet cheeks. It might make you a trifle unpopular if you arrest the community leaders. Some of them are grandfathers."

"My name is Laura," she gritted out. "Don't worry. I know politics and rules and how they're bent to suit the individual, especially if said individual has connections in the right places." Bitterness tinged her words and stirred Jonno's curiosity. There was a story here, and he'd wager it related to her employment in Dunedin. She gave the impression of a woman with ambition. A job in small town Middlemarch screamed of a sidestep rather than promotion.

"This is a country town. Everyone knows each other—the usual residents at any rate. With the balls and other functions the town is organizing plus the tourists from the Tairei Gorge train, there are more strangers around the place. Saber and the rest of the council are concerned locals are involved because the thieves seem to know when the homeowners will be away and have inside knowledge of what to steal."

"Did they think to report it to us? Stopping thieves is in our job description."

"No offense, Laura. You're new. Charlie hasn't been here much longer than you and you're both unknown quantities. The crimes were reported to you."

"What about tonight? Did you see anything?"

"The thieves had left by the time I arrived. I don't understand why the Millers didn't have an alarm," he added. "Their safe comprised of a locked cupboard. No trouble for the thieves to break the lock." He made a mental note to mention this to Henry Anderson and Gerard Drummond who ran a local security business. They were both away, working on a big month-long job in Dunedin, but they'd probably appreciate more business.

"Thieves? There's more than one?" Laura considered him carefully and decided he held something back. "There's something else."

"You're good." Admiration filled Jonno. His mate didn't miss a trick.

"Changing the subject won't help. Spit it out."

"Yeah, more than one. A gang perhaps. Although I didn't see them, I caught their scents." He expected skepticism and received it.

"Come on! What are you? A sniffing dog?" Laughter curled across her lips, lighting her face and enticing him to share the joke at his expense.

When Jonno didn't so much as crack a grin, her humor faded to confounded.

"You're serious."

"Yes." His feline made a protesting sound, irritated by the laughter. Jonno had known she'd doubt him. He set his beer on the ground near his chair and stood. "Sit there and don't move. I want to show you something." This might rate as a stupid move. Too bad. Laura was his mate. Instinct told him he could trust her. Besides, if she tried to tell people around Middlemarch, they'd laugh at her. As a newly arrived cop, spreading tales of cats might come close to professional suicide. No, he'd calculated the odds and figured showing his feline wouldn't cause any problems, not unless she hated cats.

With deft movements, he slid off his socks and straightened to lift his T-shirt over his head.

"Wait a minute," Laura said. "What's with you and the stripping?"

"I like to show off my body to you," he said, knowing it was nothing less than the truth. "But this time I want to show you something else."

"Okay, I'll just sit back and enjoy the show. So far I see nothing objectionable. A warning though—I will report violations to the relevant authorities." Glints of humor twinkled in her expression, and he found himself charmed over again by this sassy woman. She sipped her beer before setting it aside in clear expectation.

Jonno shivered as her fascinated gaze ran over his upper body. His feline pushed at him hard, eager for both mating and release. He wanted truth between them. He wanted Laura to know what she faced by sleeping with him. Yes, he'd be putting himself at risk. He wanted to embrace that risk and go with his gut instinct. Laura was a cop, not easily frightened. Already she'd shown her fighting spirit and willingness to listen, even if it went against her professional training. Jonno unzipped his jeans and shoved them down his hips.

Laura clapped her hands with enthusiasm. Her lips pursed in a sharp whistle of appreciation. "Don't I get any fancy moves?"

"All in good time." Jonno kicked his jeans out of the way and couldn't stop from striking a pose for her viewing pleasure. He flexed muscles and got a real buzz out of the entire situation, even knowing things could head south fast.

"Very nice," Laura approved. "Can I touch?"

"Soon." Taking a deep breath to settle the onset of nerves, Jonno pictured a spotted leopard in his mind. Discomfort flashed through him as his body fought the first stages of the change. This gave way to complete upheaval as fur rippled across his skin and bones reshaped. Vaguely aware of Laura's sharp gasp of horror, he fell to all fours, his jaw reshaping and sharp canine teeth flashing into prominence. He watched her reaction. Shock—yes. At least she hadn't run. Feeling as possessive as he did, he wasn't sure he'd let her leave. Perhaps this hadn't been a good idea.

The magical glow of the change faded, and Jonno turned to face her squarely, unable to prevent the lash of his tail through the air. He knew he appeared scary because of his sheer size. But hell, he was a pretty feline with a glossy coat and cute spots. It wasn't all bad news. Jonno padded toward Laura, taking it easy and giving her time to process.

"Jonno?" His name sounded scarcely louder than a whoosh of air from her lips.

Moving closer still, he rubbed his head against her knee and let out a soft purr as the gingerly stroke of her hand ran along his back, ruffling his fur. Elation fueled the next purr since her touch held more confidence. Everything would work out. Now that he'd exposed his true self there were no other alternatives.

Chapter 3

Show and Tell

"Are you the cat burglar?" The words burst from Laura before good sense quashed them. The hairs at the back of her neck stirred while her heartbeat took flight.

A leopard.

He was a bloody big leopard, and while the great lug purred now, nothing guaranteed he'd continue in the same vein.

Her gaze dropped to his claws—lethal weapons capable of great harm. Sharp white teeth gleamed, and her breath caught in her throat. *Holy crap.*

Jonno—the cat—drew back a fraction with an indignant snarl. Damn, he'd turned into a cat right in front of her eyes. Surreptitiously, she wiped them and blinked to refocus. A big leopard still rubbed against her, regarding her in a regal manner. Every single bit of her education and upbringing told her shapeshifters didn't exist, yet she'd seen him change from man to beast. And she hadn't been drinking—well, not much.

She forced herself to breathe slower, her nerves to settle. He hadn't hurt her. *Yet.*

"If you're not the cat burglar, then who is?" Somehow concentrating on the thefts helped her stay calm. Her instinct to run passed, replaced by curiosity and fascination along with a healthy slice of unease. "Can I stroke you again?"

Jonno let out a purr, sounding full of pleasure. She stood, almost losing her knees. Maybe she wasn't as cool as she'd thought. It wasn't every day a woman discovered her beliefs regarding fact and fiction needed amendment.

He rubbed his head against her thigh, and Laura crouched beside him to run her hands over his back, treating him much as she did the family cat. She scratched behind his ears and petted him, glorying in the plush fur beneath her hands while keeping an eye on his teeth and claws. He purred before pushing her aside and backing away.

Laura let out a started cry as she found herself sitting on her butt. A glow surrounded the cat, and she watched in fascination as he shifted again, seconds later, appearing as a naked man in front of her. A very aroused naked man.

With two long strides he reached her side and scooped her off the ground.

"Are you okay? Did I hurt you?"

"I'm fine," Laura said, dazed, her nerves still doing a number on her knees. A girl didn't find herself fully clothed in the arms of a naked man often either.

He strode into the house and headed away from the kitchen without bothering to turn on lights. Seconds later they entered a room, and she found herself in the middle of a large bed. With rapid moves he unfastened the uniform shirt and divested her of it. Her bra followed, his competent fingers brushing the straps down her arms and releasing her swollen breasts. He groaned. The masculine sound of appreciation worked magic on her body, her nipples drawing to taut crests.

Laura did nothing to protest or to help. She couldn't do a thing, mesmerized by his eyes. They glowed, and while she couldn't see much in the dark room, she could imagine all too well. A leopard. The reality kept rearing up to tease her mind. This wasn't such a good idea, having sex...

"Could we have light?" she asked, picturing many things, including being split open by a forked cock. Yeah, she'd seen him earlier. She'd tried not to look then. This time she'd scrutinize him in case of barbs or anything else alien and alarming.

Seconds later a bedside lamp softened the darkness, allowing her to see him. Her stomach turned in a slow somersault when she focused on his erection. It seemed huge.

He glanced up on hearing her gasp, and she knew he'd notice her wide-eyed and apprehensive expression, although he didn't stop removing her clothes. Excitement laced with trepidation raced the length of her body, sensitizing nerves and bringing a tremble.

"What are we going to do?" *Stupid question, Laura.* One glance at his swollen cock provided the answers she needed.

"We're going to have fun. Mutual pleasure." He unbuckled her belt and worked the buttons and zipper free, a slight smile of anticipation on his lips. She wondered again if she should protest. Her breath eased out in a soft pant. Yeah, like that would happen. She didn't want to halt him. Sleeping with a man who transformed to a cat should've scared her silly. Something in Jonno encouraged trust, in his human form at any rate. It was clear Emily Mitchell knew him, liked and trusted him.

"Is Emily the same as you?" Emily ran the local café. She cooked. The locals liked her so she didn't present a danger.

"No," he said without hesitation, urging her to lift her hips so he could remove her trousers. He tossed them aside before returning to her side.

"Oh." There went that theory. "Are there others like you?" *Someone I might know already so I have a rational reason to continue down this track without freaking...*

"Yes. Do I frighten you?" Warm hands slid her socks off her feet, leaving her dressed in skimpy black panties.

"No...a little bit." At this point honest reactions were good.

Jonno nodded, serious for once. "I prefer honesty, which is why I demonstrated my special skills. I don't like starting off a relationship with lies." He stroked his hand across her bare breast, coming close to her nipple but stopping short of touching it. She quivered, the need in her building to urgency and unlike anything she'd encountered before.

"We don't have a relationship." The truth, besides she didn't know about this cat thing. It might work in the movies or in a book, but real life? Not so much.

"We will. You've wanted to fuck me ever since we first saw each other."

Heat suffused her cheeks. Had she been so transparent? And worse, had Charlie noticed? He knew of her disgrace in Dunedin and the reason for her placement in Middlemarch, although he didn't seem one to gossip. Laura shifted a fraction on the bed and registered the burning arousal in her body continued to grow rather than dissipating.

Large hands, capable of harm, stroked her hair. "It's no need for embarrassment. I craved your touch from the minute I saw you. There's a reason for that."

"There is?" She suppressed a shudder at the stroke of his finger across her cheek. *Yeah, she was stark, raving mad. Got it in one.*

"Felines mate for life. You are my mate."

Whoa! No way. She didn't believe in love-at-first-sight shit. "It sounds like a corny romance. I don't believe you. You've done something, performed weird magic."

"Not magic. It's more hormones. The desire between us, the electricity whenever we touch. I dare you to lie and say you feel nothing." His expression held frustration along with heat and a longing so palpable she wanted to rub against him, to placate him and stir the hunger to greater depths. Like a...like a cat in heat.

A flush moved across her face, and she couldn't hold his intense gaze. She had to glance away, each breath coming in a harsh pant.

"It's not magic or compulsion?"

Jonno nuzzled her neck, his warm breath making her squirm. "No magic," he repeated. "It's hormones and the yearning to mate."

"Not like any hormones I've encountered before." She twisted away from him to study his face, battling both fear of the unknown and her own desires. Something told her if she gave in to the compulsion to touch all would be lost. "I don't understand. Why did you show me? What if I go around telling everyone you're a cat?"

Jonno smirked. "I doubt they'd believe you. Besides, I don't want secrets between us. I believe in candor right from the start. Lies are no way to start a relationship."

Laura scowled. He kept mentioning relationships. The man had rocks in his head if he thought this was about anything other than scratching an itch. "I don't do relationships." No way, no how. Not after the travesty with Mike.

"Okay. We can stick to sex and friendship at the moment." And with that he pounced, caging her with hands placed either side of her shoulders. His eyes, full of laughter, glowed, and now that she knew he could shift forms, she could see the feline in him—the power and grace whenever he moved.

Uneasy still, her focus shifted to his mouth. His sensual lips curled as they drew nearer to hers. Just sex, she told herself. She

41

sucked in a breath, her heart thudding faster. Then their lips touched, a subtle brushing. A shiver shot through Laura, a sense of excitement that scared her. It had never been this way, so hot and intense, not even during the initial days of her fling with Mike. Warmth suffused her body as Jonno pressed her farther into the mattress.

"I enjoy kissing you," he whispered against her lips.

The brush of their naked chests shot a jolt of electricity clear to her toes. A fine sheen of sweat bloomed on her skin when he took the kiss deeper. His tongue pushed into her mouth at the corner, igniting nerve endings and making her think of the sexual act. She shivered, and with a sigh wrapped her arms around him, giving in to the urges clamoring inside, his solid weight welcome and desirable. Magic, she thought. Definitely magic.

Jonno continued to kiss her, rubbing their lips together and using the perfect amount of pressure. Warm, wet suction drew her bottom lip into his mouth, yet he never overwhelmed her with too much tongue or too much moisture. Perfect. She wrapped her arms around his neck and clung, turning her head to the side to let him nuzzle her neck. For a moment she considered his dual nature before letting her trepidation disperse. He held her with care, not using brute force but offering pleasure, each move slow, as if he didn't want to frighten her.

"I love your scent. Sexy. Very enticing." He trailed a line of kisses across her jaw before nibbling at her earlobe. Sensation spiraled down, and when she shifted her body weight, a trickle of moisture seeped from her pussy, dampening her panties. He kissed her neck, pausing to lick as he reached the fleshy part where neck and shoulder met. His tongue lapped back and forth across the same spot.

"Jonno," she whispered, a moan falling from her lips as he used a hint of teeth.

Her thighs clamped together briefly before she melted into him, pliant and open to his desires, her disquiet gone, shoved aside by the growing heat and madness suffusing her body. If he kept this up, kindling her pleasure, he could do anything he wanted.

"Please. Please." Laura pushed her neck against his mouth, unsure of what she wanted, only knowing he could satisfy the yearnings, the need roaring through her body.

His tongue rasped across the spot again, the surface rough and abrasive, calling up shivers of extreme pleasure. Silently, she pushed into him, encouraging him to repeat the move. He did—a lash of moist tongue and the faint scrape of teeth.

"That feels so good," she murmured, her voice thick with pleasure.

Jonno jerked away, his gleaming chest rising and falling as if he'd run a race. "Damn, I didn't realize it'd be so hard to stop. I'm having trouble holding my feline at bay."

Laura's gaze glided across his chest and lower to his straining cock. Thankfully, his shaft seemed normal despite his large proportions. If he were about to change back into a cat, she couldn't see it. She licked her lips, her palms fair tingling with the need to touch his chest.

"What do you mean?" Probably best if she didn't use her imagination at this point.

"When a feline shifter finds his or her mate they have an urge to mark them. The mark acts as an anchor."

"So what is it?"

"I bite you on the neck until you bleed. My saliva mixes with your blood and a small scar will form." Jonno cupped her face with his hands. His expression stalled her heartbeat for an instant—full of longing and passion, yet with a primitive power that called to her. Despite knowing little of him, she wanted to bare her neck and let him mark her. The urge pulsated through her, tempting and powerful. Her pussy clenched while her breasts throbbed and her mind yearned for more.

"I want to mark you so bad," he admitted. "Except it's not the right thing to do."

Laura opened her mouth to speak, and he placed his fingers across her lips.

"I want you, never doubt that. I have never wanted a woman the way I want you right now. Instead I'll make love to you, and we'll use condoms so there's no chance of pregnancy."

"I'm on the Pill." She frowned. "Why? Would I have kittens?" Laura couldn't contain her horror at the thought. And she'd thought a barbed cock was bad.

Jonno chuckled. "No kittens. Any children we have will appear human, but they'll be able to shift to feline. You—you'll have to observe while we play in cat form. Laura, I'm sure of what I want for my future—from the moment I saw you. I want you to have time, to think about what it will mean mating with me."

"Pardon?"

"I want to spend my days and nights with you, make love, and we could even catch the cat burglars. I want you to get to know me better, to learn the little things, my good and bad points. What do you say?"

Laura recalled her past, the mistakes she'd made with men. It was true she'd acted impulsively in the past and had suffered for it. Hell, tonight rated as impetuous. After a couple more seconds, she nodded. "Friends first and see what happens?"

"I know what's gonna happen," Jonno drawled. "My mind is made up on the situation. We're discussing you, not me."

"Friends and lovers," she said.

"Friends and lovers." Jonno's mouth lifted in satisfaction. With a final glance at the creamy skin of her marking site, he shifted his attention to her breasts. They tingled. Her mouth went dry at the yearning in his expression. Desire. Pure and simple. It pushed aside the inhibitions that had returned during their discussion, bringing a surge of wetness between her thighs.

He traced a finger down her cleavage and around one breast, leaving a path of fire in its wake. She swallowed, her breathing harsh.

"You're beautiful, Laura. I love your breasts." He weighed one in his hand, his palm rough against her sensitive flesh while he learned her shape. Hazel eyes glittered, and a purr erupted, a tinge of heat showing in his cheeks.

"Use your mouth," she whispered.

"Good idea. Tell me what you want, what you need to make this good." His face shone with sincerity, making her feel treasured and needed. Important. A partner instead of a mere participant. He rasped his tongue across the curve of one breast before moving his mouth to lick around her areola. The texture of his tongue differed from Mike's—rougher and more abrasive. "Like this?"

The tip of his tongue, dragged across her skin, sent tiny electrical currents skating along her nerve endings while the flat brought warmth.

"Yes." She burrowed her hands into his hair and clasped him closer in silent encouragement. Instead of upping the pace, he took his time, savoring and learning her responses.

Once again Mike slipped into her mind—deceitful bastard. He'd been about speed because he'd needed to get home to the little wife—not that she'd known at the time. Laura pushed the man from her mind. *Past history*. She'd learned and moved on, determined never to make the same mistake.

Her fingers slipped through Jonno's hair, pads massaging his scalp while she gave in to the sinful pleasure of his talented mouth and hands. "Yes, perfect."

Without haste, he stirred pleasure, taking her higher and giving her a hint as to what would come. His mouth contained magic, shooting heated arrows the length of her body.

"Jonno. Oh! That feels *so* good." She arched, lifting into his touch and finally he closed his mouth around one nipple. With a seductive rhythm, he sucked and frissons of excitement streamed to her clit. One callused hand crept across her belly and she willed it to move lower, stirring restlessly in silent encouragement. A finger traced along the elastic band of her panties, and a shiver swept her body.

"You have a talented tongue," she whispered.

Jonno lifted his head, the relish in his hazel eyes inviting a smile. "Wait until I get to the good bits. I bet you'll taste spicy."

"Now?" she asked with clear hope, a shiver of pleasure skating her body at the thought of his tongue running the length of her slit, probing and teasing her clit. "Now would be perfect."

He chuckled, the rich sound reverberating through her body and making her beam widen. "Not the first time. My control is nil. I need to fuck you a couple of times just to take off the edge. Babe, I'm not sure if I can go slow this time. I promise to make it up to you."

Each of his breaths sounded more and more catlike, and for a moment, she thought she saw actual canine teeth. Luckily, a slow blink dispersed the vision, or perhaps it was because he'd closed his mouth. His words should have scared her and irritated her since she had as much right to climax as him. Instead, she thrilled to the knowledge of the power she held over him.

"Take me," she said, sure and confident even though her experience with Mike should have made her wary. And for all she knew, he'd split her asunder with his cock. Nah, an overactive imagination. Besides, if Emily knew his true feline identity and wasn't one herself, possibly her husband... Emily hadn't appeared in fear of her life.

"Are you sure? You're not going to get pissed at me later if I last about two seconds and fall asleep?"

A burst of laughter filled the room. "Is that what you'll do? Fall asleep? Because that will get old fast. I could stay in my bedroom and get myself off just as easy, if that were the case."

Jonno stood, at ease with his nakedness. He smirked and gripped his cock with one hand, pumping it in a lazy motion. "I could get myself off, except it's not as much fun."

Laura couldn't stop her amusement bubbling to the surface. "We won't know until we try. You'd better grab a condom and show me action."

Jonno moved so fast she blinked. The crinkle of the condom wrapper sounded as he opened the packet. He unrolled the latex onto his erect cock and turned to her in one smooth move. Laura lifted her hips and started to peel her panties down her legs. He stopped her with a hand on her abdomen.

"Let me." He ran his finger along the elastic waistband again, wringing a gasp from her. Her stomach muscles trembled as she met his intense scrutiny.

"For someone who is in a hurry, you're moving awfully slow."

"Complaints already? That doesn't bode well for the future."

They didn't have a future. Despite the driving need to spend time with Jonno, she doubted this fated-mate shit. She'd play along even though she didn't believe in love at first sight.

Lust—yes. Her sexual urges were always getting her in trouble. A flaw in her character. She met his direct stare with one of her own. "I need sex. Please don't go slow on my account."

He scrutinized her for a long, drawn-out moment before giving a clipped nod. The laughter faded from his face, and with another quick move, he ripped her panties away from her body.

Laura's mouth opened to protest until she saw his expression and any thought of words died. Hunger. Determination. Erotic fear lashed her mind. What had she done? The tight cast of his features and the feral gleam, the elongated pupils of his eyes reminded her of his alien nature. Part man and part cat. Surely he wouldn't hurt her?

"Last chance," he whispered in a dark voice, as if he could read her mind.

Laura just stared, flinching as he parted her legs. He drew a lone finger the length of her cleft. A strum of his finger across her clit told her she still wanted him, or at least her body did, even if her mind wasn't with the program. Before she could second-guess herself, she inclined her head.

"Good girl," he said, his voice ringing with approval as he moved over her. "Normally, if we were mating, I'd fuck you from behind. Right now this is better."

Laura signaled compliance by spreading her legs, worry edging into her mind. With his veiled hints of feline behavior, he was doing a great job of building her nerves.

Jonno lined up his cock and pushed into her with one seamless thrust. Her eyelids drifted closed as he pushed inside, concentrating on the glide of his cock, tunneling and parting sensitive tissues. The first stroke. Wow. Always the best. Her breath eased out when he paused, fully seated. God, he was huge, stretching her to capacity, the weight of his large body covering her—perfect. She gripped his shoulders and pressed a kiss to one bulging biceps.

The kiss seemed to act as a signal and he stroked his cock in and out of her pussy. Each thrust plunged into her smoothly, without a shred of hesitation—a man going for gold. She curled her fingers into his hard, masculine contours and held on, letting him take what he wanted. Her inner muscles contracted around his cock and familiar low pressure gathered.

"Laura," he said on a groan, increasing the pace of his strokes.

The scent of his soap filled her nostrils along with the distinct aroma of sex. The sounds of fucking increased, and she could feel her wetness, how much her body needed this. Beneath her fingers, his sweat-dampened skin gave off powerful heat until she burned both inside and out.

She nipped at his earlobe and he went crazy, pounding into her body, not getting the angle right with his digging strokes.

He grunted. "Damn, I need this so bad. Need you, Laura."

Arching her hips, she strained to get the stimulation she needed. Her orgasm shimmered just out of reach as he pistoned his hips a final time, his big body convulsing with the force of his release. His cock pulsed and he groaned, freezing, fully impaled while he rode out his climax.

Disappointed and aching for fulfillment, she hid her face against his neck, biting her lip to hold back her complaints. After all, he'd warned her. His body surrounded her, becoming heavy while heat seared into her. She struggled, trying to draw a breath.

Jonno must have realized because he shifted his weight, moving enough to stare at her face.

"Aw, babe. You're disappointed." He pressed a tender kiss to her mouth, making it slow and easy until craving prickled through her again. She ached and moved a fraction, to no avail.

"You warned me," she said, tears inexplicably flooding her eyes.

"I did, but I'm not a total bastard." He pulled out of her and stood to deal with the condom before returning to her side. Moving down her body, he parted her legs, openly studying the swollen folds of her pussy.

"Jonno!"

"What?"

"It's not polite to stare."

"You're so pretty, and you gave me so much pleasure." His lips curved into a sexy grin. "Actually, it was fuckin' incredible, and now that I have better control, I'll return the favor."

Laura glanced at his cock and wrinkled her nose with clear doubt. "Are you sure about that control? You seem to be rising to the occasion again."

"Shush," he whispered. "We'll get this right soon." He pushed his hands under her bottom and lifted her to his mouth.

One long, luscious stroke of his tongue shut her up. Pleasure fired to life again, and she relaxed, deciding that this might work. He slipped a finger into her, filling the emptiness while he licked and nibbled. He teased her until intense bursts of heat swirled from her clit. Her eyes fluttered closed and her other senses rushed to fill the void. She heard his breathing and the noisy lap of his tongue as he collected her juices, smelled his musky scent and the spicy tang of sex. The feelings...they cascaded through her, growing and layering one on top of another. His raspy tongue. The friction of his finger stroking her internally.

"Jonno," she wailed, balanced on a precipice of pleasure.

He pushed a second finger into her and intensified his assault on her clit, using direct strokes instead of grazing the hard nubbin. Her heart lurched as she strained for release.

"Harder," she demanded.

Luckily he meant what he said about direction. He increased the pressure on her clit. A bolt of liquid fire started at the point where he stroked, quickly gaining in mass, spreading out and shooting to her legs and up her torso. A strained groan squeezed past her lips, the clench of her channel squeezing his fingers in a series of hard spasms as her body exploded in pleasure.

She groaned, swimming in the aftermath of the fiery heat until the waves decreased and receded. Wow! She sucked in a hasty breath, her heart still thudding erratically. Never had she experienced such intense pleasure. How was it possible?

Gradually, Jonno reduced his strokes over her clit and removed his fingers from her. "Are you okay?" He sounded worried.

Laura forced heavy eyelids open. "Wow. Thank you."

Relief showed on his face followed by a smile. "Why don't we start over and do that again? We might even get our timing closer. What do you say?"

"Do you have rocks in your head?"

"No." His reply sounded a trifle uncertain.

"For sex like that I'd do anything. Anytime, anyplace, Jonno. Just say the word."

Chapter 4

Sweet Progress

J onno woke in the early hours of the morning, wrapped around Laura. He breathed in her scent and satisfaction filled him. *His mate*. Knowing he'd wake her yet unable to halt the impulse to explore her silky skin, he ran his hand down her bare arm and across her hip. Instant reaction roared through him, his cock lengthening and his feline pushing him to take her again and complete the mating process.

Damn, she had to be sore since they'd made love several times before falling asleep, none of them gentle. He could give her gentle and loving now, show Laura he wasn't just a rutting beast. At least he'd imprinted her with his scent. Other shifters would know she belonged to him, despite the lack of a mating mark.

He leaned over to kiss her, sweeping her brown hair off her cheek and baring her neck. His gaze caressed the curves and angles, lingering on the place where he'd mark her. Soon, he hoped, wondering how long this courtship might take. He was impatient now that he knew what he wanted. She moaned, drawing a smile from him. *His mate.*

"Wake up, babe." He kissed her again, biting her full bottom lip and tasting her. This time he steered clear of the marking site, knowing better than to test himself again. The feline snarled in displeasure. He ignored it, instead concentrating on pleasuring his lady. His fingers tangled in her hair while he drew agonizingly slow circles around one nipple with his tongue. When he glanced up, he caught the flutter of her eyelashes.

"Jonno," she whispered.

"How are you?"

"You expect conversation before I have coffee?"

Amusement vibrated in his chest at her dismay. "I'll make coffee for you soon. I even have the real stuff instead of instant."

"Promises, promises." She yawned before stretching, arching against his naked body. She paused as he licked around her nipple again. "Oh, did you have something else in mind? What's the time?"

"Just after five."

"It's still nighttime," she said with a horrified gasp.

"We're in bed and that's the perfect place to fuck."

"It's also the perfect place to sleep."

Jonno moved up to trace her lips with his finger and tried not to laugh. "I'm willing to do all the work."

Her brow wrinkled while she pretended to ponder his proposition. "Well, as long as I get an orgasm, I suppose."

"I promise you'll leave this bed satisfied." He kissed the smooth vulnerability of her throat before heading to her breasts, thrilling at the free rein he had on her body, the sense of intimacy. With one hand he pinched her nipple, twisting and tugging hard enough to give her the edge of pain. She groaned and turned toward him, sliding one leg between his and bringing their bodies together. His cock jerked at the intimate contact. *Yes*. But more, he wanted to see her expression, to watch her breasts bounce as she took her pleasure. Suiting action to thought, he rolled, untangling their limbs and lifting her so she straddled his body. She peered through the darkness at him, her features quizzical.

His lips curled upward in approval, even though she likely wouldn't see much in the dim light. "I thought you might like to explore my body, unless you're certain I have to do the work."

"You won't take over again?" she asked. "I didn't get a chance to explore last night. You kept growling at me and taking control."

"I'm all yours." And he meant it. He belonged to her in every way apart from the mating mark. That would come in time. Despite his feline's displeasure, he knew his decision not to mark her until she understood the consequences was the right one.

"Put your hands above your head and hold on to the headboard."

"I enjoy you in this mood."

"If I'm woken at this time of the day and don't have coffee, you get a stroppy woman."

"I can deal."

"Are you sure?" Even in the darkness, he could discern the cheeky grin on her face. The thought of waking up with her in his bed every day, teasing him like this and even complaining about the earliness of the hour brought delight.

His mate. Damn.

Excitement raced through him in a rush—a kid at Christmas. He couldn't stop thinking how lucky he was with his new toy. Not that he'd verbalize this aloud because she meant way more than that to him. She was his future, the mother of his children and more.

Without taking his attention off her, he stretched his arms above his head and grasped the rail of the wooden headboard with his fingers. At first she touched, using hands and fingers to explore his face, almost a massage of sorts. His lids closed to enjoy the novel experience. She traced his cheekbones and jaw and the outline of his mouth.

Unable to resist, he opened his mouth, taking her forefinger inside. His tongue stroked over her fingertip and traced around her nail. She stilled, her astonishment written into a hasty gasp. When he sucked on her finger, her soft moan echoed in the bedroom. His cock jerked, ready for more intimate action.

"Hey, my show," she chided, removing her finger to replace it with her lips. Lazily they kissed, as if they had all the time in the world, lips stroking and sucking, brushing together. Need roared to life. He attempted to bank it down and let Laura set the pace. He'd have thought a night of fucking would appease his feline yet still the urge to mate propelled him, a constant factor at the back of his mind. His fingers curled around the headboard in a white-knuckle grip, determined to maintain control and let Laura set the pace.

She continued to kiss his mouth, taking small bites, nipping and soothing. A fine sheen of sweat covered his skin, and he trembled as she moved her way down his body. The moist lick along his collarbone almost did him in. He twisted his hips, grinding his cock against her hipbone. Pleasure flickered. A hiss of air whooshed through tight lips, the sensation so good he rocked his pelvis upward again.

Laura laughed. "Now, now. Enough of that. Stop trying to hurry things. I will handle our pleasure this time. Is that clear?" The bark of command in her voice brought diversion despite the taut, almost painful sensation of his cock and balls. He liked the tough streak and could imagine her in work-mode.

"Do you behave this way while you're apprehending criminals?"

"You should know."

"What? You treat all the men you arrest like you did me?" His tone emerged hard and terse, and it matched the flash of jealousy burning his mind. For a moment red rage fogged his vision. He hated the idea of Laura touching another male. Loathed it.

"Hell, no! I'd have the police complaints authority on my case in no time. You're the first." She cast him an enigmatic glance. "Are you going to report me?"

A lock of hair fell over his forehead as he shook his head. He ignored it, studying her instead and trying to impart his sincerity. He'd do nothing to hurt her, either emotionally or physically. She didn't understand what mating meant. Not yet. "Not likely. I don't have a single complaint."

The slight narrowing of her eyes and the furrow of her brow told him she didn't believe him. The knowledge didn't sit well. Was it him who caused her caginess? His feline? Or someone in her past? She moved, distracting him as she took the head of his cock into her mouth. He hissed. Sweet, silken heat surrounded him and his world narrowed to one of hot sensation. Complete masculine satisfaction because his mate lovingly tended him. Her tongue glided across the head, exploring curving glans and the sensitive underside. Pleasure roared through him, blood cramming into both his cock and his balls. Her mouth was hot. Wet. The lazy stroke of her tongue dragged a groan from deep in his chest, and he couldn't prevent the upward surge of his hips to drive his cock deeper into her heated mouth.

"Laura." He tightened his grip, fighting the need to take control. Instinct told him Laura needed this, needed to set the pace and control the pleasure between them. "Damn, that is great. Too good."

He should ask her questions to distract himself. Why she'd become a cop? Why she'd moved to Middlemarch? And her interests—he'd need to learn about those. He wanted to learn everything. A twin-edged situation.

As if she knew how close he hovered to release, she increased the pace, pushing him relentlessly toward orgasm with both hands and mouth.

"Laura, please. Let me come inside you."

Lifting her head, she glanced at him, lips swollen, hair ruffled and hanging loose around her shoulders. Beautiful. Absolutely beautiful and breathtaking. His. That was the best part of all.

"Condom?"

"On top of the dresser." He indicated the packet with a jerk of his head, releasing his hands, intending to grab one.

She stopped him with a hand in the middle of chest. "Stay. I'll do it." Leaning across the bed, she grabbed the packet and pulled out a condom. "Hands back where they were. I'm not doing a thing until you obey."

Her warning caught him by surprise. "You sound as if you mean it."

"I do."

Judging by her harsh breaths, she wasn't immune to the chemistry between them. Her skin appeared flushed and dewy, a pulse at her throat beating a rapid tattoo. Her tongue flickered out to lave her bottom lip. Slowly, her tongue glided across the plump pink curve, leaving it glistening and shining. Tempting. Against his feline's demands, he returned his hands to the headboard while she ripped the condom open. Sharp nails sliced into the wood, evidence of the feline coming to the surface.

He obeyed because his mate asked, the give-and-take intriguing him, even though his feline hated the delay.

She rolled the condom onto his erection, the heat from her hands searing his hard flesh. As she leaned over, her hot breath caressing his tight, achy balls. Enthralled, he watched her full lips part and her tongue glide out to moisten his sac.

"Are you trying to kill me?"

"If I wanted to do that, I'd use my gun."

His pulse jumped and a rusty chuckle emerged. "I'll remember that. It's hot having a lover who's a cop. Do you enjoy the job?"

"I don't want to discuss work." She straddled his body and guided his cock into position. Taking her time, she sank downward, and he savored every increment of the impalement. "I much prefer concentrating on sex."

"Making love," he protested. Didn't she understand? This was the real thing.

"Whatever. It's good, almost as good as coffee." Her head dropped forward, hair sliding across her face and screening her expression from him.

"We can't be doing it right if you're still thinking of coffee."

"Stop talking," she ordered, rising and falling so slowly he felt his cock part her inner tissues, delving and separating, gliding with exquisite friction.

He wanted to protest, the words of chastisement already forming when her head fell back and a soft, needy sound vibrated in her throat. Yeah, she was right. The lovemaking

61

should come first. Lovemaking, not sex or fucking. He wouldn't call it that again. She rose and fell on him with easy strokes, one hand creeping down her body to finger her clit. On each upward stroke he saw his cock, glistening with her honey, and he couldn't stop watching. So stunning. Sexy. Her breasts bounced as she increased her pace. Her beautiful face tautened with passion while heat blossomed between them. He drove upward to meet her next stroke, slamming flesh against flesh.

"Yes! Yes! Perfect," she cried, and her vaginal walls pulsed, squeezing his cock. She cried out. His shaft bucked, and the tension snapped inside him. Semen spurted from his dick in pulsating waves. A loud groan rushed up his throat, the pleasure ripping the length of his body, stealing this breath. He released his grip on the bed to wrap his arms around her pliant form. *His.* She might not accept it yet. By the time they'd made love a few more times she would. They were meant to be together. Each touch seemed so right. Perfect.

His hand smoothed over her sweaty back, happy and replete in a way he'd never experienced. "Are you ready for coffee yet?"

"Don't you believe in a postcoital cuddle?" She sounded tired, and her words made him chuckle.

"If we stay here, you'll get more than coffee."

"Coffee," she stated. "I want to walk into work."

Jonno rolled and separated their bodies. He dealt with the condom and padded from the room to the bathroom on the other side of the hall. Five minutes later he'd set the coffeemaker in motion and returned to the bedroom.

"What's our plan of attack for today?"

"I am going to work. You will stay well clear and keep a low profile."

"I won't do that." She might as well know up front he had no intention of backing away. He became involved the minute Saber and the council had asked him to help. The presence of at least two feline shifters amongst the thieves meant he needed to stay in the loop.

And then there was Laura. He wanted to spend time with her.

He sat on the edge of the bed and smoothed the hair off her face, loving the silky sensation as it trailed through his fingers. "I want to spend time with you. Besides, my special skills will come in handy. I can try to track the thieves. And I'd like to visit the scenes of some of the other robberies to see if I can find the same scents."

"You're a civilian. I'm already in troub— I have to stick to the guidelines."

Jonno's attention focused on her body language, searching for clues. Already in trouble. That was what she'd intended to say. He wanted to push even though instinct told him to wait. He'd learn the details soon enough, just as Laura would accept his presence in her life.

"Who is going to tell? Coffee won't be long. I'm off for a shower. I'll leave a towel for you in the bathroom. Come through to the kitchen once you're ready." Normally he'd have invited her to shower with him. He refrained, sensing she needed time to think. He just hoped she made the right decision.

Jonno forced himself to move away and leave the bedroom. After a quick shower, he prowled back into his bedroom to pull out a clean pair of jeans and another T-shirt.

To his frustration, Laura pretended sleep. Once he left the bedroom again he heard the rustle of sheets and the squeak of the bed as she moved. He continued to the kitchen, deciding to give her space. On automatic pilot, he pulled two mugs from the cupboard and retrieved a bottle of milk from the fridge. After pouring coffee into one mug, he added a dash of milk and one sugar. Idly stirring in the sugar, he let his mind drift to the thieves. Felines. Who the hell were they?

Hesitant footsteps broke into his musing, and Laura appeared in the kitchen, dressed in her police uniform.

"How do you take your coffee?"

"White, no sugar."

Jonno poured the coffee for her and shunted the mug across the table. They needed to ease this uncomfortable morning-after atmosphere before any damage occurred, such as him breaking his coffee mug, he thought ruefully, easing his grip and setting it on the table.

Work, he decided, to put her at ease. "Have the other towns around Middlemarch had any burglaries?"

"I don't know. I haven't been here long enough to think about checking. Charlie hasn't mentioned other towns, and I didn't see the policeman I replaced. He left two days before I arrived."

Good riddance, according to Saber and everyone he questioned. The retiring cop had all the skill of a brown paper bag.

"Yeah, well, it occurred to me they might hit the other towns. Hell, they might even be a professional group of thieves or a gang coming from Dunedin."

Laura sipped her coffee, tossing around the possibilities he'd raised. "I'll check first thing this morning. That's a good idea, and if that's the case, we can pool our resources and knowledge to put them out of business."

"Most of the stuff they've stolen from the Middlemarch region is jewelry. If they've hit other areas, it will be interesting to see if they've stuck to that or if the jewelry theme is coincidental."

"Yes." Laura inclined her head again, her gaze sliding across his chest. When he caught her in the act, she flushed and rushed into speech. "Good coffee."

He tried to smother his grin and failed. "Worth waiting for?"

"Maybe."

His amusement faded, replaced by chagrin. Way to burst his bubble. "Don't forget we're invited to dinner at Emily and Saber's place tonight."

"I...I'll ring Emily and cancel," she said, dropping her attention to the tabletop.

A burst of anger hit him and his hand clenched his coffee mug again. This time the mug didn't stand the strain. Hot coffee and china sprayed in all directions. Jonno cursed, low and fluid words that did nothing to relieve his frustration. He should have known a relationship with a human wouldn't go smoothly. Standing, he crouched to pick up the biggest of the china pieces before retrieving a small broom and dustpan from the hall cupboard.

Patience, he counseled himself. Despite his natural inclination to grab her and kiss her senseless, he needed to take his time. He'd frightened her with his intensity, and the knowledge of feline shifters wandering around her patch hadn't helped things. Humans saw things differently, didn't understand.

Jonno grabbed a cloth and swiped at the spilled liquid. "Want more coffee?"

"No, thanks. I need to stop by my place before I head into work."

Jonno chucked the cloth aside. "I'll grab another T-shirt and drive you back to town."

"Thanks."

After a deep breath, Jonno strode away from his mate, his feline snarling in protest. It looked as if he'd returned to step one. Hell, it felt like minus one. He should have guessed things were working too smoothly.

Chapter 5

Regrets

The drive back into town would never be one of her better memories. Uncomfortable didn't come close. Laura stared straight ahead, trying to concentrate on the job at hand—her work and catching the thieves preying off the folk of Middlemarch. Work had helped her through difficult times in the past. This time—not so much. Jonno's gaze drilled into her, shared between her and the road ahead.

"How old are you?" Suddenly it became important to break the taut silence between them.

"Twenty-four," he said.

"Twenty-four? I'm twenty-eight!"

"And you're telling me because?"

"We're not doing this again. I don't sleep with younger men."

"Because?"

Laura's teeth clacked together. Her mind blanked. Why? Heck, she couldn't think of a good reason. Recalling the previous evening, she knew she couldn't tell him he lacked experience. The man knew what to do with his equipment and seemed clued up on hers. "Because...because..." Her brain scrambled for reasons and came up short.

"You can't give me a reason." Satisfaction echoed in his words. "There is no reason we can't have a relationship."

"No, last night was a one-off. Just sex."

"It wasn't just sex," he snarled. "Admit it. It was way more."

Laura remained silent because she couldn't refute his charge. She'd experienced something last night she'd never had with Mike. A sense of completeness that scared her. Things with Jonno were too new, too raw. She didn't need another man in her life. "I don't know you."

"Fine." He shot her an intensely masculine glare of annoyance and frustration. "Ask me anything. I'll do the same with you. We'll get to know each other."

He wasn't going to back off. That was as obvious as the nose in the middle of her face. "Okay," she said. *Fine.* She'd pretend and gradually back away, putting space between them. Besides, her superiors had warned her to follow every rule and law in carrying out of her duties. Allowing Jonno to take part in the investigation could leave her open to chastisement and possibly the loss of the job she loved. Her mouth tightened. No, not possibly. Definitely. The head honchos had been angry after the incident, and Mike, the weasel, had made sure the blame fell on her.

"We're mates."

"Enough with the mates stuff." As if she believed his stupid spiel. No such thing.

His muscular shoulders lifted in a careless shrug as he pulled into the driveway of the house she shared with Charlie. Hopefully, she'd sneak in without Charlie realizing she'd stayed out all night.

The front door flew open and Charlie stood in the doorway.

His pale blue eyes widened in surprise. "Laura, hobnobbing with a criminal?"

"He's not a criminal. He has an alibi, which means we're back at the start," she said. Please don't let him notice anything out of the ordinary. *Please.*

"Someone rang for you. A guy. He refused to leave his name or number," Charlie said.

"Strange." She turned to Jonno. "Thanks for the ride."

"Does this mean I don't get a kiss goodbye?"

Laura glanced over her shoulder at Charlie before jerking her head in the negative.

Jonno scowled. "I'll pick you up at quarter to seven."

"No! I'll—"

"Quarter to seven," he repeated before taking off with a screech of tires, leaving Laura staring after him.

"You slept with him. I thought you'd be more careful," Charlie said, his blond hair was still wet from the shower.

"My private life is none of your damn business," Laura snapped.

"You should tell that to the man who rang four times last night. He made it my business when he accused me of lying about you not being here."

Mike? He was the only one who knew her location. And she'd thought she'd seen the last of him...

"Jonno asked me whether other areas were having the same problems with robberies. Have you considered there is a gang of thieves rather than the one person we'd assumed?"

"Good point," Charlie said, looking excited. "More than one thief. That's a possibility. I've been so busy investigating the local complaints I haven't considered alternatives yet. I'm heading over to the station now and will check with the nearby towns."

"Be there in ten minutes. Any other problems?"

"None relating to business." His words held questions, and Laura didn't know him well enough to confide her problems. Best she kept quiet.

"Good. I'll see you soon." She pushed the front door open and stepped inside. Heading straight for her bedroom, Laura held it together until she closed her door and sank onto her bed. Then she trembled in reaction to both the night and this morning's events. And even worse, the moment Jonno had driven away and disappeared, she'd wanted him back at her side.

Weird. Plain weird.

Moisture filled her eyes, and she wiped it away with an impatient swipe of her hand.

No matter what Jonno said, there was no such thing as mates. In books and movies, not in real life. In the first place, men were incapable of committing to one woman, and secondly, they lied whenever it suited them, fitting their words to the situation.

But Jonno had told her—shown her his big secret after knowing her for mere hours. Laura frowned, trying to reconcile his revelations with her trepidation about moving into new relationship territory. No, she didn't want a relationship. She wasn't ready. She needed time to heal, then she'd consider another man. Baby steps.

Laura hurried to grab a change of clothes. Although Jonno had suggested she have a shower at his place, she'd waited. The pipes in the old house clattered to life when she flipped on the shower control. As usual, it took a few minutes for the water to heat. She hadn't jumped into the shower without testing the water after her first day of living in the police house. Charlie had thought her yelp of shock funny.

Fifteen minutes later, five extra than she'd told Charlie, Laura strode into the police station.

"Laura, you were right," Charlie said, showing more enthusiasm than she'd seen from him the entire time she'd been in Middlemarch. "This seems like an organized operation. Thieves have hit most of the surrounding towns. They're taking jewelry and money and seem to have inside knowledge."

"Great!" At last something to sink her teeth into and take her mind off her problems. "Let's grab a map and mark the areas where the robberies have occurred. We can try to work out where they'll hit next."

They worked together well, and once they'd finished, it became clear Middlemarch was one of the last towns on a large stealing spree. So far they'd had three burglaries, which was on the light side compared to the other townships.

"There are two towns the thieves haven't hit," Charlie said. "We should warn them. It mightn't make a difference, but, if the residents are aware and increase security, it won't hurt."

"Why don't you take care of that, and I'll ring around the residents here."

"What are you going to tell them?"

"I might tell them we're doing free security checks for everyone. What do you think?"

"It's a pity Gerard Drummond and Henry Anderson are away on a job. I met them just after I arrived in Middlemarch. They have a security company and could have taken care of this for us." Charlie studied the map before turning back to her. "I think the free security checks are a good idea, but the last thing we need is mass panic."

Laura stood. "Do you want anything for morning tea?"

"Sure, I'll have a steak and cheese pie and a chocolate chip muffin. Do you want money?"

"You can buy next time." Laura headed out of their office, pausing to answer the phone. "Middlemarch police station," she said, her mind on the approach she'd use with the residents.

"Laura." The familiar voice brought her back to the present with a nasty jolt.

"Mike. What do you want?" She didn't want to deal with him now.

"I've missed you, babe. Where were you last night?"

"I don't want to talk to you."

"Where were you last night, babe?"

Laura counted to ten. "Because of you they transferred me to Middlemarch and placed a mark of censure on my record. I don't want to talk to you. You're married. Talk to your wife."

"Sweetheart, we can get past..." He started to refute her charges, trying to spread his charm.

She hung up with him midsentence. "Bastard," she muttered, sending a glare in Charlie's direction since he was a handy male. "I'll be back soon."

Jonno drove straight to the Mitchell homestead, his gut roiling with anxiety. Never had a woman tied him up in knots like Laura. Last night had been wonderful, the best experience of his life. But this morning...this morning he'd slipped into a nightmare. She'd backed away, blown him off, as if this thing between them didn't exist.

Her coworker had mentioned a man ringing her during the night. He'd eavesdropped without guilt because she was his mate. His fingers curled around the steering wheel in a tight grip as he roared into the Mitchells' driveway. He pulled up with a shriek of brakes, sucked in a deep breath before slapping his open palm on the steering wheel in a burst of temper.

The small sting of pain made him realize something. They'd had one night together. She had to be scared and confused because fear filled him, and he'd known what to expect. Yeah, he'd try to cut her some slack and court her. That couldn't hurt. With another deep breath, he exited his vehicle and strode to the front door, calmer now that he had a plan.

Saber opened the door as he raised his hand to knock. His friends' brother took one look at his face and stood aside to let him enter. "Everything okay?"

Jonno hadn't been going to say anything, his confusion about Laura rushing out in a single word. "No."

"You eaten yet?"

"No, I haven't had a chance."

"Emily said you spent part of the night in custody."

Jonno snorted. "That was the easy part."

Saber led the way into the kitchen, the scents of toast, coffee and bacon bringing back memories of his happy childhood.

Emily turned to glance at him and smiled. "How was your night?"

"Confusing."

"Oh?"

Saber gestured at an empty seat and sat himself. "You might as well tell her. She'll worm it out of you anyway."

"The new cop is my mate. Laura." Both pleasure in the fact and anxiety about Laura's reaction this morning combined to squeeze his heart in a tight grip. He swallowed and coughed. When he glanced at Saber, he saw the older feline smiling.

"That's great. Joe and Sly might take the same step and put me out of my misery."

"No sane woman would take on those two," Emily said with a grin.

"My worry exactly," Saber said, his tone dry.

Emily placed a mug of coffee in front of him, and Jonno reached for the milk jug. A plate of bacon, eggs and grilled tomatoes appeared in front of him. Saber placed a rack full of toast in the middle of the table.

"Did you learn anything at the Miller house?" Saber asked.

"Yeah, or at least I think I did. The Millers are human, right?" Saber nodded. "Why?"

"I picked up the scent of two different shifters. The Millers might have friends who are shifters, but I'd have recognized the scents because I've met most of the locals since my arrival in Middlemarch. I didn't. I need you to come and check it out with me. Besides, I'm not looking forward to facing Mr. Miller on my own."

"Just wait until you meet Mrs. Miller." Emily smirked as she joined them at the table. "She's the scary one."

Jonno sipped his coffee before applying himself to breakfast. He loved how Emily made him feel like part of the Mitchell family. "You know, Saber, if I hadn't found my mate, I'd be after Emily."

Saber winked at Jonno. "She's always misbehaving. Believe me, you'd give her back damn quick."

"Hello?" Emily clicked her fingers in front of her husband's face. "I'm here. Right in front of you. I can hear everything."

Jonno chuckled, enjoying their byplay as he always did. He hoped to have that sort of relationship with his mate. His smile faded, replaced by concern. It didn't appear too promising at the moment.

"We'll visit the Millers once we've finished breakfast," Saber said. "Hopefully the scent tracks will give us a lead."

"I didn't investigate because the police showed up and dragged me to the station. We can follow the scents, or if you recognize them, it will give us something to follow up."

"Good," Emily said. "That's settled. Now we can discuss Laura. What went wrong?"

"I don't know," Jonno said, taking Emily's questions with scarcely a blink. He'd guessed they wouldn't be long in coming. "Last night seemed fine. This morning..." He trailed off with a shrug.

Emily sniffed. "Feline males are always in a hurry. It's not so bad if the woman you're chasing is a feline. She's more prepared than us ignorant humans who are a bit slower. We like to contemplate things, and then there's the fact you're feline. That's something else again."

"She knows I'm a feline shifter," Jonno said. "Once I knew she was my mate I decided it might be best to show her up front."

Saber shot him a sharp glance. "You're taking a risk."

"I don't think so," Jonno said. "I don't think anyone would believe her and besides, I'm not even sure she'd tell anyone since she's one of the town cops."

Emily cut a slice of bacon. "I think you're right. She'd be risking her career to go public with something like that. People would laugh. Remember the reactions to Tomasine's newspaper article. Some of the locals still treat her as a pariah."

"How did Laura take it?" Saber asked.

"She seemed okay. A bit nervous. She didn't freak out or anything. It was fine, and she stayed the night at my place. This morning she backed away. She considers last night a one-time thing."

"You need to give her time," Emily said.

"Yeah, I've already worked out that." A rueful smile shaped his lips. "It's not gonna to be easy."

Saber grunted. "If you think I had an easy time with Emily, think again."

Emily sniffed before grabbing a piece of wholemeal toast and scraping butter across the surface with noisy swipes. "Feline men are bossy. They think they know best when they know nothing!"

"Put in our place," Jonno said with a smirk. "Okay, I'll give her time, although my feline is pushing me hard. I wanted to mark her. I still want to."

"You will not mark that girl without her agreement," Saber snapped.

"No," Jonno said. "Of course not. I explained the marking process to her."

"Good," Saber said. "I know it can't have been easy to restrain the feline urge to mark her. The urge to mark affects some felines worse than others. Emily and I are here to talk if you need us."

"You should talk to the twins too," Emily suggested. "They're giving Saber gray hair along with his worry."

Jonno laughed, the sort of laugh that ripped right to his belly. "Joe and Sly are my friends. If they get up to mischief, I'm usually right beside them."

"That's what worries me," Saber said, his voice wry. "The three of you encourage each other in your hijinks. It's just as well they spend so much time in Dunedin."

Emily cocked her head in a quizzical manner, reminding him of a curious bird. "Are they going out with anyone serious? Could we have two more matings in the future?"

Jonno thought about Maggie. Even he didn't know what was up with the twins and Maggie. They always had women around the place. "You should ask them," he said, deciding on tact rather than truth. "Great breakfast, Emily. Thank you."

"We'll go to the Millers now," Saber said. "Just as well we persuaded Mr. Miller to substitute the diamond necklace for a fake."

"Knowing him, he'll still be angry because people broke into his house. Do we know if anything else is missing? And who tipped off the police?"

"I don't know. I didn't think to ask, and it's a good question because the house doesn't have an alarm," Jonno said. "You suggested I stake out the place because most of the locals have heard of the Miller diamond necklace and it seemed the obvious choice. I'll check with Laura when I see her again."

"We can discuss that with Laura at dinner tonight," Emily said.

"Ah, you might want to give her a ring and remind her," Jonno said. "Because I got the feeling she might try to wriggle out of dinner, using work as an excuse."

"Saber or I will call her, using work as an excuse," Emily assured him.

Jonno grinned, marginally more confident. With Emily on the case, Laura didn't stand a chance.

Emily stood to remove their empty plates. "Courting her might help. A woman likes romance, a fact which most men forget these days."

"What? You mean flowers and romantic dates?" Jonno asked, willing to listen to anything. A twitchy sensation crawled over his skin making him desperate to move. His mind kept returning to Laura and the previous evening. His cock stirred,

79

pushing against the denim of his jeans and his feline gave a silent snarl.

"Every girl needs a little romance, even married ones," she said with a meaningful glance at Saber.

"Yes, Emily," Saber said, reaching to tug her onto his knee.

Envy flashed through Jonno. They seemed so together, so happy. He knew from the twins their courtship had been fast with a few roadblocks on the way. It didn't show now. His mind drifted to Emily's suggestion. That he could do, because even though he didn't have experience in romancing, he'd watched enough movies and listened to enough radio discussions to imagine the things he should try. "Thanks for breakfast, Emily. Saber, are you ready to head out to the Miller place?"

"Yeah. Thanks, sweetheart. I'll see you later at the café." He brushed a kiss over her lips.

Emily said, "I'll ring Laura and make sure she can't wriggle out of dinner tonight. I might see if Felix and Tomasine can come. Leo and Isabella as well."

"Great," Jonno said. "I haven't seen everyone since Leo and Isabella's wedding celebrations." He followed Saber from the house, glad he was taking action. Hopefully it would take his mind off Laura.

They took his vehicle and arrived at the Miller place ten minutes later to find a police vehicle outside. Jonno's heart jumped, jolting against his ribs before settling, and his feline pushed, a snarl bursting from him. He scented his mate and badly wanted to touch her. Now.

"Easy," Saber said.

Jonno wanted to curse. Out of respect he refrained. Saber might not be very old by feline standards, yet everyone in Middlemarch respected the man. He climbed from the car and sucked in a deep breath. *Laura*. The sweet scent of soap and laundry powder and woman greeted him even before he could see her. He prowled away from his car, not waiting for Saber because his feline had taken firm control.

When he turned a corner he found Laura deep in discussion with Miller.

"Hello," he said, straining for politeness when all he wanted was to touch.

"You were meant to protect my property," Miller growled. "They took money and jewelry. Susanna is hysterical because strangers touched her things. I have to buy her new lingerie," he said in disgust.

Jonno wanted to point out that new lingerie might help the man's temper. He held his tongue. On the other hand, lingerie might come into his romantic equation with Laura. He visualized her in a corset with stockings and had to swallow.

"We saved the Miller diamond necklace," Saber said from behind him. "If we hadn't persuaded you to replace it with a fake, you would have lost that too."

"Mr. Miller," Laura said, ignoring both Jonno and Saber. "I need you to write me a complete list of the missing items. You'll need to do that for insurance anyway."

"I want my property back," Miller snapped, his face turning redder by the minute.

"We're doing our best," Laura said. "Unless we receive cooperation we won't be able to help you. The sooner you give us the information the quicker we can circulate details of the missing jewelry in the surrounding towns as well as Dunedin and Queenstown. The robbers might try to sell the stolen items."

"Very well," Miller said.

"I'll help you with that, Dan," Saber said. "Can we do it inside?"

Miller dragged his hand through his thick gray hair. "In my office is best. I don't want to upset Susanna any more than necessary."

"Of course," Saber said, moving away with the other man and leaving Jonno with Laura.

"What are you doing here?" Laura snapped.

"I told you Saber and the council want to catch the thieves as much as you do." Jonno moved closer, pushing into her personal space. She took a step back and another, trying to retreat without making it obvious.

"Don't." Jonno lifted his hand to smooth across her hair. In the morning sunlight, the red highlights danced and glittered. Sexy. Touching her soothed his feline while the man wanted even closer contact. "You won't forget dinner tonight, right?"

"It depends. I might be too busy."

"Emily will be very disappointed. So will I," he added, his voice low and husky. He trailed one finger over her smooth cheekbone and caught the faint shiver that sped through her body. Unable to resist, he bent his head, his warm breath feathering across her cheek and lips. He took great satisfaction from the second shiver. Then his lips bumped against hers. He tugged her pliant body closer and folded his arms around her in a silent dare for her to object. She gave a small moan, her body tense. Jonno coaxed her with a soft kiss, pouring every emotion he underwent into the kiss. Hope. Passion. Connection. Longing. *Love.*

Laura moaned again and relaxed against him, her arms creeping around his neck as she gave in and participated. Their lips slid together in an easy kiss, a lazy joining of mouths cocooning them in a sensual bubble for two.

When they pulled apart, the play of emotions over her face told Jonno he still had more work to do to prove they belonged together. But he'd awakened her hunger. He sensed it in the pressure of her fingers now clutching his shoulders.

"I can't do this while I'm working," she said.

"I know, and I'm sorry. Will you come to dinner with me tonight? I can pick you up."

"I—okay." Her shoulders slumped, and he caught the tail end of an inner battle that showed briefly in her eyes before she glanced away. "I should finish work around six. You said quarter to seven, right?"

"Yeah." Jonno tucked a lock of hair behind her ear. "Do you drink wine? I thought I'd buy a couple of bottles to take with us."

"Yes. I don't understand what's wrong with me. I wanted to jump you the moment I saw you."

"You hid it well," Jonno said with a smile. "I'll pick you up, okay?" He wanted a firm commitment from her.

She nodded. "It's possible I could run a little late."

"No problem. I'm a big boy. I can keep myself amused until you're ready." He kissed her again, harder this time, making sure she knew how much he wanted her.

"Are cats sex machines?" she asked when they parted.

"I enjoy sex as much as the next guy. It's because we're mates that we're both on edge and desperate. It will keep happening until we formally mate."

Laura sighed, her frown highlighting her unhappiness with the situation. "I didn't ask for this."

"I know. It's not fun for me either." Time to change the subject. He'd extracted a promise for her to go to dinner with him. He'd leave it at that for the moment. "Laura, Saber and I wondered how come you and Charlie were at the Miller place last night. Why were the police there? How did you know?"

"One of the neighbors called. The woman said she saw strange lights when she drove past and knew the Millers were away. Charlie and I checked it out, and we found you on the premises."

"Strange," Jonno said, unable to resist running his hand up and down Laura's arm. Just being with her eased the torment and restlessness he'd experienced after driving away from her this morning.

"I was about to check the outside of the house. We didn't do it last night," Laura said, pulling her hand from his.

"I'll come too." Jonno reclaimed her hand and swung it back and forth. He tugged her past two fragrant rose beds, the bushes covered with white and red blooms. Roses—the traditional flower of love. "Did you know that red roses mean love and white roses mean I am worthy of you?"

Laura laughed, tense shoulders relaxing. "And what happens if a rose is both colors?"

"It means passion," Jonno said, hearing the huskiness in his voice. "That's what my mother told me when I was a boy." The memory brought back others—of his parents laughing and whispering together and going to bed early. By all rights he should have lots of siblings.

"How do I know you're telling the truth?" she teased.

Jonno decided he liked Laura in this mood, so full of laughter. Relaxed and carefree. "Check it out on the internet if you don't believe me." He stopped and smiled at her, unable to resist running his finger over her velvet-soft lips. "I never lie. Ever. You'll always get the truth from me, even if it might hurt. If there's one thing that gets to me more than any other, it's a person who lies."

"Um...that's...why?"

"Because lies cause pain."

"There's no such thing as black-and-white, Jonno. Sometimes people lie with good intentions. They don't mean to hurt anyone."

Jonno thought of his parents, his father and the way he'd forced him from their home. His father had lied to him about the reason, and it still ate at him. Jealousy. He hadn't liked a mature male in the house. Sure, they'd argued. What family didn't? "Lies hurt people, which is why I decided I'd travel a different path." As they rounded a topiary bush, he came to an abrupt stop. "Wait."

"What is it?"

"The scent. I can smell the thieves."

"How do you know it isn't one of the Millers or their family?"

"Because I'd recognize their scents. A group of people stopped here. See, two of them stepped into the garden bed in the dark. Do you see the footprints?"

"Good spotting," Laura said. "I have the digital camera in the car. I'll take photos of the prints. Anything else?" Her eyes narrowed in concentration while she surveyed the vicinity.

"I think there were four people, perhaps five. It's difficult to distinguish the scents since time has passed. At least one or two are shifters, which was what I thought last night. It's possible some of the Middlemarch residents are part of the thieves' gang."

Chapter 6

Investigation

E xcitement pulsed through Laura. This was the part of police work she enjoyed—the detecting. She found it way better than the usual mundane duties of a community cop in Middlemarch. "I'll be back in a moment. Wait for me."

She hurried around the rose beds and past a formal garden of red and white petunias. Someone had a definite liking for structure with precise planting and strict use of red, white and green throughout the garden. Although beautiful, she couldn't help thinking a blaze of different colors could work just as well.

Laura grabbed her camera and a small crime scene bag before speeding back to where Jonno waited. He appeared big, solid, and she liked that he didn't quibble talking about the meaning of flowers. She smiled and realized happiness filled her for the first time in weeks. Even knowing a relationship with Jonno might be wrong—it was too fast for a start—and she wanted more from life than a job at a country police station where nothing happened. Usually, she amended as she came to a halt by Jonno.

"Any other clues, Sherlock?"

"Yeah, Watson," he drawled, pointing to a small light green object the size of a credit card lying under a sprawling red-and-green bush. "One of our thieves has dropped his driver's license."

"No!" Laura peered more closely before backing up and bumping into Jonno. "It is. It's someone's license. Man is he gonna be pissed."

Laura placed small yellow-numbered plastic disks near the footprints and snapped several shots before doing the same with the license. Photos taken, she found a glove and pulled it onto her right hand. She picked up the license by the edges and placed it inside a plastic evidence bag. "Do you know a Max Abraham?"

"No. If he's local, Saber will know him."

"Great." Laura spied another partial print and photographed it.

"Did you know you're very sexy in cop-mode?" Jonno's husky voice lowered a register, and to her despair, she shivered, her pulse speeding without warning. The urge to jump him came to the fore. It had hovered in the back of her mind ever since she'd seen him stride over to her and Mr. Miller. Saber Mitchell looked good in his T-shirt and dark denims, but it was Jonno who she wanted to drag to the nearest flat surface. Her breath puffed out in a soft whoosh as she imagined his naked body spread in front of her.

"Are you okay? You have a strange expression on your face. Are you thinking about me?"

Laura's mouth dropped open. She recovered to curse under her breath. *Well, that was professional.* And she'd been trying so hard. "I'm just thinking ahead to decide what to do next," she hastened to explain, although, judging by the secret smile on his lips, he didn't believe her for a moment.

"Is Mr. Miller in sight? I'd like to shift and try to follow the tracks."

"They had a vehicle." Laura glanced at the house where Saber and Mr. Miller had disappeared. When she turned back, Jonno had already peeled his shirt over his head. She couldn't help it. She stared. Bronzed magnificence summed it up nicely. "What about Mr. Miller?"

Jonno offered a wicked grin. "I can hear Saber discussing his prize-winning sheep. The man will rattle on for ages. And I catch a whiff of scones. I'd bet Mrs. Miller will offer us morning tea." He bent to remove his boots and socks before unzipping his jeans and taking those off. "I've been thinking about you, Laura," he whispered.

"That is obvious," she muttered, trying and failing not to glance at his erect shaft. "Is sex all you men think of?"

"Pretty much. It's worse for me at the moment because my feline is pushing me to mate with you."

Laura had to terminate the traitorous urge to move closer and run her hand over his bare shoulders and flanks, to kneel before him and take his cock into her mouth. Yeah, that would cross the lines of professionalism. She wore her uniform! "You sunbathe in the nude."

"Guilty," he said. "Sometimes my friends Joe and Sly and I go for a run and lie around in the sun afterward."

A frown creased her forehead. Did he...did they?

"Hey, get that look off your face," he said coming closer. "We're just friends. None of us swing that way, not that I have a problem with same-sex loving. You have nothing to worry about. You're the one I'm interested in touching."

"I...um...you'd better hurry and do your thing before Mr. Miller comes looking for us." It was difficult to concentrate and portray professional when he stood in front of her naked. Where would she touch first? It was like trying to decide what to choose from a chocolate dessert buffet.

He laughed and hauled her into his arms to steal a kiss, releasing her again before she had time to formulate a plan of where to grope the man. Jonno stood back and transformed to leopard in front of her, a faint glow surrounding his body during the change. He dropped to all fours and lashed his tail, prowling to her side to rub against her legs. He seemed a tactile sort of man, always touching and stroking.

The loud vibration of his purr reverberated through her body, and helpless to his feline charm, she ran her hand over his glossy fur. No doubt about it. The man made a beautiful cat, and his markings were striking with small black rosettes covering his tawny coat. His tongue stroked across the pulse point on her wrist, the abrasive lick bringing a shiver. Jonno gave a last purr of satisfaction before trotting away.

Laura picked up his clothes and boots, plus her bag and hurried after him. The man's skills might come in handy if they could follow the tracks. They passed a grove of trees, the roots pushing out of the earth in places. Dry leaves crunched under her boots before they burst into the sunlight again. A tall hedge edged the road, and they passed a small maze and a series of potager vegetable gardens. A vehicle chugged along the road and Laura glimpsed a bright yellow tractor. Jonno slowed, waiting for it to pass. Since they'd almost reached the road, the tracks would come to a halt soon because the thieves must have a vehicle. Traveling on foot wouldn't make sense, not if the gang needed a quick getaway. As she suspected, Jonno slowed near the road, waiting for her to catch up.

He shifted, grinning in approval. "You brought my clothes. Thanks. They parked their vehicle here. See, you can make out the faint footprints on the side of the road. That set there is almost identical to the ones in the garden."

"You're very observant. Have you ever considered joining the police?" She set his stuff and her bag down before taking more photos.

"No, I enjoy working on the land."

"Are you sure?" Laura smirked at him as she put the camera away. "You're better than a police dog because you followed the tracks and gave me a verbal report."

"I have lots of talents," he murmured, his voice without inflection, although his eyes glittered with sexy promise.

Boom. Straight back to sexual tension with a few words and a roguish smile. Laura's breath caught, and she couldn't help but notice his erection. Ready for action again. "That's gonna hurt when you try to force it into your jeans."

"How about helping me out then?"

No mistaking his words for anything but a challenge. "Here?" Laura swallowed and glanced up and down the road. There wasn't a vehicle or person in sight.

"Not right here," Jonno said, his mood buoyant and catchy. "Did you notice the hedges we passed on the way out to the road? They will work for privacy."

Laura swallowed again, fighting her sexuality and the temptation standing right in front of her. A brief battle. "Okay." Heck! Mouth and brain not connected. "That was not what I meant to say," she whispered, averting her gaze from Jonno's naked body, away from enticement.

"Too late." Jonno swept her off her feet and into his arms, striding over the grass verge to the hedge maze.

"Wait, I need to get my bag of tricks. Don't you want your clothes and boots?"

Jonno came to an abrupt halt and with long strides returned to where her bag sat. He set her on her feet, waiting while she collected their belongings before seizing her again, cradling her in his arms.

Instead of fighting or protesting as she should have, Laura rested against his chest, breathing in his musky scent, enjoying the flex of masculine muscles and the show of power. When she glanced up, she noticed the banked passion flickering in his hazel eyes. Even though she was working and should know better, she was powerless to resist his charm and the flattering desire shining in his face. Damn it all!

Once Jonno reached the privacy of the hedges, he let her slide down his body and his heat seared her despite her layers of clothing. She gasped, aching for a more intimate touch, her insides jangling with excitement. With trembling hands, she set their belongings near the hedge.

"This had better be quick. Saber and Mr. Miller will expect us back at the house."

A reality check. Time for her to tell him they couldn't do this. She opened her mouth, ready to tell him, but he sealed her words of protest with his lips. Warm and tender, his mouth caressed hers, tempting her with drugging kisses. A whisper of pleasure sounded—hers. Damn, she was easy. Laura melted into him.

"I don't know what's wrong with me. I can't stop myself where you're concerned. Dammit, I don't even know you." Her voice came close to a wail and held clear frustration.

"You sense the mating bond," Jonno said, his lips catching one earlobe and giving her a hint of bite.

"I don't want to. I—" Laura gnawed on her bottom lip, aghast at the way she'd almost blurted out the stupid mistakes she'd made with Mike, following her impulses instead of using her head.

"Shush, we don't have much time. Tonight, okay?" With competent hands he unfastened her blue uniform shirt and slid his hand inside a cup of her bra. The slight friction against her nipple brought a moan. Weak. So weak. "Jonno." The steady pinch of his fingers brought a strangled groan of pleasure, nerve ends sizzling at his touch.

"Steady, sweetheart."

"You make my thoughts fly from my head whenever you touch me, so hands off."

"I'll make it up to you tonight."

If she were smart, she wouldn't go home with him tonight. She'd stay far away. Although, she suspected her willpower was faulty after a few hours in his company. Her hand wandered across his collarbone and over one pectoral muscle, fascinated by the silky skin and underlying hardness of his form. Her fingernails scraped over a flat nipple. Back and forth until it stood erect and Jonno growled at the back of his throat.

"We have no time for exploration."

"We'll do this my way," she said.

"And her tone is implying her way or not at all."

"Got it in one, buster." Her fingers trailed across his stomach. Taut muscles. Sexy muscles. Gripping his hips, she knelt in front of him, running her lips over the smooth skin of his stomach. His cock brushed against her cheek and she turned her head, sticking out the tip of her tongue to run along his length.

He groaned, his hands gripping her head. "Please. Do it faster. My control isn't too good with you."

Laura wanted to take this slow. She wanted to watch his every reaction and search out places to touch that gave him the greatest pleasure. She felt the impatience in his tense muscles and knew he was right. They needed to hurry. Laura pulled back a fraction to glance at his cock. Large and rigid with a deep red head. With a light touch she ran her fingers along his length. He jerked and a purr sounded, bringing a smirk to her lips.

"You're easy. I always know your mood because of the sounds you make."

"You make me purr," he said, totally serious. "No one else."

"Never? You haven't purred before?" That was hard to believe. When a man was so tactile like him his story seemed hard to believe. Nothing special with her—Mike had proved that.

"Never."

The thing about not lying—did that apply to this as well? Aware of passing time, she decided to debate it later. "All right. Let's see if I can push the purrs up to groans." Holding on to his muscular thighs for balance, she licked across the mushroom-shaped head of his cock. He stilled, a rough growl vibrating in his chest.

She glanced up at him in amusement. "Not quite a purr. You're easy, Jonno."

"Yeah." His hands laced in her hair, dragging strands out of her ponytail, directing her mouth back to his cock.

Laughing, she took him inside and loved him in earnest. With one hand, she massaged his balls and the skin behind while she licked, probing the tiny slit at the top with her tongue. His fingers opened and closed on her head in silent encouragement. His loud purrs made her smile. She gripped his thighs harder and used pressure on them to encourage him to move.

Jonno massaged her scalp and pushed his hips forward, feeding her his cock. "Damn, that is good. Can you take more?"

Laura flicked her tongue over the head and relaxed her jaw, taking more. She licked the sensitive underside, forcing a groan from him. His musky flavor and scent filled her mouth and every inhalation, fire running through her body to come to rest at the apex of her thighs. The velvet flare of his cock grew damper, freely oozing pre-cum while she worked him. Moisture pooled between her own thighs, surprising her. Damn, his purrs and groans were hot. Jonno's soft, appreciative sounds grew louder. He flexed his hips and the muscles of his ass, his groan coming from deep in his chest. His cock pulsed and thickened, then after one final lick, he trembled, a harsh sound of animal enjoyment ripping from him.

"Laura," he groaned with a convulsive heave of his muscles. His cock pushed deep into her mouth and semen shot to the back of her throat. Gradually the spurts ended, and he seemed to come back to himself. He smiled at her, alight with approval and pride. "Thank you, Laura. That was incredible."

Laura eased back, unable to resist one final swipe of his softened cock before releasing him. Gripping his legs, she stood to kiss him. Their lips moved together in a lazy kiss of mutual pleasure.

"Tonight," he said, pulling away to grab his jeans. His eyes glowed with heat, sending silent messages to her with ease. Her body softened and tensed as she thought about what another night spent with Jonno might entail. Sex—yes, and it'd be hot. She already knew that. It was the underlying *other* that concerned her, the inherent promises that came along with repeat sex with the same male. Every instinct told her to run now, before it became too late, yet all she did was nod her head in agreement. What was with that? Why couldn't she say no to this man, even though she knew walking away might keep her out of trouble?

"We'd better head back to the house," Laura said. "I need to check out the owner of the driver's license. I'll say goodbye to Mr. Miller before I leave." She turned to pick up her bag. Jonno stayed her with fingers curling around her upper arm.

"Wait."

When she looked askance at him, he grinned. "There's evidence at the corner of your mouth."

Laura gave a horrified groan, hot color staining her cheeks. Damn, would she ever learn? Work and sex didn't mix—not at all. She stuck two fingers in her mouth to wet them and scrubbed at her face.

"Don't panic. Let me. I'd never embarrass you in company, which is why I told you." His humor faded, replaced by a maturity she hadn't seen in most men she dated. Jonno might be

97

young, but he did care and act with great responsibility. "Shush. Tilt your head for me."

Silently, she complied, sexual awareness thudding to life again at his first touch. His damp fingers swept across the corner of her mouth, pressing firmly. Back and forth three or four times. Laura lost count, drifting in the pleasure of his fresh scent and his nearness. The pulse at her throat hammered when the strokes of his fingers slowed. The rapidness of her breathing eased as well until she seemed to inhale in time with his strokes.

Magic. There must be magic involved, she thought. Damn, if she didn't want to purr.

His hand dropped away from her face and dazed, she stared up at him, his tawny hair and strong, determined face. Hot hazel eyes, full of passion and need. Her stomach turned in a slow somersault while they stared at each other, neither hiding their emotions in this unguarded moment.

Right then and there, Laura knew she'd been fooling herself. This man had burrowed into her heart, her soul, and there was no way on earth she'd stand him up tonight.

"One kiss before we go," he said, already dipping his head to claim her lips.

Laura stretched up on tiptoes to meet him. Soft pressure met with her lips before he drew her close, flattening her breasts against his hard chest. Laura clung, opening her mouth to let him explore while enjoying his attentions. Her fingers speared into his thick hair and their tongues tangled and twined together, tasting each other, the contrasting sensations of soft and smooth. Her heartbeat roared in her ears, and when they pulled apart, both were breathing fast. Jonno's cock thrust into her stomach and his smile appeared rueful when he grinned.

"I meant to keep it casual and friendly, but something about you pushes me hard." He kissed the tip of her nose before putting several feet between them. "You'd better head back to the house first while I sort out my control issues."

"Okay," Laura said, picking up her evidence bag.

"Laura?"

"Yeah?"

"You'd better remember to refasten your buttons. You're mine, and I don't want other men to see your breasts."

Laura muttered a succinct curse and buttoned her shirt. "Am I presentable now?" *She was not his.*

Amusement danced across Jonno's face and, after an intense inspection, he agreed. "Perfect."

With a curt nod, Laura set off toward the house, passing the vegetable gardens and closer to the house, the rose beds. Once she was out of sight of Jonno, she slowed to take a deep breath. Crazy. Away from him her mind functioned like a rational human being, yet one touch or look at him and she became a yes-girl, pliable and agreeing to everything he suggested.

Everything.

Hell, sucking him off here of all places. The big brass in Dunedin were right to ship her off to the country where she couldn't do any damage. Their words. Not hers.

Shaking her head, she forced her mind back to work, robberies and discovering more info on Max Abraham. Jonno Campbell was a very perplexing man—a distraction she didn't need.

Dinner with Emily and Saber Mitchell turned out much better than she'd expected. They made her welcome, and she enjoyed meeting the other Mitchell brothers and their wives. Jonno made no secret of the fact he was with her. She'd thought it would place pressure on her. Instead, for the first time in her life she felt part of the group. They accepted that she and Jonno were mates.

"How long have you been with the police force?" Isabella asked.

Laura glanced across the table at the blonde-haired woman. "I went to the police college in Wellington at twenty. They prefer the recruits to have work experience under their belts before they join the force."

"You're not joining the police force," Leo, Isabella's husband, said.

"Can I help it if I like to kick butt?" Isabella asked. "A few months ago I might have asked to help Laura at the police station and get work experience. Luckily, I now have stuff to do, but if I could aid you in any way, I'll fit it into my busy schedule." She winked at Leo. "I have a schedule."

Leo patted her hand. "You do."

Everyone turned to scrutinize Laura. "I'd love help with the burglaries taking place, except I doubt the top brass in Dunedin would agree to pay more wages," she said. "Or approve of civilian help."

"I'd work for free," Isabella said.

"Do you have experience?" Laura asked, trying not to let her doubt show.

Tomasine and Felix both sniggered, and even Leo couldn't contain his smirk.

Their amusement did nothing to ease the sinking sensation in Laura's stomach "Is something funny? Have I said something wrong?"

Saber glanced at Jonno, and Laura caught Jonno's imperceptible nod. Saber scanned her face before speaking. "Isabella is...was a trained assassin. I'd say she's very qualified to help you track our robbers."

"An assassin?" Laura asked in a faint voice, taking in Isabella and measuring her in light of the new knowledge. "You shoot people for money?" She had to be joking. *Of course she was*.

"Used to," Isabella said with a toss of her head. "I'm retired, but it took time to find something to fill my day. One can only have sex so much of the time."

"Tell that to Jonno," Laura muttered. How did Isabella manage to keep such a straight face?

The moment of stunned silence made her realize what she'd said. Laura didn't know where to look and settled for concentrating on her clasped hands.

Emily laughed and leaned over to pat her on the shoulder. "Don't worry. Isabella, Tomasine and I know what you're going through. Feline males can be very inconsiderate while in the grips of mating. They think they know everything."

"Not me," Saber said.

Emily coughed, unconsciously scrunching her brows together. "Think what you like, Saber. We females know what we know."

"One-track minds," Tomasine agreed.

"So," Isabella said, pinning her gaze on Laura. "Can I help with your investigation in an unofficial basis? I like a busy schedule."

"You won't shoot anyone?" Laura asked, deciding to play with the joke. Isabella couldn't go around taking the law into her own hands and butting into their investigation. Jonno was bad enough.

"Not unless they shoot at me first," Isabella promised. The twinkle in her eyes sort of counteracted the promise.

"You might as well give in and say yes," Leo said.

"Okay," Laura said, thinking that the Mitchell brothers were similar in appearance. According to Jonno, they were all shifters apart from her and Emily. She'd thought the fact would scare her. In reality having dinner with this group was like dining with friends. They laughed, they debated and argued, and the males and females ganged up on each other. For a few seconds she felt like an outsider peering through a window into a forbidden room, then Jonno took possession of her hand underneath the table. The warmth and security he communicated went a long way to easing her discomfit.

"Would anyone like coffee?" Emily asked.

"Not for us, thanks, Emily," Jonno said. "Laura and I need to get going."

Emily's brows rose. "Are you sure?"

"Yes," Jonno said without the slightest bit of embarrassment.

Laura glanced around the circle of Mitchell faces and saw that not one of them smirked. Interesting. It seemed they took this mating thing as seriously as Jonno.

Chapter 7

The Past Intrudes

T he trip from the Mitchells' house to Jonno's didn't take long. By the time they arrived, Laura's gut danced with knots of alarm and excitement. The longer she spent with him, the more her emotions seesawed.

The sharp rings of her satellite cell phone were a relief since it meant she could concentrate on something else. "Hello, Police Officer Adams speaking."

"Laura, why haven't you returned my messages?" Mike's husky voice rumbled down the line. Once she'd have thrilled to the sound of his voice. Now he irked her.

"I've been busy. How did you get this number?"

"I have contacts."

Huh! The very contacts who had torpedoed her career and left her taking the blame for Mike's indiscretions. She hadn't realized he was married. "I'll lose my job if our bosses discover we're in contact. Leave me alone." Laura hung up, her shoulders tense while she sent a wary glance at Jonno. She could see the glint of his eyes and the outline of his face, the rest of his expression shrouded in the darkness.

"Problem?" he asked, pulling up outside his house.

"Nothing I can't handle." Uneasiness crept through her again. Was she trading one man for another? One problem for another? Feline shifters were a mystery to her. Other than they seemed to mate for life, or so Jonno told her.

"Okay then. Are you having second thoughts about this?" His intense gaze seared her, even in the dimly lit vehicle.

"Yes." Uncertainty throbbed between them.

"Do you want me to take you home?" He stared at her, waiting for her decision.

Laura's heart pounded while she tried to think. She had to decide, and she had to stop with her indecisiveness regarding Jonno. It wasn't fair on either of them. Her next breath exited on a whoosh, and she admitted what she wanted to herself.

Jonno.

Despite every reason to the contrary, every bit of experience she'd garnered from her past relationship with Mike, she still wanted Jonno.

"I'm coming inside with you," she said on a rush. And later she'd second-guess the decision. Too bad. It was the one she intended to go with right now.

Jonno didn't reply. The glow from his eyes winked out and reappeared. She presumed he'd shut them briefly, although he didn't say a word, merely climbed from the car and walked around to her door.

Damn, he was such a gentleman. If he'd been an arrogant ass, she could have said no. She found the small things he did unconsciously so incredibly sexy, and they made her feel cherished. Dangerous, she thought as she stepped from Jonno's vehicle. Very treacherous and seductive.

Taking her arm, he led her to the front door, opened it and ushered her inside. The door slammed shut and Jonno prowled into her space, forcing her against the wall. Her hands slid behind his neck and their lips met in an urgent kiss. Hands struggled frantically with buttons and zippers as they tried to get to skin. A button pinged to the floor.

"Fuck, sorry."

Laura giggled and yanked up Jonno's shirt, burrowing her hands beneath. She aimed for his mouth, wanting another kiss and missed. Her lips brushed his jaw as he released the clasp of her bra. He lifted her shirt and grinned at her before lowering his head and taking one nipple into his mouth.

"Jonno." She gripped his head, enjoying the hard suction, the hint of pain. "Jeans off. Now." She kicked off her shoes as she issued the order.

He lifted his head and made short work of her jeans, shoving them down her legs while Laura attempted to remove his jeans. She managed the button and to slide down the zipper. Difficult to concentrate with him stroking along the leg of her panties.

A gasp escaped as he slipped his fingers beneath into her damp core.

"Damn, you're so wet."

"Only for you," she murmured, and it was true. No one else made her this hot so fast. "Jonno."

His fingers slid across her clit, telegraphing pleasure throughout her body. She shuddered, trying to get closer. Their lips met.

"The hell with this." Jonno dragged off her panties, tossed them and her jeans aside, and yanked down his jeans farther. His cock sprang free, and seconds later, he was inside her. They both groaned. Laura wound her legs around his waist and held on tight while he pumped into her with deliberate, long strokes.

"Jonno." She gasped, arching back and trusting him to hold her. Spasms took her despite her wanting to prolong the encounter.

"Damn. Laura." He buried his face into the crook of her neck, thrusting once before he climaxed with a hoarse groan. A fierce kiss seared her mouth. They both panted, trying to regain their breaths. She opened her mouth to him, stroking his tongue with hers and tasting him. Warmth drifted through her body as his hands caressed her hair and back. One masculine hand swept along her spine and came to rest on her butt, pressing her to his lower body again. His scent, a combination of his natural musk and soap, filled every breath. When Jonno lifted his head, his eyes did the same glowing thing she'd noticed previously.

"Should we take this to the bedroom?"

A bolt of lust hit her then, and she bit her bottom lip in consternation. "That was almost too quick."

He stroked the tangle of hair from her face. "Sorry."

"I wasn't complaining, although slow is good."

"Slow we can do." Jonno stripped off his footwear and removed the jeans pooled around his ankles along with his shirt.

Without turning on lights, Jonno led her to the bedroom and bent to switch on a bedside lamp. This time she paid more attention to the contents of the room. Like the rest of the house, the furniture appeared scarred and battered from constant use. A large chocolate-brown carpet square covered most of the wooden floor and the curtains were a suitable masculine green and brown, albeit faded. Whoever had chosen the bed linen had continued the color theme, using a chocolate-brown duvet cover and a lighter browny-beige color for the sheets.

"You're tidy," she observed.

"No one else to pick up after me. I like to know where to find things. Sly and Joe Mitchell keep things neat as well, so it was easy to share a place with them. Evidently Saber used to be a tyrant and made sure they kept their rooms tidy. They said he's more laid-back since meeting Emily."

"So that's what love does to a man," she murmured. "It mellows them."

"Not all men," Jonno said with a lopsided grin. He smoothed her shirt and sagging bra off her shoulders, leaving her naked. The intense concentration on his face brought a new surge of awareness. It was almost as if he touched her physically.

Laura shivered at the idea of his hands running over her bare skin. Instantly her nipples tightened, and she gave a soft laugh of embarrassment once she saw Jonno noticed. "You make me hot."

"You make me lose control. All I can think about is getting inside you, touching every part of you." He cupped her cheek and smoothed his thumb back and forth, warming her tender skin. A look of concentration in place, he outlined her mouth with one finger. They stared at each other, the atmosphere turning sultry and full of expectation, their lust a living, breathing thing.

Laura's heart gave three hard thumps before starting to race. She swallowed in a small show of nerves. This felt like a step away from casual, a step into serious. Glancing away, she shifted her body weight, still unsure if she was doing the right thing.

"Love touching you, the way you respond to me." Jonno moved his hands through her hair. It slid over her shoulders and he let out a sound of approval, smoothing the reddish-brown locks from her face and tucking them behind her ears. Then Jonno slid his hands over her shoulders and cupped her breasts.

Too intense. She moaned at the touch of his lips, lost in the pleasure of his mouth, the way his erection ground against her hip. Her teeth sank into her bottom lip as she struggled for control. They were casual lovers. Nothing more. "We worked on the case."

"How did you go with the background check on Max Abrahams?"

Laura coughed to clear her throat, glad of the topic change since it gave her something to concentrate on instead of how he made her feel. The acute temptation. "I meant to tell you earlier. Max Abrahams is twenty years old and his last known address was in Christchurch. His family hasn't seen him for four months and, according to them, they have no idea of his location."

Jonno traced the curves of her collarbone, dragging her attention back to him, to sex and the pleasure his touch engendered. "So he's homeless?"

"I don't know. Maybe. They gave Charlie a list of his known friends, and he's working his way through them. So far nothing unusual has jumped out."

"The license might be unconnected."

Laura considered and disregarded the thought. "Millers live on a quiet road. There's no need for tourists to travel down there since it's nowhere near the bike trail."

Jonno ran his finger along the upper curve of her breasts, eliciting a shiver, and her nipples drew hard. Her stomach clenched tight while she waited for his next move.

"Lift your arms for me."

She obeyed, and he blew a stream of warm air over her nipples.

"Beautiful," he said, and she could tell he meant it. In his eyes, she was beautiful. Mike had always complained her breasts were too small. Sometimes, she'd bought into his criticism while at other times she'd ignored him. Some of the tension inside her lessened and Laura determined to relax and enjoy the seduction. Because that was what it was—seduction, pure and simple.

His hands skimmed her body, lingering at her hips, and when he cupped her breasts, each breath came quicker and dampness bloomed between her legs.

When he continued to stare, she shifted her weight in a giveaway of her discomfit. "Stop staring at me."

"But you're gorgeous. I'm fond of your sleek curves and muscles. You must exercise."

"I used to run. I haven't had time since I've arrived in Middlemarch."

His hazel eyes gleamed with sudden mischief. "Ah, a frustrated feline at heart. That's good because I love to run. On your days off we can go to a secluded spot and run to our hearts' content."

Something told her he wasn't speaking of exercise. "I'll consider it," she said, not wanting to think about anything beyond the present. Besides, once she'd served here for a couple of years, she'd have a chance to return to Dunedin. If she kept her head down, she might even work toward detective.

"Turn around for me," Jonno instructed in a low voice, standing back to put several feet between them.

Without haste she turned, feeling the weight of his attention the entire time. Her skin heated and tingled, her breasts becoming tender and heavy. Prowling toward her, he dipped his head and licked across one creamy mound, pausing at her cleavage to inhale deeply. His tongue darted out to lick the light sweat on her skin and her fingers dived into his thick hair, holding him closer while he made sweet, agonizing circles with his tongue. Heat spread from each part his mouth touched and the heavy pressure of arousal sank to her pussy.

"You taste good," he said, trailing tiny kisses up to her collarbone. He licked the fleshy part where neck and shoulder met, in the same way he had the previous night, seeming to enjoy teasing her in this way. Her head tilted to allow him better access, and he purred. The bite of teeth tormented her, in a good way. She seemed to float through the air before the cotton at her back made Laura realize Jonno had lifted and placed her on the bed.

"Jonno, no more teasing," she murmured.

"What should I do?" He bit one nipple and she felt the rough, sensual play of his teeth. Instinctively, she arched her body, wanting more. Instead, he teased her with fingers and mouth, driving her crazy with need.

Finally she gasped. "I want you to fuck me." Blunt words.

On hearing them, he halted and lifted his head to stare at her. "You don't want me to make love to you?"

"Is there a difference?" A trace of bitterness came through in the unguarded moment.

Jonno frowned. "Fucking is something casual, something hard and fast for physical gratification. Making love is giving and receiving. It's an expression of feelings between a man and woman who care for each other. There is nothing casual about what I feel for you."

She'd disappointed him. It was easy to discern in his chiding words, his definition of making love. Laura half expected him to send her away, to tell her he didn't want her anymore because she'd disappointed him.

He didn't.

Instead, Jonno pressed a gentle kiss to her lips and smiled. "You look confused. I guess I'll have to show you."

Jonno fought to keep his emotions level, fought his feline and the change. Someone had done a number on Laura. Although she projected confidence with her job, in her personal life she was anything but self-assured. Gradually he'd learn the details of her past. He badly needed to show her how much he loved her. Yes, it was quick. They didn't know each other well. This was right though. He hoped he'd control the cat and not scare her because she didn't realize how deeply he cared for her. Not that he blamed her. As a human, she didn't understand the concept of fated mates.

It was up to him to show her.

Moving closer, he traced the faint blue veins visible on her breasts, watching her for each little reaction. Her body radiated tension. A challenge and one he'd win. He cupped a breast, noting the contrast in colors in her creamy skin and his tanned hand. His heart thundered, a low snarl building at the back of his throat. Jonno fought the instincts his feline bombarded him with, determined to show her the difference between mere sex and love.

"Do you like it when I touch and kiss your breasts?"

"Yes." Her blue eyes were wide with apprehension.

"And if I pinch your nipples? Do you enjoy that?"

"Very much."

At least she'd decided on honesty with her responses. Ignoring the heaviness and throbbing at his groin, he set out to seduce her to his way of thinking. He measured her breasts in his hands, stroking and kissing as he learned their shape and what she liked best. At first he ignored her taut nipples, since he already knew how sensitive they were and how much she enjoyed the slight bite of pain. With delicate precision, he teased and explored, stoking the sensations one on top of the other until she cried out, murmuring her enjoyment and gripping his arms in a quiet show of urgency. Her responsive body wanted him, her musky arousal driving him to action.

"Jonno," she pleaded. "Please suck my nipples again. Please. You're driving me crazy."

Smiling, he licked one finger and circled her nipple, repeating the same move on the other one. He followed this with the glide of his tongue, duplicating the journey, making the pleasurable trail damp enough that she'd feel the contrast between warm and moist. "Do you like that?"

"Yes," she hissed, arching eagerly against his body to hurry things along.

"Patience."

"But I want you right now."

Pleased with her open and eager responses, he decided it was time to ramp up the action since the slow exploration demanded a price from him too. Moving his head a fraction, he took one nipple into his mouth, sucking hard while he pinched the other. She cried out, a dark sound of pleasure and gripped his head tight.

"Yes, perfect," she said in encouragement. "The one thing that might feel better is if your cock filled my pussy and you stroked my clit." Her words brought a shiver, and his cock gave an involuntary jerk.

Urgent hunger fueled the feline's demands, molten fire ripping through him. Jonno lifted his head to study her while he continued to pluck and pinch her nipple. It turned a deep rose color. Beautiful. Jonno moved down her body, stroking her calves and feet, silently encouraging her to spread her legs. With his mouth he teased the insides of her knees. Sliding higher, he kissed the tender skin of her inner thighs.

"Please don't tease me anymore."

"Ah, but you don't need me enough yet. You're not desperate."

Laura's hands fisted in his hair and her breath whooshed out in frustration. "I am ready, so ready you wouldn't believe it. Touch me. Touch me and tell me I'm not ready."

Amusement filled him at her impatience. "Soon. Very soon," he promised, allowing his fingers to wander close to her moist folds, smiling when she shivered. "You're right. You want me. So wet."

"*Touch me.*"

He contemplated making her wait, stringing out the pleasure for even longer before deciding he'd never last the distance. With that in mind, he stroked her cleft, skillfully teasing her swollen flesh. When his finger grazed her clit, her entire body jerked. Jonno repeated the move in reverse, trailing his finger over her swollen nub and down to her entrance. This time he pushed a finger inside. Instantly her warmth and tight flesh surrounded his finger, making him think of the pleasure to come and the snug feel of her sheath pulsing around his cock.

"Does that feel good?" As he spoke, he pushed a second finger inside her, pumping in and out while a thumb teased her clit.

"You know it feels good." Laura fingered one nipple and teased herself. Her body arced as she strove for climax, her eyes fluttering closed.

"Turn over for me." He pulled his fingers from her body.

"Why?" Her blue eyes flew open to stare at him in puzzlement.

"I want to give all parts of you equal attention."

"You don't need to."

"Turn over." This time his voice held a tinge of insistence.

Laura frowned at him but obeyed, rolling over and arranging her head on her hands.

Jonno's breath exited on an appreciative sigh. Her hair hid one shoulder, leaving the marking spot visible. A shiver racked his body, longing thumping him in the gut.

Soon, he told himself. Soon.

Determinedly, he concentrated on her back. Slim and feminine. Her buttocks, smooth and sexy tempted him next. The tiny quiver that shimmied through her body made him smile. She sensed his close attention, and it pleased her. He leaned over and placed a kiss in the middle of one creamy cheek. Laura jumped, and when he licked then nipped her, she turned with a reproachful glare.

"What? You didn't enjoy that?"

"Remind me to bite your butt, and we'll see how you like it."

"Bite me?" He chuckled in real amusement, the rich sound increasing as she rolled her expressive eyes at him. "You can bite me any time you want."

"Huh." Ignoring him, she turned her face away.

Still smirking, Jonno parted her legs, revealing the swollen pink folds of her sex. Glossy juices coated her, and the sudden stillness of her body told of her investment. He'd bet if he listened he'd hear an elevated pulse, and when he touched her she'd cream for him even more. To test his theory, he leaned closer and blew, directing the stream of air along her slit.

After repeating the move twice, Jonno gave in to the need to pet. He ran his hand down her back in a firm sweep, enjoying the warm, smooth flesh beneath his palm. His hand came to rest on her buttocks.

Laura wriggled, reminding him of a kitten or a puppy eager for affection. A wave of satisfaction filled him. She wanted love and tenderness, instinctively sought it from him even though she denied it. He stroked the firm globes, parting them to tease her perineum and the sensitive nerves at her puckered entrance.

"Jonno, what are you doing?" She sounded curious rather than alarmed.

"I promise I won't do anything to hurt you." Back and forth his finger stroked until Laura relaxed again. "If I do, it will be unintentional and all you need to do is tell me. I'll stop. Okay?"

"Okay," she whispered, and he continued with his furtive seduction.

He grabbed a couple of pillows and placed them beneath her so her body was raised and more accessible. Her soft sigh brought pleasure for him. She might have difficulty trusting his words, yet she enjoyed his care and attentions. He made himself a promise never to abuse her trust because he realized how much it meant to him. Not that he would anyway. He believed in truth between a couple.

Leaning closer, Jonno lapped delicately at her juices, smoothing them upward toward her anus.

"Jonno."

"Shush, relax. Let me make you feel good."

With a finger, he smoothed the juices over her rosette. Usually, he'd use lube, but since he intended only a little play and the merest introduction of his finger, he thought this would be enough today. He lapped downward toward her clit, giving her the merest pressure while he continued to stroke and finger the nerve endings of her rosette. Soon she parted her legs farther, straining upward and giving him easier access to her clit. He lapped around it, loving the taste of her and her fragrant scent, so feminine and decadent. Gradually he pushed the tip of his finger past the puckered ring. She gasped, tensing.

"You okay, Laura?"

"Yes." She didn't sound too certain, so he let his finger rest where it was and lapped at her swollen nub, letting the pleasure build. Gradually she relaxed, and he gave her more of his finger while continuing to rasp his tongue over and around her clit.

"Jonno," she wailed. "More. You're driving me crazy. I've never...I need...more."

He gave her more, pushing her harder, feasting on her flesh while moving the tip of his finger in and out of her rear entrance. She shuddered and shook, her body straining for release. It was thrilling, both watching and being the one to give her pleasure. She thrashed a little, groaning and muttering his name. *His name.* That pleased him.

Jonno moved fast then, deciding he'd rather fill her with his cock than his fingers. He pulled free of her trembling body to yank open a drawer and grab a condom. With shaky fingers he rolled the latex onto his weeping cock and moved behind her. One seamless stroke was all it took. Balls-deep in her, he savored the silken heat surrounding him.

"Laura, you feel so damn good, so hot and tight."

"Please move."

"I need that too, before my cock bursts," he muttered, rueful at the thought of how his teasing had backfired to net him. He pulled back, pressing her spine against his chest and stroking as smoothly as he could given the urgency throbbing through his veins. His thrusts grew harder. Faster. Soon they both gasped. Jonno's feline rose to the surface, urging him to lean over, to bite the smooth skin of Laura's shoulder. Giving in to temptation, he slid his lips across the creamy flesh, deepening the caress by giving her the sting of teeth. Her entire body jerked.

"Jonno," she screeched, surprising him with the shout.

Her pussy clenched and squeezed his cock sweetly. He slammed into her. Once. Twice. His semen seemed to bubble inside his tight balls, the prickle of pleasure growing intense and painful. His loud shout filled the room. Then, one final hard, deep stroke pushed him over the edge and he jumped into climax with Laura's pussy still compressing around his hard length.

Once his heartbeat slowed, Jonno pressed a kiss to her shoulder and separated their bodies. He removed the condom and wandered from the bedroom to the bathroom to wash his hands before grabbing a warm cloth for Laura. Part of lovemaking involved taking care of his mate, and he intended to show her he was capable of both pleasure and nurturing.

When he returned to his bedroom, Laura had turned away and lay on her side. He knelt beside her, chucking the pillows they'd used back to the head of the bed.

"Part your legs for me, Laura."

Without lifting her lashes, she obeyed, rolling to her back. He stroked the warm cloth over her sex while he studied her face. It was an oval shape, bearing a soft flush at the moment. Her dark lashes swept across her cheekbones while her straight nose turned up a fraction at the end. He loved her mouth with its full lips and the determined chin. It looked so pretty as she glared at him, her eyes flashing and color high, her straight hair spread out in a red-tinged halo.

Oh yeah. His lover. His mate.

Jonno returned the cloth to the bathroom and went to join his mate in bed. He tugged back the sheets and lifted her underneath before covering her and joining her in the bed. He fell asleep with a smile on his face and Laura tucked securely in his arms.

Chapter 8

Another Robbery

"There was another robbery last night," Charlie said as soon as she walked into the coffee-scented police station. Jonno had dropped her off at home before returning to the farm to help muster cattle for drenching. She wouldn't see him until later this evening.

"Damn, I shouldn't have taken the night off," Laura said, her stomach roiling because she'd failed at her job. "We should have staked out the houses or at least driven around to show our presence. Where was it?"

"The Peterson property, right at the other end of Middlemarch." Charlie scowled. "I drove around a couple of times and saw nothing out of the ordinary."

"Jonno and I drove through town on the way back to his place. We didn't meet a single car."

"Things are serious between you and Jonno." Charlie stood to refill his coffee mug.

Laura snapped her head around, scrutinizing him to discern his meaning. His ruggedly handsome face, the pale blue eyes didn't tell her a thing. "We haven't known each other for long."

"There's no need to act defensive. Jonno seems like a great guy. We talked yesterday while he was waiting for you."

She still wasn't sure what he meant and decided to shift the discussion. "We need a plan." Laura grabbed a mug and poured herself a cup of coffee before returning to her desk. After taking a sip she wrinkled her nose. The coffee at the café...heaps better. No wonder they spent so much time and money there. "Any suggestions?"

"You asking me?" Charlie's left brow quirked and a playful smile lingered on his lips.

"We're a team. Of course I'm asking you." A week ago she'd have informed him what to do, quoting seniority as her reason. Gut instinct and Charlie's reaction told her this new way would work better. Confusion filled her. In a short time she'd changed, and she didn't understand the urge to do things differently.

The door to the police station opened and Isabella Mitchell prowled inside. "Reporting for duty," she chirped. "Oh good. You have coffee. Leo—" She broke off when she noticed Charlie gaping at her. "Probably goes in the too-much-information category," she said.

"Isabella has experience in law enforcement," Laura said, choosing her words. She'd heard rumors of the cops they'd replaced. Isabella might help gain the trust of those locals still bearing suspicions of the new police officers. The goodwill would help everyone. "She offered to fit us into her busy schedule. I'll get you a coffee."

Charlie stared at Isabella before shifting his focus to her. "Is this official?"

"No," Laura said. A huge mistake. Too bad since she'd done it now. "Let's call her an independent expert, should anyone ask. You cool with that?"

"No problem," Charlie said. "Middlemarch and the surrounding areas are too big for the two of us to handle. We need help."

"One of us had better visit the Petersons," Laura said. "There was another burglary last night," she added to Isabella, handing her a mug of coffee.

"You know what you need to do is set a trap." Isabella sipped her coffee, pulled a face and walked over to the coffeemaker where she spooned two sugars into her mug. The energetic stir of the teaspoon rattled against the thick china. "At the moment the best we can do is employ a needle-in-a-haystack method and hope we get it right. What if we spread rumors that Saber purchased Emily a valuable necklace? Between all of us we could cover one house and wait for them to come to us." The metallic clack sounded as Isabella finished with the spoon and set it aside, highlighting the sudden hush in the police station.

"That's a great idea," Charlie said. "What do you think, Laura?"

A frown creased Laura's forehead as she measured the pros and cons of a sting. It would help their investigation if they only had to focus on one place. "What about the danger? No one is hurt yet, though it's a matter of time. Will Saber and Emily be willing to help?"

Isabella's joyous laugh rang out, bringing a smile to Laura despite her inner concern. "You've met Emily. What do you think?"

Laura reflected on Jonno's protective nature and just knew Saber would feel the same way with Emily. They were actual mates, according to Jonno, so they'd have an intense bond. "Saber might take more convincing."

"Possibly. It's still a good idea," Isabella said. "Do you want me to ask him?"

Laura shook her head. "No, I'll do it."

"I'll drive out to the Petersons now. Mrs. Peterson sounded hysterical and her instructions fell into the garbled category. If I don't return, you'll know I'm lost," Charlie said.

"I can go with you. It might be a good idea for me to go because Mr. Peterson is strange." Isabella glanced at Laura, her eyes saying way more than her words. She meant her shifter abilities might turn up something Charlie missed.

"Is that okay with you, Charlie?"

He shrugged, although expectation shone in his eyes, as if he anticipated excitement. "Sure."

"Just don't hit on me," Isabella warned. "I'm a happily married woman and my husband is big."

Charlie chuckled and snapped his fingers. "Damn, the good ones are taken."

"I'm going to continue checking with the surrounding police stations and see if there were any new robberies last night. Hopefully I'll be able to follow up on this Max Abrahams and his known associates. I'll check with Saber to see what he thinks of Isabella's idea."

Charlie and Isabella left and Laura rang around the other police stations. An hour later she knew the thieves had struck only in Middlemarch the previous evening and so far they seemed to have worked from Queenstown, hitting properties in the tourist city before moving closer to Dunedin. If the thieves continued to schedule, they'd hang around Middlemarch for a couple more days before moving to Mosgiel, Milton or maybe Lawrence, which seemed to have escaped their notice.

Charlie and Isabella arrived back at the station while Laura was running down leads on Max Abraham.

"Hey, Charlie. How did it go at the Petersons?"

Isabella wandered over to her desk and perched her butt on the corner. "The thieves got a pair of diamond earrings and a matching ring. Mrs. Peterson is distraught. They gave us photos of the missing jewelry. She said as soon as Gerard and Henry return to Middlemarch, she's ordering an alarm."

Charlie dropped into the black office chair behind his desk. "The thieves entered via a window."

The phone rang and Charlie answered it. While the call occupied him, Isabella leaned closer. "Some of your thieves were shapeshifters. I didn't recognize their scents, which means they're not local."

"Did you see any footprints?" Laura had told the Mitchells about the footprints the previous evening before conversation turned more general, the subject of the burglaries put aside.

"No. They must have been careless at the Millers."

"I'll ring Saber to ask if I can visit him," Laura said.

"Why don't you ask if he can meet us for lunch at Storm in a Teacup? That way we can eat and Emily will help talk Saber around. You might need her help."

"Noted." Laura's satellite phone rang.

"I'll go and see Emily and prep her before you call Saber," Isabella said.

"Thanks." Laura picked up her phone. "Hello."

"Laura, I miss you. Come back to Dunedin."

"I told you not to ring me. I'm busy and I need to keep this line open." She disconnected before Mike could reply, distaste sitting uneasy in the pit of her stomach.

"Problem?" Isabella had paused at the door, and Laura suspected the woman's feline hearing had enabled her to catch the conversation, not just her side.

"Not at all. I'll see you later." Not quite the truth. Mike's persistence was a predicament, especially since he'd acted the bastard in Dunedin, throwing her into the thick of the mess and stepping aside so he didn't dirty his shoes. She wasn't stupid enough to go through the same experience again. Besides, now Jonno interested her...

In a thoughtful mood, she dialed Saber and waited for him to reply. Keeping in mind Isabella's advice, she asked if they could meet at the café to discuss developments. Once Saber agreed to the meeting, she returned to researching Max Abraham and his friends.

Charlie finished his call. "What do you think about involving the Mitchells? I thought you'd go more by the rules."

"I don't like it, not that we have much choice. They've already involved themselves." Laura picked up her pen and thumped it three times on the top of her desk. Her brow furrowed while she studied Charlie. "What do you think?"

"I think it's a great idea, although the head brass won't approve. I think we should set up the sting."

Laura struck the edge of the desk with her pen again. "I agree." *Tap. Tap. Tap.*

Charlie stood and walked over to her desk. He grabbed the pen mid-tap. "That is irritating."

"Sorry. Let's do it. If it works, everyone will be happy."

"And if it fails?"

"Let's just hope everything goes right, and no one gets hurt. Everything depends on Saber Mitchell. If he doesn't agree, we'll think of another strategy."

Charlie returned to his desk and settled into his chair with a soft sigh. He leaned back, making the chair creak. "The window of opportunity isn't big. We don't know how long the thieves are planning on staying in this area before they move to another town."

"True." Laura glanced at her watch. "I'd better go. Do you want me to bring you back anything for lunch?"

"Surprise me," Charlie said.

"You'd better hope I don't come back with a bean sprout sandwich." Laura grabbed her phone and wallet and left for the café.

By the end of the day, with Saber Mitchell's full approval, she and Charlie had a plan in place. Now they needed to dangle the bait and wait for the trap to spring.

Jonno paused in the doorway of the police station, taking pleasure in watching Laura work. She hadn't noticed him yet. The last rays of the sun reflected through the window, bringing fire to life in her hair. It glowed fiery red for an instant before the sun disappeared below the line of the trees. "How's my girl?"

Laura started, lurching back in her chair while nailing him with an accusing glower. "Don't stalk me."

"Darlin', it's my nature to stalk. Don't you know half the fun is the thrill of the chase?"

"Huh! I'm not sure I like the implications."

"Are you ready to leave? I'd kiss you hello, but I need a shower. It's been a busy day."

"I wondered about the smell," Charlie said, entering the main office from the rear storeroom and delicately sniffing.

His feline took offense. Jonno growled low and deep in his throat, stopping Charlie in his tracks. Jonno wanted to laugh at the incredulous widening of the cop's eyes, his wary stance and quick glance at Laura.

"Jonno," Laura chided, but he heard the silent laughter in her voice and couldn't restrain a snicker.

"Sorry."

"Cool party trick," Charlie said.

Jonno noticed he detoured and kept a desk between them.

"Yeah, I'm ready to go," Laura said. "Why don't you head home too, Charlie? I'll switch the phones over to my mobile. We'll be working late tomorrow. Probably for the next few days." She stood and flicked the switch on the phones.

Jonno held the door open for her, taking pleasure in the small service. With the sun gone, darkness approached. In silence they walked to his vehicle. Jonno seated her in the passenger side before jogging around to climb behind the wheel.

"Charlie's right. You are a bit ripe."

"We'll get you out on the farm and see how you smell after a day's work." Jonno switched on the headlights, started his vehicle and pulled away from the curb. "So how was your day? Any luck locating the thieves?"

"Nothing much to speak of, although we have a workable plan now. We're setting a trap, spreading the word that Saber is purchasing Emily a new diamond-and-sapphire ring." Laura grinned at him. "Emily cracked me up. She said she preferred colored stones, but she could live with a diamond on the ring, if that was what Saber decided."

"He's buying her a ring?"

"It sounded like it. I've never seen a couple so suited to each other."

He and Laura were perfect for each other. Early days for Laura to admit it yet. "Good plan. Who came up with it?"

"Isabella suggested the idea."

Jonno nodded, driving along the main street of Middlemarch, past the grocery store, the post office and the petrol station. Vehicles lined the road near the primary school. "There must be something on at the school."

"A parent-teacher's evening, according to Emily. Tomasine and Felix are going."

"I noticed a few strangers wandering around the town when I drove down the main street. More than usual."

"Yeah, Emily said there were a lot of people doing the rail trail this week. She seems to know everything happening in Middlemarch."

"I know. She's made it her home. The locals love Emily." *The ones who weren't idiots, at any rate.*

Jonno left the small township behind, turning onto a country road. A car approached, its headlights on full. "Wish they'd dip their damn lights."

"Do you recognize the car?"

"No. I haven't been in Middlemarch much longer than you. Prior to that I've spent the odd weekend. That's all. Damn, I couldn't see the license plate. Did you get it?"

"No, too much glare. Besides, they're not doing anything illegal or suspicious, apart from not dipping their headlights."

"True. I don't want to think of thieves tonight. I presume you need to work on your plan and spread the word via the local gossip line before we stake out Saber's house."

"Yeah. Emily and Saber are heading to Queenstown tomorrow morning and returning with a flashy ring."

"A real one?"

Laura chuckled. "No, Emily has a friend in Queenstown who makes costume jewelry as a sideline. She says it appears real enough to fool most people. Meantime Isabella and Tomasine will spread the news to the locals who visit the café. Emily says Storm in a Teacup is always full of tourists and locals. It's an excellent plan."

Jonno pulled onto his driveway and parked.

"Emily and Saber will go out for the evening and hopefully the thieves will strike. Emily is going to say she needs to cater for a special function coming up the following week."

"Wouldn't Emily take the ring with her since it's new? Most women show off their bling." Jonno unclipped his seat belt, glancing across at his woman. God, he loved watching her, knowing she belonged to him. It was almost as good as touching her skin, wringing responses from her—shivers, moans and hot, wet arousal.

"We discussed that. We decided Emily wouldn't want to wear the ring while working in the café, and if anyone asked, she'd say she intended to wear it for special occasions. Since she's working at the café, hopefully the thieves will assume the ring is in the house."

"Not a bad plan." Jonno enjoyed the enthusiastic sparkle in her blue eyes, the passionate need in her to catch the thieves. "But right now I need a shower. Wanna shower with me and help scrub my back?"

"You are stinky." She wrinkled her nose.

Carefree humor bubbled up inside Jonno. "Better watch what you say. I might take offense."

Laura cocked her head, a teasing glint he hadn't seen before lighting her features. "And do what?"

"I don't think you'll approve. I'd lock you inside my bedroom and not let you come out again for a month."

She opened the vehicle door and climbed out. "I should have asked you to stop by my place so I could pick up clean clothes."

"No problem. I'll drop you there tomorrow morning before I start work on the drenching."

"Are you going to stink again tomorrow night?"

"You'll have to get used to it."

They walked inside together, both removing their footwear at the door.

Jonno's stomach let out an earthquake-sized rumble. "Shower first," he said, despite the empty sensation in his belly. There was one other appetite he intended to fuel first. Grasping Laura's arm, he marched down the passage to the bathroom. Laughingly she protested, digging in her heels, to no avail.

"Noooo!" she wailed, giggling and struggling at the same time.

With one hand, he turned on the shower, using the other to restrain Laura's thrashing. He pushed her under the stream of warm water and held her struggling body until she was sodden.

"Jonno, I don't have clothes to wear tomorrow morning." Ire replaced the former humor, and she pushed past him, tracking water over the gray tiles on the bathroom floor.

"Hey," he said, catching her hand and holding her fast when she would have ripped away from his grasp. "I said I'd take you to your place tomorrow morning to get more clothes. Why don't you move in with me? You're spending a lot of time here already. It would be easier for both of us and will give Charlie the run of the police house."

"I've known you for a few days. I'm not moving in and openly living with you. How's it gonna look to my employers? These things have a way of getting back."

"They can't run your life. I'm sure they've had unmarried employees living together before."

"Ah, but they don't have my reputation. Do you know what they were calling me? The black widow spider. Word is I eat my prey."

Huh? Jonno studied her indignant face, the storm in her eyes and the set mouth. She believed what she was saying, that moving in with him could harm her reputation.

"I don't give a fuck what people say. You're my mate. It's what we think that's important. Black widow? Why do they call you that? You don't kill people."

"No, of course I don't kill people. They call me Black Widow because I seem to break up couples. I never set out to do it." Laura's shoulders slumped, and she stopped trying to pull away from him. "The nature of police work means we hang out with each other, go out for a few drinks after work. Outsiders don't understand the close bonds we have. I got myself entangled in a couple of romances where the cop dumped his girlfriend for me. I...heck...I didn't even know these guys were with long-term partners. I was new to the force and when they told me they were single I believed them. You'd think I'd learn. The romances ran their course, and we remained friends. The last time I hooked up with Mike. I fell for him hard, and he spent lots of nights at my apartment."

Jealousy gnawed at his gut and a rumble in his throat warned Laura of his agitation.

"See, even you're judging me." She tried to turn away. Jonno grasped her upper arm, using brute strength to hold her in place, facing him.

"I'm not judging you. I know you're with me now. Hell, we both have pasts. They're the force that's shaped us, made us into better people. The past has prepared us for each other."

Laura snorted. "We're sleeping together, nothing more."

Instinctive words of denial tickled the tip of his tongue. He bit them back. Not the right time. "Let me help you out of these wet clothes." Jonno unfastened the first two buttons of her shirt before she batted his hands away.

"I can undress myself."

"Tell me about Mike. What happened?"

At first he thought she'd refuse. Her fingers slowed, and she glanced up, ducking her head when she noticed him watching her. When she slid the next button from its hole, her fingers trembled.

"Laura?"

"Mike is married. I truly didn't know. I believed him when he said he was divorced, and because of my earlier relationships, I wanted to keep my new romance to myself. At work we spent little time together. Outside of work we saw each other a lot. Mike moved into my apartment."

Jonno frowned, trying to picture the situation and not judge. Laura wasn't stupid. Surely there must have been signs. "When did he see his wife?"

"He's a detective, and I understood when he said he was working a case. It turned out he told both of us the same story. Sometimes he had to work, but he'd arrange his schedule to fit in both of us."

"How did you find out?"

"His wife turned up at the station one day. She didn't know until she saw charges for two Valentine's Day gifts on the credit card, and she received one. And that should have been it." Laura shivered, and Jonno closed the distance between them. He skimmed her damp panties down her legs and helped her balance while she stepped out of them. A twist of his wrist unclipped her bra, and he smoothed it off her arms. With a gentle push, he directed her beneath the warm water. He stripped and joined her in the shower, shutting the glass door to enclose them in privacy.

"What happened?"

"She's related to the police commissioner, and I got shunted sideways to Middlemarch, my hopes for promotion to detective shafted."

Jonno reached for the soap and ran it over his chest, arms and legs to help remove some of the stench of work. The brisk scrub of a washcloth helped him complete the job before he settled in to enjoy the novelty of Laura in his shower.

"If you hadn't come to Middlemarch, you'd never have met me."

The mulish set of her mouth gave away her opinion. "I've dreamed of being a police detective since I was a teenager. It's all I ever wanted, why I joined the police force in the first place."

"What about a transfer to another city? Wellington or Auckland."

Jonno picked up the soap again and ran sudsy hands over her shoulders and breasts, pinching a nipple in the exact manner he knew she liked.

"I could, but I enjoy Dunedin. My friends are there, my family, even though we're not close."

"I like Dunedin," Jonno said, nibbling along the cords of her neck. "Have I told you I used to share a house with Sly and Joe Mitchell?" Somehow he had to get her to see Middlemarch wasn't so bad. It wasn't a sideways step. Maybe he should discuss Laura with Saber because a connection on the local police force might make things easier for the feline community. Often the felines had to handle things themselves rather than involve the police. Laura could help with that, and it might make her feel more at home, more involved and part of the town. Perhaps it wouldn't be so hard to get her to stay.

Laura cocked her head, allowing his lips better access to her neck. "Yeah, you've told me. Are they the same as Saber and his other brothers?"

"They're younger, more impish versions of Saber. Saber had to grow up fast and raise his younger brothers when their uncle died. You'll like Joe and Sly." Not that he intended to introduce them to Laura until he'd put his mark on her. "Enough about the Mitchells and the burglaries. This Mike, is he the same one ringing you all the time?"

"Yes. I wish he'd leave me alone."

"You could always give the phone to me next time he rings. Or Charlie if I'm not available. We could tell him to piss off, and if you have problems later, we'd be your alibis."

Laura closed her eyes, her mouth compressing to a flat line of irritation. "Mike's wife is vindictive. I didn't know he was married, and once I did, I tried to break it off. He kept bothering me. His wife kept hassling me until I left. Thankfully, that seems to have stopped."

"So you'll let Charlie and me handle him if he rings again?" Although he didn't know Charlie well, he instinctively liked him, his dry sense of humor. From what he'd seen, Charlie was a decent bloke. Contacts on the local police force never hurt.

Laura slipped her arms around his neck, pressing close so the water pooled between their bodies and made a funny sound. "Thank you."

"There's no need to thank me. I care for you."

"Jonno, you can't care for me yet. What we have now qualifies as friendship, that's all."

The feline within loosed a possessive growl, incensed at her insistence on calling their relationship casual. There was nothing casual about it. Despite his inner turmoil, he kept his thoughts hidden, not wanting to create friction.

"I'm a grown male. I know my mind." He swept his hands over her back, letting them come to rest on her butt. He squeezed, lifting her to rub against his groin, groaning under his breath. "Damn that feels good. I don't wanna talk anymore. Let's make love." Suiting actions to words, he ducked his head to capture her lips with his. A punch of heat swept through him, heading straight for his balls. So damn good. Every time. He traced his tongue along the seam of her lips, swallowing her quiet sigh of surrender and pushing for entry to the interior of her mouth. Their tongues stroked in a seductive rhythm, and when he lifted her, pressing her body against the cool wall of the shower, she acquiesced eagerly, parting her legs to allow him closer.

"I've never fucked in a shower." A very non-cop twinkle appeared in her eyes.

"Best we extend your education then." With easy strength, he lined up his cock and pushed inside, her welcoming flesh parting easily, aiding his invasion. Balls-deep, he paused when all he wanted to do was pump into her with frenzied and choppy strokes, grasping his pleasure with both hands. Instead he forced himself to thrust with leisurely strokes, pushing inside halfway, teasing them both, taking care to drive her pleasure to great heights where she soared. He surged into her and retreated, building passion, building heat. Making love to her, determined to show her by his actions the difference between simple fucking to climax and love between mates.

"Laura," he whispered, the sound not much more than a fevered groan. "I love the way your pussy feels. Hot."

"Just for you."

"Mine, huh?" Teasing both of them, he pushed inside her hot sheath and stroked his tongue into her mouth at the same unhurried pace.

"Oh yeah." Her fingernails cut into his shoulders as she ground against him. "You're so good at this. You make me so hot."

The passion soared with each stroke into her molten pussy. The iron control he held over his feline eased and urgency gripped him. Jonno trembled, his face tightening into a grimace.

"Laura." He buried his face in the crook of her neck, teeth biting before he even realized what he was doing.

Her shout of pleasure and the tight clasp of her pussy, dragged him back, made him realize the possible consequences. Hurriedly he lifted his head, the close call sobering him. Damn. It wasn't right to mark her this soon. She didn't understand now, but soon. He'd mark her, and she'd understand they were a couple, a mated pair.

Gritting his teeth, he pressed her into the shower wall and increased his stroke rate. He dipped his head and took her mouth in a dominating kiss, something to appease his snarling feline. His cock swelled, becoming increasingly sensitive. His balls ached, drawing up high and tight while he plundered her mouth. Fire lashed him, burning bright and consuming, each time he buried himself in her wet core. Then orgasm approached, crashing in on him. He pistoned his hips, thrashing into her with hard and choppy strokes. The flames licked along his cock and his body convulsed with the force of his release, satisfaction releasing in a rough growl.

Once Jonno came back to himself, he realized Laura was pushing at his shoulders. "The water's gone cold."

And it had. He hadn't realized, so caught up in the sensations and coming apart in her arms. With a last bruising kiss, he separated their bodies and let her fall against him.

He soaped his hands and slipped them between her legs. Laughing, she tried to bat them away.

"Let me," he said as she squirmed. "I love touching you." He stroked her folds, washing away the evidence of their lovemaking. "Your scent is addictive and the way you respond to me...I like you so much I'm willing to do this over again. We'll try the bed this time."

"I'm clean," Laura said, batting at his hands again. The laughter in her voice reassured him, told him she was just as enthralled with the relationship. Time would improve things between them.

Jonno straightened and gave her a slap on the arse, smirking as she squeaked. "Out you go. Dry off and wait for me in the bedroom."

After a long beat, she lifted her right hand in a snappy salute. "Yes sir."

The door rattled when it opened and closed. Jonno stuck his face under the blast of the shower and grabbed for the shampoo bottle. With deft moves, he washed his hair. It was at that moment he realized they hadn't used a condom.

Chapter 9

Call Out

J onno stalked into the bedroom, water still dripping off his nude body. "We didn't use a condom. We missed using one the first time last night as well."

"No problem. I'm on the Pill, remember? Don't you think you should get a towel? You're dripping everywhere."

"Shit." Jonno swiped a hand over his face and strode from the room, returning seconds later with a towel. With brisk rubs, he toweled dry. "Does it make me a bastard that I was glad we didn't use a condom? I forgot you're on the Pill. All I could think of was your belly swelling with my child." His voice cracked with emotion. "I liked the idea. Very much."

They stared at each other for a tension-filled moment.

The picture he described filled her mind with a clear visual. She saw them together, instinctively knowing Jonno would love being a father and be a good one. For the first time in her life the idea of marriage and a family didn't send her running in the opposite direction. She liked the idea. When had she changed?

"I...okay," she whispered.

"Okay, what?" He'd stilled, face tight with concentration, but she thought she caught a flicker of longing.

"Um, I'm saying maybe we have more than a casual friendship."

The flash of his smile reminded her of a bright and vivid spring flower after a long winter. "Good."

"Is that all you're going to say?"

"For the moment. You already know what I want. I don't want to scare you any more than necessary."

His words were a revelation for Laura because his honesty shone from his gaze and stamped his features. Nice. Especially after the fiasco with Mike.

Jonno stalked toward the bed where she sat, his attention on her. The intent glint in his hazel eyes brought a quick protest.

"Oh no you don't. I need food—sustenance—before we go another round in this bed."

He paused and dipped his head in a quick nod. "All right. Can we go without condoms from now? Felines can't contract sexually transmitted diseases from humans."

Laura took what she'd learned about him and didn't have a single qualm. She believed him. "It's fine by me."

"Good. I'm hungry. Do you want a sandwich?"

"Hell yes. I'm starved." The loud rumble of Laura's stomach punctuated her words.

The insistent peal of her phone interrupted their dinner foraging.

Laura's mouth squeezed into a moue of disappointment. "I hope that's not anything serious." After retrieving the phone from the bedroom, she stabbed the on button.

"Police Officer Adams speaking."

"Laura, I have to see you."

She stiffened, her shoulders twitching in irritation. "I can't talk to you now, Mike. Too busy."

"I'm going crazy not seeing you, touching you."

A low growl was all the warning she had before Jonno plucked the phone from her hands.

"Laura is busy. She's not interested in you. Don't call again." Jonno hung up on Mike, turning to her with a grim expression.

"Don't look at me like that. Do you think I encourage him? I've told him to leave me alone, to stop calling. I've told him several times. He refuses to listen. The man railroaded my career. Any feelings I had for him died the instant I learned he'd lied about his marriage."

"If he rings again, give the phone straight to me. I'll deal with him."

Anger exploded deep inside her, tensing her muscles. She sucked in a noisy breath and bared her teeth at him. "I don't need you to handle him for me. I'm capable of dealing with him myself."

"Then why does he keep ringing back?"

Laura jerked as if he'd struck her in the chest. "It's none of your damn business." All the closeness they'd built during their lovemaking dispersed in a few heated words. Tears stung, and she fought to keep them at bay.

Stunned silence bloomed between them. Laura dropped her gaze, too hurt to focus her attentions on him. His hand under her chin gave her a fright. She flinched, flinging her arms back and knocking her hip on the corner of a chair. A pained cry escaped.

"Are you okay?" His hands closed on her shoulders, drawing her away from the chair.

A lone tear escaped and rolled down her cheek.

"Laura?"

"I'm fine. Just a bit clumsy."

"I'm not trying to take over. I want to help." His husky voice throbbed with concern. "And I'm jealous," he added ruefully. "I hate to think of you with another man."

"Believe me, you're three times the man. Mike is a self-centered asshole. He doesn't respect women. I don't know why his wife didn't turf his butt out the door. I would've if I'd been her."

Jonno smoothed a strand of hair away from her face. His lips curved up into a tender smile that tugged at her heart. "That's my girl."

"I'm not your girl," she said with a sniff.

"No, you're my lover. My mate." Jonno's voice held certainty while the heat in his hazel eyes hinted at much more.

146

"Are you going to feed me?"

The phone went again. Immediately the tension ramped up between them. Jonno took a step toward the counter. She stayed him with the touch of a hand.

"Let me. It might be something work-related."

With a curt nod, he stood aside, but she noticed the tension in his body. It vibrated through him, reminding her of a big cat ready to jump its prey.

"Police Officer Adams." Relief rippled through her once she realized it wasn't Mike. "Loitering strangers? Address? Okay, I'm on my way." She hung up and glanced at the masculine robe she wore. "Do you have clothes I can borrow?"

"We can make a quick trip to your house if you like."

"There's no 'we' about it. You can't come with me."

Jonno picked up his keys. "Why?"

"I knew I should have brought the police car."

"We can argue this later."

"This might be the gang of robbers. I want to catch them red-handed." Laura balked at the door. "I can't go home wearing your robe. I'll grab my uniform."

"Don't be silly. It's sitting on the bathroom floor in a sodden heap. No one will see you in my robe, apart from Charlie if he's at home." He slipped his arm around her shoulders and propelled her to the door, shutting it once they were outside.

The drive to her house didn't take long. Laura climbed out of his car and scuttled to the door while Jonno followed.

"What's up?" Charlie asked. "I thought you were staying the night at Jonno's place."

"Call out," she said in a terse voice. Heat seeped into her face when Charlie's gaze scanned the masculine robe. She hurried past him and along the passage to her bedroom, shutting the door with a firm click. "You'll need to come with me," she called through the door.

"How do I get myself in these situations?" she muttered, letting the robe fall off her shoulders. She rifled through her drawers and pulled out a pair of white cotton panties and a matching bra. Aware of the need to hurry, she scrambled into jeans, a T-shirt and jacket instead of a uniform.

A tap sounded on her door and it opened. Jonno stepped inside just as she tugged on a pair of boots. Her phone went again. She picked it up, listened, her stomach twisting.

"Mike, if you don't stop ringing me, I will report you for harassment." She stabbed the phone, disconnecting the call.

Jonno growled at the back of his throat. "The man needs to back off. If he rings again, I'll talk to him."

"Okay," Laura agreed, deciding it was a good idea.

Jonno appeared surprised and she couldn't help a chuckle. "I'm not stupid. Besides, Mike isn't listening to me." She checked her watch. "Thanks for bringing me home. I need to leave. I'll see you tomorrow."

"Not so fast. I'm going with you."

Laura brushed past him, urgency thrumming through her body. She had a good feeling about this call out. They needed to move fast. "This is police business. Charlie will come with me."

"I'm coming." Jonno grabbed her upper arm, dragging her to an abrupt halt. "It's not safe for you." The hard light of determination glinted in his hazel eyes.

A spluttered laugh of disbelief escaped Laura. "Don't be silly. I'm a cop. This is my job. It's what I do. Look, I don't have time to argue. Let me go."

"You're my mate. It's my job to protect you," Jonno countered. "I'm coming with you."

They stared at each other, fighting an inner battle. Aware of the passing time, Laura gave in. "Fine, if it's so important to you, but you will sit in the back and keep your opinions to yourself."

Charlie met her at the front door, dressed in a police uniform—obviously more organized than she was in the laundry department. A woman could hate a man like that. A pity since she'd started to feel comfortable with Charlie.

"Where's the call out?" Charlie asked.

Laura grabbed the keys for her police car. "Gerathies Road. Do you know where that is?"

"No idea," Charlie said. "You have a map?"

"I'll drive," Jonno said. "I know where it is."

Charlie and Laura exchanged a glance. Laura's brows rose and Charlie shrugged.

"Okay," she said, handing Jonno the keys. "Drive fast and safe. Don't have an accident because although Charlie and I enjoy our jobs, we hate paperwork."

"That's true," Charlie said as they hustled to one of the two police cars in the driveway.

To Laura's relief, Jonno drove well and true to his word, he had them at the Fitzroy property on Gerathies Road in record time.

Laura scanned the shadows at the side of the road. "Anyone see anything?"

"No. Do you want me to stop here or drive to the house?"

"Pull over here. We'll walk to the house. I don't suppose you'd consider staying in the car?" Laura asked him.

"Nope." Jonno pulled over and coasted to a stop in the dark shadows cast by a seven-foot hedge. He switched off the ignition.

A gunshot sounded, audible even in the interior of the car.

"Fuck," Charlie said.

The three exploded from the car.

"Charlie, you go to the driveway. I'll cut across the paddock," Laura said.

Nodding, Charlie sprinted across the road and slipped into the shadows, silent despite his size.

"I'm going in feline form," Jonno said, ripping off his clothes. "Be careful," he growled as she dashed across the road and vaulted the fence.

With Jonno's words echoing through her head, Laura crept through the paddock, almost tripping over a sleeping sheep before gaining her night vision. Cursing under her breath, she waited for the startled animal to quieten before striding toward the house. Another gunshot increased her pace to a sprint.

Laura slipped through another fence, scanning the house. It was ablaze with light and a skinny man dressed in baggy blue pajama pants waved a rifle. She caught sight of the silhouettes of two or possibly three figures before they blended with the shadows.

"Get the fuck out of my house, you bloody thieves!"

Mr. Fitzroy, she presumed.

The rifle fired again and someone yelped. In the background a woman cried and a small dog yapped hysterically.

"Police!" Charlie shouted. "Everyone freeze right where you are."

Good thinking, Laura thought. "Police," she shouted. "Mr. Fitzroy, put down the weapon."

"No bastard will come sneaking into my house to steal my property," Mr. Fitzroy roared.

Laura stalked closer, no longer trying to keep out of sight. At this point she thought it safer to stay visible. She didn't like the way the rifle wavered in Mr. Fitzroy's hands.

"You! Freeze right there," Charlie hollered.

The person ignored the order. The rifle went off and someone screamed, his sprint faltering before he disappeared behind three bushes.

"I've hit the thieving bastard," Mr. Fitzroy hollered.

Laura stepped into the light. "Police, Mr. Fitzroy. Put the weapon down now!"

"Let her have the rifle, Henry," a tearful woman cried. "Before someone gets hurt."

The instant Henry Fitzroy lowered the rifle, another of the lurking thieves made a run for cover. Charlie sprinted after them, leaving Laura to deal with the Fitzroys. She took custody of the weapon, knowing she'd have to charge the man, even though she felt sneaking sympathy for his plight. He was attempting to protect his property. The law didn't see things the same way.

"Mr. Fitzroy, perhaps we can go inside. I need you to tell me what happened."

"They stole our chicken dinner," the man snapped. "Damn thieves. They should be shipped to Botany Bay."

Laura choked back a laugh. Somehow she didn't think Australia would welcome a new wave of convicts. "Okay, Mr. Fitzroy. Can we discuss it in your house?" She kept her voice low and soothing, having learned from experience that calmness went a long way toward soothing upset victims. "Mrs. Fitzroy, I don't suppose you could make a cup of tea? I haven't had dinner either."

"Oh, you poor girl," Mrs. Fitzroy said. "This way please."

"What about the thieves?" Henry Fitzroy demanded. "Aren't you going to chase them?"

"I have two colleagues with me. They're in pursuit right now." Jonno's special skills might come in handy, although she shuddered to think what Charlie might say later.

"They'd better catch them. With all the tax I pay I deserve better protection." The wiry man stomped into the doorway where his wife had disappeared, and with a sigh Laura followed. She prayed either Charlie or Jonno captured some of the thieves, although she didn't hold too much hope. The two were on foot, and if the thieves reached the car before they did, they never have a chance to grab them.

Laura settled at the breakfast bar with Mr. Fitzroy, placing the rifle beside her after checking it wasn't about to fire. She wished the man would don a shirt because his scrawny chest was mighty distracting. She sought diversion by asking questions.

"Can you tell me what's missing?" A petite fox terrier trotted over to sniff at her ankles before wandering off again. Thankfully it had stopped the frantic high-pitched yapping once Mrs. Fitzroy calmed.

"I told you! Our chicken dinner. They took the whole bloody chicken."

"And a loaf of bread," Mrs. Fitzroy added. "Oh, it looks as if they raided the fruit bowl. It was full of apples and oranges earlier this evening."

"So the thieves took food, and that's all?" Laura asked.

Mr. Fitzroy vibrated with irritation. "Do you have a hearing problem, young lady? I told you they took the chicken intended for our meal."

"Is anything else missing?"

"No. Henry caught them in the kitchen ten minutes after he rang you," Mrs. Fitzroy said. "I'd left the side door open. I presume they came in that way."

"Laura?" Charlie shouted.

"Okay." Laura stood. "It sounds as if I'm needed. I'll come back tomorrow morning to take your official statements. Mr. Fitzroy, I'm taking your rifle with me. We will discuss its possible return tomorrow."

"Laura!" Charlie hollered again. "We have to go. Call out."

"Tomorrow," she repeated.

"What? You're just leaving?" Mr. Fitzroy demanded.

"This sounds like an emergency, Mr. Fitzroy."

Charlie had the police car in the driveway. There was no sign of Jonno. Her heart flip-flopped, banging against her ribs. Laura grabbed the rifle and took off at a sprint, not liking the panicked tone of Charlie's call. She dropped the weapon into the trunk, taking a mental note to lock it. Hopefully it'd be okay there until they could deposit it at the police station. She jumped into the vehicle. "Where's Jonno?"

"He has the thieves with him. He told me to come and get you. There's a teenager and a bloody big black cat. It looks like it should be in a zoo. What the fuck is going on?"

"I've no idea, but I suspect we're going to find out," Laura said.

"Your boyfriend isn't wearing any clothes. Is this a new fashion I've missed while living in the country?" Charlie asked as he did a three-point turn and sped down the driveway to the road.

"Just as well you're not gay, Charlie," Laura said, unable to prevent a smirk. "I'd have to hurt you."

"There's Jonno. Grab his clothes, will you?" Charlie said. "He said they were in the backseat of the car."

Laura reached over to grab the shirt and jeans, bumping her head when Charlie fishtailed to a screeching halt. "Ow, drive carefully, will you?"

"Your boyfriend just turned into a fuckin' big leopard."

Oops. Charlie shouldn't see that.

"And now he's naked again. What. The. Fuck."

"I'm sure Jonno has an explanation." Or at least Laura hoped he did because she didn't think the Middlemarch feline shifters wanted gossip filtering to the human residents. She climbed from the police car, grabbing Jonno's footwear before striding over to where Jonno stood naked on the edge of the road beside a quivering teenager and a panting black leopard. She shot a quick glance at Charlie before saying, "What's going on?"

"These are our thieves. We need to take them to Saber's house," Jonno said. "And I need to call the vet. Do you think we can squeeze in the car?"

"Yeah. Okay. What about Charlie?"

"I want to know what's going on here," Charlie said, coming to a halt by the injured leopard. The feline snarled, its lips curling up to reveal sharp white teeth. He took a rapid step back, tension radiating from his pale face.

"Leave my brother alone," the teenager said in a quivering voice, stepping between the leopard and Charlie.

Laura studied the kid with a distinct frown, scrutinizing his face. He was young.

"They won't hurt him," Jonno said. "Clothes?"

"Oh. Yeah." Laura handed over the garments. "Sorry. I was enjoying the view."

Jonno dressed, shoved his feet into his boots, forgoing socks. He stuffed them into his jeans pockets instead. "Charlie, I'll explain everything to you once we get to the Mitchell homestead and call the vet. Terry, get into the police car." Jonno walked over to the panting leopard. It snarled and tried to get up, falling back with a pained bark. "Steady there. Ramsay, I won't hurt you. I've promised both you and your sister. I'm going to take you to someone who will help."

"Sister?" Charlie asked.

Now that Laura examined the kid closer she could see the feminine features and mannerisms, the nervous licking of lips and fine frame.

"Come on, Terry. Are you hungry? I know I am. The sooner we get to the Mitchells, the sooner we'll eat. We can help Ramsay there," Jonno said.

"I don't believe you," the girl muttered, her manner sullen and rebellious. "I bet you're gonna lock us in jail." A tear rolled down her cheek. She wiped it away with an impatient hand.

"Go with Laura." Jonno scooped up Ramsay, striding swiftly to the car. Terry followed and slipped into the car after Jonno and Ramsay.

"Are you coming?" Laura asked.

"Oh yeah," Charlie said, shaking his head in astonishment. "I wouldn't miss this for the world."

Chapter 10

Progress

This time Laura drove, heading to the Mitchell homestead, even though she was a cop and knew they should bypass Saber and go straight to jail. Not a single light shone from the house when she pulled up outside.

"Wake them," Jonno said. "Bang on the door. Walk inside if the door's open and shout for Saber. Tell Emily to ring for the vet."

Charlie leaped from the car and ran to the front door, thumping on it. Laura watched him try the handle and step inside, disappearing from sight.

"Won't they get upset with Charlie—a human—barging into their house?"

"Not Saber. He's calm under pressure, which makes him a great leader. He'll gather facts before he acts, except with Emily, then things are different," Jonno said. "He's protective."

"What are you going to do with us?" The sullen voice from the rear of the car jerked Laura back to professional.

"What were you doing in the Fitzroys' house?" Laura speared the girl—Terry—with the intent gaze she reserved for interrogation. "What were you after?"

Terry's bottom lip jutted out in a sullen glower, making Laura wonder why she'd ever thought the girl a male. The pout was pure female and combined with an indignant sniff. "We were hungry. We haven't eaten today."

Laura could believe it. She'd heard the empty rattle of the girl's stomach and seen her slight body. "How old are you?"

Terry's chin shot upward. "Eighteen."

"Try again, kiddo," Jonno said. "The truth this time."

Terry slumped into the seat. "Fourteen."

"And your brother?" Laura asked, glancing at the prone Ramsay. The kid—leopard—looked in even worse shape than his sister, all skin and bones.

"Eighteen. Okay, seventeen," she said as Jonno raised his brows in disbelief. "All right! Sixteen."

"What's up?" Saber asked, appearing beside the car.

Laura started, holding her girly shriek back to a harsh intake of breath.

"Gunshot," Jonno said, taking over. "Has Emily called for Gavin?"

"Gavin is on his way." Saber took in the panting leopard and his clear distress. "Let me help you." He bent to take Ramsay from Jonno.

"Don't hurt my brother! He hasn't done nothin'. We were hungry."

"My wife will give you food. How about coming inside while we get Gavin to tend your brother's wound? He'll give him something to help with the pain. Has he shifted since being shot?"

"Once," Jonno said. "He had little control, so I told him to shift back to feline."

With long strides, Saber carried him into the house. Terry darted from the car, following closely, as if she didn't believe Saber wouldn't hurt her brother.

A car pulled up and a man not much older than Jonno climbed out carrying a black bag.

"Your patient is inside, Gavin," Jonno said.

With a nod, the new arrival hurried into the Mitchell house.

"Why a vet?" Laura rounded the car to meet Jonno on the other side.

"They're shifters," Jonno said, as if that should explain everything. It didn't, just raised further questions. "Come on. We should supervise Charlie."

"Good point." She'd had longer to assimilate the existence of feline shifters. There was no telling how Charlie might react.

Apprehension bounced in the pit of Jonno's gut as he walked into the homestead. Not only had he endangered the Middlemarch shifters by telling Laura about their existence, he'd brought Charlie into the equation. Saber might discipline him for the action. An ache speared his chest at the thought

160

of rejection. Jonno reached for Laura's hand, taking comfort from the warmth of her touch. He loved living in Middlemarch, socializing with other felines. Although the concept seemed foreign to his parents, Jonno found he needed the contact. It filled a hole in him, one he hadn't known existed until he'd moved to Dunedin.

Jonno thought over his actions and sighed. There was nothing he'd have done different. He hoped Saber saw things in the same light.

They found Charlie, Terry and Emily in the kitchen. Emily, bless her, had Charlie busy chopping tomatoes and slicing cheese while she rinsed lettuce and made sandwiches.

"Trying to make sure we eat our vegetables again, Emily?" Jonno asked, feeling the weight of tension lessen.

"Everyone requires a balanced diet," Emily said without even turning around. "Pass this over to Terry, please." A heaped plate of chicken salad sandwiches appeared in front of him. "Laura, there's milk in the fridge. Please pour Terry a glass of milk."

Laura sprang into action, and Jonno smiled. Emily held a power all of her own. Ten minutes later they were sitting around the table eating.

"Should I check on things?" Laura asked.

"No need." Saber entered the kitchen with Gavin on his heels.

Terry shot to her feet, an empty plate flying off the edge of the table, knocked by a careless hand. "You've killed him."

"Not me," Gavin said. "Your brother is asleep. The bullet is small caliber and there's not much damage. I'm more concerned about his physical well-being. Haven't you been eating?" He strode over to Terry and took her chin in one hand, turning her face left and right. "You look as if you've been starving yourself."

"We have no money," Terry said, her tone back to sullen.

"Sit," Saber said, his quiet authority working well on Terry. She slipped back into her seat. "Tell me what you're doing in Middlemarch and why you broke into the Fitzroys' house."

"We came with Ramsay's friends." She snuck a quick glance at Charlie in his uniform before speaking so fast the words compressed into nonsense.

"Slower," Saber said, taking a seat beside Emily.

"Ramsay's friends steal jewelry and other things to sell in Dunedin and Christchurch. They needed someone who could climb into buildings. Ramsay is good at that stuff. He refused to do it unless I could hang with them too. Ramsay and I had nowhere to live. We needed the money."

The girl's guilty expression told Jonno she knew they were doing wrong. They'd done it anyway because they were out of options. "Where is your family?" Even though his father had kicked him out of the home at a young age, he'd still supported him financially for a couple of years.

"My parents died in a fire last year. My father got Ramsay and me out before going back for my mother. They died," she whispered, her eyes haunted and much too old for a feline of her age. "We were in foster care. It…" She trailed off, her attention centered on her clasped hands.

Emily patted her arm. "A foster home can't have been easy for you and Ramsay."

"Did they hurt you?" Gavin asked, his meaning clear from the tone.

Bright color flushed Terry's face before receding to leave it ghostly pale. "No! No, nothing like that. They were kind but never understood our need to be outside. We couldn't shift. We couldn't talk to them—well, it's not a good idea to tell people. Confinement made us miserable, so we ran away."

"So you're telling me you people are like that kid," Charlie said.

Jonno couldn't restrain his grin. He'd wondered if the cop would get over his shock and ask questions.

"You knew?" Charlie demanded, turning his attention to Laura.

Laura frowned, raking a piece of hair off her face in impatience. "Yes. Does it matter? They're decent people who contribute more to our community than most ever will. Is it such a hardship to work with them? By all accounts they've lived here for a long time with no serious crimes. Do you need to tell people what you've learned?"

Jonno knew the exact moment Charlie realized his vulnerability. His face paled. To his credit, the cop held his ground, remaining in his seat next to him.

"I want to know what's going on so I can do my job. Both Laura and I need to do our jobs to protect the citizens of

Middlemarch. I guess it doesn't matter what...um...race you belong to," Charlie said, straightening his shoulders.

Emily clapped. "Good. I'm glad that's settled. I need to get Terry into bed before she falls asleep at the table. You'll be in the bedroom right next to Ramsay so if he needs you during the night you'll be handy. We'll check on him before you go to bed." She stood, ready to usher Terry from the kitchen.

"No, just a sec," Laura said. "Terry, where is the rest of the gang? I want to know where they are now."

Terry's gaze darted left and right, then hit the floor. "Dunno."

Laura stood and approached the girl. "You must know where they are."

"I don't. They left us," the girl snapped tearfully.

"I don't believe you. It's not too late to lock you up," Laura threatened.

"They left us, I tell you. They didn't tell me where they were going. They left."

"Ramsay's friends left him, left you?"

"Yes!"

Laura frowned at Charlie, and he shrugged. Emily directed a sobbing Terry from the kitchen.

Jonno frowned after them. "Our cue to leave."

"No wait." Saber halted their departure. "You don't believe her."

"I'm not sure," Laura said. "Her body language says lie."

"I agree," Saber said. "If it's not a lie, she's bending the truth. We have to decide if we're going ahead with the plan."

"There are other people involved in the thefts. We found footprints." Laura glanced at Charlie. "She must know where they've gone. Can we question the boy?"

Saber's brow furrowed. "Not tonight. Maybe in the morning. I'd like to keep to the plan."

Charlie glanced around the table. "If the kids are here and get word to the gang, telling them they can get the thieves inside the house without difficulty, I think we'd have the perfect trap."

"I hate using the kids in that manner," Saber said.

"They are, or were, hanging out with thieves," Laura pointed out.

"The boy will take a few days to recover," Gavin said. "It's not a bad wound, but he's undernourished. He'll need rest and good food. He's not in any shape to climb through windows."

"He'll get rest here," Saber promised.

"What do you think about continuing with the plan?" Laura asked, directing her question to Saber.

"It might be the one opportunity we have to nab this gang before they move on to another area," Charlie commented. "Our research says they've been on quite a crime spree. We have to hope we haven't spooked them by catching these two kids."

Saber issued a heavy sigh. "I think we should continue with the plan."

Jonno thought over their plan and saw one possible hitch. "And Mr. Fitzroy? He was pissed, and I'd say he'll want to press charges."

"Charlie and I will do a deal with him," Laura said. "We're within our rights to press charges for use of a firearm. We'll offer to drop them if he'll waive the breaking and entering charges. I wouldn't tell the kids though. We might be able to still pressure them into telling us where the rest of the gang are hiding out."

"The two kids can do farm work for Mr. Fitzroy once Ramsay is healed," Jonno said. "I'll be happy to supervise them."

Charlie nodded approval. "That might work, although police supervision might work better. I don't mind supervising them if Mr. Fitzroy takes up the offer."

"Good food and exercise should see the kids right in no time," Gavin said. "I'm heading back to my bed. It's been a long day." He stood and offered his hand to Laura. "I'm Gavin Finley, vet and feline doctor."

"Laura Adams," Laura said.

Gavin turned to Charlie, and Jonno noticed the spark of interest on the vet's face. It piqued his curiosity, and he watched both men.

"Charlie McKenzie," Charlie said. "Pleased to meet you. I guess we'll see more of you during the coming days."

Gavin grinned and with a wave left the room.

"We'll leave you to it," Jonno said.

Saber regarded them with quiet confidence. "How about you work out the plan with Laura and Charlie and let us know what we need to do? We'll have to stay clear of the police so the thing doesn't reek of a setup."

Jonno rose, his chair squeaking across the floor tiles. He hesitated then spoke his mind, knowing it'd eat at him all night if he didn't speak with Saber. He respected the man that much. "Did I do the right thing bringing the kids here?" He glanced at Charlie and Laura. "It was too late to hide their existence when Charlie and Laura arrived."

Saber squeezed Jonno's shoulder. "You did the right thing." He smirked. "If Charlie tells everyone about the existence of cats, we can spread rumors of his drinking problem."

"I don't have a drinking problem," Charlie said, puffing up with indignation.

"Exactly," Saber said with a trace of smugness. "We had a similar circumstance with Tomasine, Felix's mate. Since she worked as a reporter, no one trusted her. She found it difficult. We take care of our own."

"I'll keep that in mind." Charlie laughed, and Jonno was glad to see the human taking everything in his stride. Not everyone had such an open mind.

"Thanks," Jonno said. "I'll contact you tomorrow once we finalize the plan. I take it Felix and Leo will be available to help keep watch?"

"Yeah, you'll have a full complement of Mitchells," Saber said. "Count on it."

When they arrived back at the police house, they were all tired.

"Stay here for the rest of the night," Laura said.

"Are you sure? What about the gossip?" Jonno asked, knowing how circumspect both Charlie and Laura needed to be.

"Charlie won't tell. Besides, as long as we keep things low-key, it shouldn't matter."

"Laura's right. Just because we're cops doesn't mean we can't have a private life," Charlie said. "Stay the night. Just don't make too much noise," he said with a suggestive rise of brows. "I'm an early riser, and I will take revenge if I'm kept awake." With a wave of his hand, he disappeared into the house.

"Jonno?"

"Yeah, okay." He followed Laura into the house and to a bedroom at the far end of the passage. She pushed open a door and stepped inside, closing it after he'd entered.

"The room smells of you," Jonno said, inhaling deep.

"Better than smelly socks, huh?"

"Much better." Suddenly his fatigue dropped away. His cock jolted to life, desire firing through his body. "Take off your clothes," he whispered, the sound intimate in the dark room. He heard Laura fumble for the light and stayed her with an arm on her shoulder. "No light. I want to feel. Let our other senses take over."

"Are you trying to seduce me?"

"I must be off my game if you have to ask," Jonno said. "Is seduction working?"

"Yes." Her reply sounded a trifle snappish and made him smirk.

"Clothes off. Now." To his great satisfaction he heard the sound of rustling clothing seconds after her harsh intake of breath. Jonno bent to untie his boots and toed them off, jerking off the rest of his clothing and leaving garments where they fell.

He prowled toward Laura, scooping her off her feet and tossing her on the bed. A single bed, he noted with a curl of lips. Cozy but rather inhibiting for a big man. Tomorrow they were spending the night at his place. Before she moved, he covered her body with his. No preliminaries or slow loving tonight. He craved hard and fast, just as soon as she was ready for him. Luckily Laura was right with him. The sleek thrust of her tongue into his mouth shot urgency straight to his cock. Tension clawed at his gut as he took over the kiss, nuzzling and sucking at her lips then stroking into her mouth with quick flicks.

"I want you," he murmured, ripping his mouth off hers to stare down at her, able to see perfectly with his night vision. With her ruffled hair and kiss-swollen lips, she called him like no other. "Can't look at you without wanting to fuck you."

"I'm glad. I don't know what you've done to me. When you're out of my sight I can't stop thinking about you. I worried when we were at the Fitzroys, with Mr. Fitzroy waving around his rifle. Damn, I left the weapon in the car."

Jonno dragged his tongue along her neck, nipping her hard enough for her to start. "The car's locked. It should be okay until morning." He soothed the small pain with the rasp of his tongue.

A pulse throbbed at her neck and he dragged his tongue back and forth over it until she moaned. His hands turned greedy, and he slid his hands over her breasts, the dip of her waist and lower to delve between her legs. Unable to resist, he dragged his tongue the length of her cleft, stimulating her clit with a careful stroke.

"No more," she whispered.

Aw, hell. She wanted him to stop. He didn't know if he could. Chest heaving, he lifted his head.

"No," she said in dismay. "What are you doing?"

"You told me to stop."

"No, I meant I wanted you inside me."

Jonno chuckled, dismay dispersing with her words. "That can be arranged." He spread her legs and slid into her heat. Taking his time, he worked his cock into her, pushing through her clinging flesh. "Damn, that feels good."

"Hmm." She arched against him, wrapping her arms around his neck and clutching his shoulders. Together they moved, rocking against each other. He feasted on her mouth, a rough growl of pleasure vibrating in his chest. His cock swelled, and he increased the rate of his strokes. In and out. The liquid sound of arousal filled the air along with the spicy scent of sex. She cried out, her pussy rippling around his cock. His hips jerked, and he pounded into her wet sex, taking what he needed while she shuddered in pleasure, milking him dry.

When the frantic jerks of his cock subsided, he rolled, arranging her over his chest like a blanket. His eyes closed, and he held her, content in the arms of his mate.

Chapter 11

The Past Again

T he phone woke them. Laura groaned, slapping a hand in the general direction of her bedside table before she realized the sound came from her phone. She pushed herself up and half climbed across Jonno's body before he seized her by the hips.

"I'll get it," he said. "Before you unman me with your flailing limbs."

"It might be business."

"Don't worry. If it's official business I'll pretend I'm Charlie."

Laura considered his suggestion and nodded. She leaned back against the pillows, a smile twitching at her lips.

Jonno winked. "Middlemarch Police." The good humor wiped from his face. "If you ring Laura again, I will make an official complaint." He stabbed the phone with a forefinger, ending the call. "You need to put a stop to this."

Laura swallowed, tiredness taking a toll. "How? No one believed I was the innocent party before. It was me who suffered and lost all chances of promotion."

"I'm sorry, sweetheart. That sucks, but he's persistent. An official complaint is the best way to stop him. Think about it, okay? On the plus side, it threw us together. My mother always searched for silver linings in everything. Is there something else you've contemplated doing?" He moved closer and rubbed his finger over her lips, his hazel eyes full of caring.

She swallowed again, his sympathy flooring her. If anything, it made her want to cry. They hadn't known each other for long, yet Jonno understood her more than her friends and family did. Her gaze drifted around her bedroom. Four cardboard boxes sat in a stack in the corner, the sum total of her possessions. Books—mysteries and detective stories. She'd always wondered if she had a book in her, not that she'd mention the dream to anyone else. Perhaps Jonno was right and she should think of this as an opportunity.

"Keep a record of each time he calls," Jonno said. "Just in case. Has he rung when I haven't been around?"

"No...once," Laura said, wrinkling her brow while she tried to remember. "That's not counting the messages he left with Charlie. What's the time?"

"Just after seven."

"I need to move."

Jonno jumped from the bed. "So do I. I'm driving into Dunedin to pick up supplies. Normally I'd stay the night with Joe and Sly. Today I'll head back here, I think."

"I'd appreciate having you here. Saber is great, but I find this feline shifter stuff easier when you're around. Besides, I figure Charlie will ask a few questions. I could do with your help in answering them."

"No problem. I loathe spending time away from you. Emily and Saber will need to leave the house for the plan. You'll need the rest of us to help with the sting."

Laura climbed out of bed, raising her arms above her head in a huge stretch. The play of muscles felt good.

"If you want to be late to work, that's a great way of doing it," Jonno said, coming up behind her. He wrapped his arms around her waist, drawing her back against his chest.

"Someone is pleased to see me," Laura said with a laugh.

"Getting it up for you isn't a problem." Jonno dipped his head and nibbled on the cords of her neck. The teasing scrape of his teeth pushed her heartbeat from calm to excited, each breath coming with a hoarse rasp. His hand slipped between her legs and thought of work drifted from her head. She needed him with an intensity she'd never felt for Mike. Resolutely she shoved her ex-lover from her mind to concentrate on the present.

He pushed a finger inside her moist pussy. She moaned, enjoying his attentions especially when he massaged across a sweet spot.

"I need you, Laura."

"Yes." Laura pulled away, turning in his arms at the same time.

Their lips met. Jonno lifted her, lowering her to the bed. Almost in the same move, he parted her legs and pushed his cock inside, impaling her.

Laura sighed, her body aroused, willing. His lips crushed hers as he filled the empty ache inside. With tormenting strokes, he pushed deep, his cock massaging her clit each time with unbearable friction. Gradually he increased the speed, flexing the muscles of his buttocks with each erotic caress. Warm, wet suction at her breast, the bite of pain and the building pleasure curled arousal through her body. Higher and higher he took her until Laura exploded in a starburst of pleasure.

Jonno caught her scream with his mouth. A hint of laughter trembled through his limbs before pleasure caught him too, his harsh sound of enjoyment echoing through the small bedroom.

A strident thump on their bedroom door made them both jump.

"That's enough of that," Charlie called. "I'm making coffee and toast now."

"We're coming," Laura said.

"I told you last night I don't want to hear your sex life details," Charlie muttered. "Especially since I don't have one of my own."

Jonno chuckled on hearing Charlie's retreating footsteps. "We'd better move." He sat, swinging his legs over the edge of the bed. "Did you notice Gavin and Charlie checking each other out last night?"

"Gavin and Charlie?" Laura said, moving off the bed even though it was the last thing she wanted at the moment. "Charlie isn't gay."

"I didn't say he was gay. Not that there's anything wrong with that, sweet cheeks." Jonno slapped his hand over her bare arse, making her yelp.

"Don't call me sweet cheeks." The rebuke came automatically. "Do you want a quick shower?"

"Yeah. We'll share. It will save time."

Laura laughed, feeling comfortable and relaxed. The differences between this relationship and what she'd had with Mike...with Mike each loving had been furtive and fast, something shoved out of sight. Secretive. She hadn't realized how much she'd craved acknowledgement and open affection. Something normal and average. She pulled clean underwear from a drawer before scuttling along the passage to the bathroom naked. At the other end of the house a current hit played and Charlie sang along.

"I hope you don't wander around naked in front of Charlie."

Laura reached into the shower to turn on the taps. The pipes clanked, and the water ran cold before turning warm. "Of course I don't. He's in the kitchen. Can't you hear him singing?"

"At least he can sing. Now if I tried to sing that might be a different story."

Laura stepped under the water and grabbed a bottle of shower gel and a massage glove, running it over her body until suds sluiced over her skin to the shower floor. "Can't you sing?"

"I'm lacking talent in that area," Jonno said, unperturbed. He squeezed into the shower, bumping limbs when he tried to wash himself. "My shower is better. It's bigger."

Laura laughed. "A case of bigger is better, huh?"

"You'd better believe it."

"Well, hurry because Charlie will come searching for us." She grabbed a bottle of shampoo and rubbed it briskly into her hair. No time to dry it this morning. She'd go to work with it wet. If she fastened it into a ponytail, no one would notice.

Ten minutes later both Laura and Jonno sat around a wooden table with Charlie.

"What's the plan?" Charlie asked. "I know we were going to set everything up so the thieves target the Mitchell house, but with the two kids there, the thieves might get suspicious."

"If the kids aren't involved." Laura scowled. "I wonder if we should move them somewhere."

"I'll ring Saber." A few minutes later, Jonno put down the phone. "They've moved the two kids to Felix and Tomasine's house. Tomasine said Sylvie wants to practice being a nurse. Heaven help the kids. They won't know what hit them once Sylvie strikes."

"That's good," Laura said. "I was wondering if the thieves might become concerned with Ramsay's and Terry's absence."

"They're confident," Charlie said. "They have a plan and stick to it. I wonder if the girl might consider going back to help them."

Laura frowned and shook her head. "We don't know if she's an innocent trapped in the situation or a willing participant. They're not forthright with information. People lie. I think it's best to supervise her while we continue to investigate."

After dealing with Mr. Fitzroy, Laura wanted to tear out her hair. Finding Mike waiting for her at the police station sent the rest of her day right into the toilet.

She paused in the doorway, torn between stalking over to the tall blond and smacking him in the nose, or turning on her heel to get a coffee. Laura did neither.

"Anything new?" she asked Charlie.

"Where have you been?" Mike demanded. "And who answered your phone this morning? Who was he?"

"Her boyfriend," Charlie said, his brows drawn together in a scowl.

Charlie stood up for her, and Laura took comfort in that fact.

"It's none of your business, Mike. You have a wife. Go back to her because I'm not interested." Laura dropped into the chair behind her desk and checked through the messages Charlie had left for her.

"Does Gavin Finley have a problem?" she asked.

"No, he rang to let us know the cat we rescued last night will make a full recovery."

"A cat!" Mike snorted. "I thought you wanted to be a detective. Reduced to rescuing cats from a tree, no doubt. You're better than that, Laura. Come back to Dunedin with me."

"I don't think so. I enjoy my job here." To Laura's surprise she spoke the truth. Since meeting Jonno and several of the community, she felt as if she belonged. She and Charlie made a great team, working well together. While at first resentment had simmered in her gut, she realized the bitterness had faded, replaced by a quiet satisfaction. Jonno was right. A silver lining.

"I won't give you a second chance," Mike said. "If you don't come with me, you'll get stuck in this country dump for years."

Laura glanced at Charlie and saw he watched her with quiet approval, almost as if he could read the thoughts racing through her mind. "Charlie and I are busy, Mike. Please leave."

"Fine. I'm going." Mike stomped from the station, slamming the front door with undue force.

"That man is trouble," Charlie said.

Laura frowned, watching Mike's disgruntled departure through the window. "I know. I wish I'd been smart enough to realize that while I was in Dunedin."

"You wouldn't have met Jonno."

"True." Laura leaned back in her chair. "What do you think of this feline shifter business?"

"Honestly? It shocked the hell out of me when I saw Jonno change forms. After having time to consider, I think it's kinda cool. It's not as if I feel threatened by any of them. They're regular people—decent and hardworking. They're better citizens than most of us. It's understandable they'd keep their presence quiet. I can imagine a scientist wanting to poke and prod at them to learn what makes them tick."

"Yeah. I'd hate the idea of them being caged."

"Plus, I'd say Jonno is serious about you," Charlie said.

The idea didn't distress her as it had earlier. Funny the difference a few days made. "It makes me curious regarding the other mystical creatures I've read of in books and seen in movies."

"Vampires and werewolves? That sort of thing?"

"Yeah. Proof of the existence of shifters is making me view the world differently. We'll have to ask Jonno." Laura stood. "Do you want anything from the café? I thought I might head over there to see how the grapevine is working."

"I heard whispers when I went to the post office to collect the mail," Charlie said. "I'm thinking the grapevine is working overtime." He checked his watch. "I'd love a coffee, but I have to go to the school to discuss road safety. Oh, Isabella Mitchell stopped in and said she was helping Emily spread gossip and working on a strategy with Saber. She suggested we meet at Felix and Tomasine's later this afternoon to go through our plan and so we could talk to Ramsay and Terry again."

"I'm redundant." Laura laughed. "That work for you?"

"Yeah, I'll meet you back here around four."

After picking up her wallet, Laura left for the café. She wandered down the footpath, daydreaming of Jonno and their lovemaking. Hopefully this'd be settled by the weekend and they could spend uninterrupted time together. She and Charlie had alternate weekends off and this coming one belonged to her.

"Laura." A hand wrapped around her forearm in a steely grip.

Mike. The next instant, he jerked her into his arms and his mouth covered hers. Funny, she'd always liked kissing and considered Mike a good kisser. This she didn't enjoy. A dominant kiss—a mashing of lips that tried to force control. A possessive kiss. Six months earlier she'd have felt elation, seen the statement of ownership as a sign her relationship with Mike was becoming closer.

Breathing hard, Laura jerked from his arms. Bigger and stronger than she, he yanked her against his chest, catching her *oomph* of surprise with his mouth. She wriggled and squirmed, trying to free herself before raising her knee and striking at his groin.

"Ow! There's no need for that," Mike said, ducking out of range. "You almost got me in the nuts."

"That was the idea. What gives you the right to maul me? In the middle of the street. Fuck, Mike! What the hell are you thinking turning up here?" She struggled to keep her voice at a harsh whisper when she wanted to holler her irritation and frustration for everyone to hear. Somehow she didn't think a member of the police should get into a screeching match in the middle of town.

"You refused to talk on the phone."

Now he looked and sounded like a sulky boy. "We're finished. There's nothing to discuss."

Mike scanned her face, his attention skimming across the faint love bite Jonno had given her during their latest bout of lovemaking. A prickle of heat swept the length of her body, coalescing in her pussy in an ache when she thought of her lover.

Jonno. He fueled her fantasies, and Mike didn't compare well with the feline shifter.

"I'm leaving my wife."

"That's what you told me when the whole mess became public. Remember? You told me you hadn't slept together for months, that you didn't sleep in the same room and barely spoke."

"Please, Laura. We are getting a divorce this time. Can we go somewhere to talk?"

Realizing they were attracting attention, Laura gave a curt nod. "I can spare you five minutes before I need to return to the station. We're busy at the moment and I need to let Charlie take a break."

Mike fell into step beside her, satisfaction tingeing his handsome face. Laura huffed out an impatient breath. She'd given Mike everything—her love, her friendship, her loyalty. He was the one who'd cheated and lied, the one who wriggled out of trouble without a speck of dirt sticking to him. She had received the punishment. Banished. Laura increased her speed, needing the physical activity to help vent her building rage. In the past, his attention had made her feel important and treasured. Now she felt dirty.

Laura pushed open the door of Storm in a Teacup. Jonno would have opened it for her. Not Mike. Irritated, she let the door go, forcing Mike to hold out his hand to stop it shutting in his face. The bell attached to the frame tinkled, reminding Laura of laughter.

"Hi, Laura," Emily said, her brows raised in a silent question.

"You know how I take my coffee. I'll wait over there." Mike sauntered over to a corner table and took the chair facing the door. Typical cop, always wanting to scan the room and its occupants.

"How's it going?" Laura turned back to face Emily, her words loaded with a silent question.

"Fine. Mission gossip is underway." Emily looked past her to study Mike. "Jonno has better manners."

"Believe me, I've noticed." Laura ordered two lattes, getting Mike's order wrong on purpose. If he refused to drink it, she'd have an extra cup. No problem. "I used to go out with Mike before I discovered he was married."

"Ouch."

"Yes. Mike is the reason I was transferred to Middlemarch."

Emily started to make the coffees, the machine hissing while she steamed the milk. "Middlemarch isn't so bad. You've met Jonno, and you and Charlie make a good team. The two policemen stationed here before you didn't involve themselves as much as the pair of you."

After a quick glance at Mike, Laura said, "I wanted to be a detective. Because of Mike they shuffled me sideways and sent me here. I came prepared to hate Middlemarch. I'll admit, the place has grown on me."

"The men have a part to play in that. Jonno is one of the good ones."

"Everything has happened so fast." Laura stepped away to peruse the food cabinet before returning to the counter. "Too quickly."

"Trust in your gut," Emily said, placing two mugs of coffee in front of Laura. "And if you want to discuss the mating aspect, just let me know. It's confusing and a little frightening at first. I fought. It took a while for Saber to win me over."

"That's just it. After Mike I'm afraid to trust my instincts."

Emily grimaced. "Yeah, men have a way of ripping out our hearts. I had the same issues with trust. My advice is to talk to Jonno. Tell him how you're feeling. I've known him for a while now through the twins. He's a good man, and if it's any consolation, in the past he's played the field, never going out with the same woman more than once."

Jealousy wrapped through her mind and a scowl curled across her lips. "Huh! I don't think I want to know about his other women."

"And doesn't that tell you something? That you're more involved than you realize."

"I'll take one chocolate brownie."

"Change the subject all you want," Emily said with a smirk. "It's still the truth so you might as well face it."

Laura grabbed a tray and placed the coffees plus the brownie on it before handing Emily a twenty-dollar note. On receiving her change, she picked up the tray and walked over to Mike.

"What took you so long?"

"Emily and I were talking about a work situation." Laura shunted a coffee mug in his direction and waited for the explosion.

"Dammit, I take my coffee black," he snarled.

"Oh, so sorry. It's Jonno who drinks latte." God, she was a bitch. She shouldn't be baiting him this way, but damn, it felt good.

Mike shoved the coffee away with distaste. "Are you sleeping with him?"

Laura picked up her coffee and took a sip while checking on the other occupants of the café. Quite a few strangers. The group to her right looked like cyclists. She'd noticed bikes outside the café. Her attention lit on the group of teens sitting outside. Now they seemed more like the ones they wanted to catch. Not wanting to attract their attention, she turned back to Mike. "None of your business."

"It didn't take you long to find a replacement."

Mike was voicing her concerns—the danger of a rebound. Still, she didn't think he rated an opinion on her personal life. "How is your wife?"

"How should I know? I told you we're separated."

He refused to listen to reason or back off. Laura sighed and applied herself to eating the brownie. Chocolate fixed almost everything. Maybe she could tune him out while she savored the chocolate hit. She drank both cups of coffee and stood.

"I'm going back to work."

"Wait! We haven't settled anything. When can you come back to Dunedin? You'll need to find a new job, of course, but I have a house. You can move in with me."

Laura laughed, his self-centeredness and selfish attitude wiping away the last traces of sympathy she felt for him at being in an unhappy marriage. "I like Middlemarch. I'm not going anywhere." And it was true, she thought with a lightened heart. She liked Middlemarch. She enjoyed the job, even though things moved slower than in Dunedin. "Have a good trip back to Dunedin." And she turned and walked away, excited about the future for the first time since the whole sorry mess started.

Chapter 12

Rainy Plan

L *ater That Evening*

"Damn, why did it have to rain?" Laura peered through the bushes at the Mitchell house, her clothes sodden from the persistent rain and her wet hair dripping down her back.

"The farmers need the rain, sweet cheeks. The land is dry."

"Yeah...ah...okay. It's just I hate doing a stakeout in the rain. Visibility is limited, and it's easy for the thieves to sneak past." Guilt lashed her. Idiot. She knew the farmers needed the rain.

"Think of all the fun we'll have thawing out."

Laura sent him a grin. "Promises, promises."

After a careful survey of the area, Jonno edged closer so they could talk without risk. "Why didn't you tell me Mike was coming to town?"

"Because his arrival is an inconvenience. Color me irked." Laura scowled into the driving rain and shivered, the raincoat not as waterproof as the label claimed. "I wasn't sure how you'd react."

"Do you still love him?"

"Hell no! If nothing else, his visit has reinforced the fact that anything we had together is over. He's self-centered and arrogant. Besides, I'm involved with you. I don't mess around with two men at the same time."

"Good." All Jonno's satisfaction and relief filled the word.

"And don't call me sweet cheeks. I don't like it."

"Yes, ma'am."

"Not that either."

"Not long until dawn. I doubt whether they'll show now. Emily and Saber arrived home ages ago."

"Yes, you're probably right. Wait." Laura grasped Jonno's wrist, her eyes straining to see. "I think I saw someone. Can you see?" she whispered. "Over to the left of the house."

"No, I can't...wait. Yeah, I see them. They're circling the house."

"Could it be one of the Mitchells?"

"I doubt it. Isabella organized us with precision. We know where the others are and I doubt they've moved." He stripped off his clothes. "I'll shift and go closer. Once I pick up the scent trail I'll know if it's the same people who broke in at the Millers."

"But—"

"Wait here. I'll come back for you." Jonno gave her a swift kiss before shifting to cat and slinking into the darkness.

"I wish I were a cat," Laura muttered. Two minutes passed before she realized what she'd said. A cat. Heck, the knowledge of feline shifters didn't freak her in the slightest. She trusted them—all of them. Interesting. She had to ask them about vampires because they sounded freaky cool. Sighing, Laura scanned the house and its surrounds.

They'd left one window open and the others shut in the hope the thieves would think they'd overlooked closing it. If the thieves didn't strike today, they'd leave a different window open or forget to lock a door, giving the impression the family was diligent and sometimes a bit lax.

Thankfully the rain eased and Laura caught another glimpse of a skulking figure on the other side of the house. Of Jonno, she saw no sign. She watched the figure circle the house until they disappeared from sight. The buzz of adrenaline sped through her veins. This appeared promising, though it seemed the thieves were more organized than they'd thought, rather than opportunists.

Ramsay had told them the thieves were in their teens and early twenties, which made little sense to Laura. In her experience someone took charge, and that someone was normally older. He'd also told them, as far as he knew, the group were finished with Middlemarch. It seemed as if he was right.

Laura waited another hour, seeing no one. She shivered, acutely miserable. This part of policing sucked. The faint rustle of a bush was all the warning she received before a black leopard crept up to her. She stiffened as she took in the size of the beast.

The cat watched her with green eyes, creeping closer once it realized she would not scream.

"Good cat," Laura said, her voice trembling. It seemed she needed to work on her confidence, but dammit, this wasn't Jonno. Had something happened to him? Her heart stalled before speeding into action again. The cat let out a rumbling purr and rubbed its head against her hand before backing up and walking toward the house. When she didn't react, the cat stopped and barked a command.

Okay. "You know, you guys need to work on your communication skills." Laura scooped up Jonno's sodden clothes and followed, wondering which one of the Mitchells this was. They sure made these cats big.

Laura moved as fast as her cold limbs allowed. Sitting in one place for a long time did little for her circulation. They entered the rear of the house and Laura found herself in the kitchen.

The cat prowled off while Emily hurried over with a towel. The rest of their surveillance crew, apart from Jonno, sat around the table nursing cups of tea. Laura peeled off the coat and the jumper underneath. Luckily her T-shirt was almost dry and after she toweled off her hair, she felt marginally better.

"Where's Jonno?"

"He's following the trail to where they're staying. At least that's what we think," Isabella said.

"Don't worry," Emily soothed. "The thieves didn't realize we were watching them."

"You weren't outside getting wet," Laura snapped, taking a seat at the table and accepting a cup of tea.

"True. I cuddled up to Saber in the warm, but things were tense for us too, wondering if the thieves would break in after we'd arrived home."

"Sorry," Laura murmured. It can't have been easy for any of them. "What happens if they leave in a car?"

"They did. Since there's only one way out until they hit the main road, Jonno had a head start," Isabella said. "Don't worry. For a spotted leopard he's good."

Leo chuckled, slipping an arm around her waist. "That's not fair. Jonno's not here to defend himself."

"Just as well I'm here now to top up the human team," Laura said. "And so you know, your communication skills while in cat form suck. I didn't know whether whoever came to collect me wanted to eat me for dinner or pass the time of day."

A startled silence ensued before Emily burst into laughter. "I think you fit in well. Jonno is lucky to have you."

Laura's phone went, and she cursed. "Damn, lucky it didn't go while I hid outside."

Isabella snorted. "Some spy you make."

"Yep, cats rule," Saber said, his green eyes gleaming with humor. He paused in the doorway before striding across the tiled floor to join the rest of them. "Despite our lack of communication skills."

With a wrinkle of her nose, Laura answered the phone. She listened for an instant before cursing under her breath. "Mike, I told you not to ring me again."

"Where are you? You didn't come home."

"On a case," she snapped before hanging up.

"Problem?" Isabella asked.

"Ex-boyfriend," Emily said. "Doesn't want to let go."

Isabella straightened, an expression of interest on her face. "I can take care of him. Do you want to hire me?"

"How much to take him out?" Laura asked, enjoying the banter and being part of the group.

"Permanently? I don't know...heck, yes I do. Let me be part of your cop team if I get rid of him for you. I'm sure I can fit it in my busy schedule."

"We need a filing clerk. Would you be interested in that position?" Laura asked.

"You're a mean woman," Isabella protested. "Sorry, I don't do filing."

"I've heard kicking a man in the nuts helps," Jonno said from the door. Water dripped off his naked body. "I don't suppose you have a towel, Emily?"

"Sure thing."

"Don't look, Emily," Saber snapped.

"Too late," Isabella chortled. "We've already seen. Very nice, Jonno. Working on a farm makes good muscles."

"Who told you I kicked—actually, I kneed him. Who told?" Laura asked, diverting everyone's attention.

"It's a small town, sweet cheeks," Jonno said, toweling himself dry. He dressed and joined them at the table. "Not many secrets here."

Laura snorted. "Apart from the fact that shifters wander the streets."

"Sweet cheeks?" Isabella said in distinct horror. She turned to Leo. "Never call me that. I have weapons and know how to use a knife."

"Never mind that," Laura said, unable to prevent the flush of embarrassment creeping into her cheeks. Jonno did that on purpose. "What happened? Who are the thieves? Where are they staying? You didn't lose them, did you?" She strove for dignity and concentrated on work.

"They're staying at the campground near the pub. Terry and Ramsay lied. They must have known because I heard the camper on the site next to them complaining of the noise levels. They told them they'd report them to the police if they made as much racket as they did the previous two nights."

"Are they part of this?" Emily asked.

Saber shrugged. "Felix said that Ramsay told him the gang had left town and good riddance. That's all he is saying. Terry is sticking to her original story. Hard to say who is telling the truth. Felix and Tomasine are keeping them away from phones and both are under constant supervision." His mouth firmed. "Terry is complaining about imprisonment. Unless they leave on foot they have no way of contacting their friends."

"They deserve a good scare if they're lying. What I don't understand is why the two kids were so hungry they had to steal food. Was that what they were there for? If they're part of the gang, why don't they have money? There has to be something else going on with them," Laura said, wrinkling her brow in a thoughtful manner. "They had no identification and we know next to nothing about them because they're so tight-lipped. Are you positive they're both shifters? I know Ramsay is but is Terry?"

Jonno grinned at her. "They're both shifters. They have a distinct scent."

Laura leaned over and sniffed him before turning to Saber and sniffing him too. Nothing out of the ordinary leaped out at her. Jonno smelled clean and damp while Saber bore the scent of soap.

"Would you like me as comparison?" Emily asked, amusement sparkling through her.

"They're no different than you or Charlie," Laura said.

"Hey, sweet cheeks. Just how closely do you work with Charlie?"

"We're friends and colleagues," Laura said disparagingly, and realized her words were true. She liked Charlie, and they worked well together. That closeness would improve with time. "We will make sure those two kids remain secluded."

"Or we could leak information to them and let them loose," Isabella suggested. "A two-pronged attack. That way we'd learn where Ramsay and Terry fit into the gang."

"I like it," Emily said. "It's plain sneaky and underhanded."

Laura glanced around the table, taking in the varied reactions. They ranged from stoic in Saber to intent and focused in Isabella. "Votes?"

"I dislike using the kids," Saber said, "but I think we should do it. It will short circuit what could be a long wait for the thieves to strike. I don't know about everyone else. I like my bed at night."

"Because I'm in it," Emily quipped, kissing his cheek.

Saber scooped her up and deposited her on his knee. "Damn straight, kitten."

"Anyone else?" Laura asked. When no one commented, she inclined her head. "Okay. Who will watch the kids and follow them if they go into town? Is Ramsay going to be fit enough to go under his own steam?"

"Tomasine said he's healing well," Leo said. "He will hurt, although he'll be able to move if he wants it bad enough."

"I'll keep the two kids under surveillance," Isabella said. "I think we should make it easy for them. Tomasine will need to pick up milk and bread at some stage. Why doesn't she ask them if they'd enjoy a trip into town for a change of scenery? Or leave them to their own devices while she goes to school. She could make up a reason for visiting the school, even if it's just to drop off Sylvie's lunch that she's supposedly forgotten."

"Sounds good," Laura said. "I'm heading home to grab a couple of hours' sleep before I have to start work."

Jonno pushed back his chair. "That's my cue."

"Let the poor girl sleep," Emily said. "She's exhausted."

Isabella chuckled while Leo snorted.

"Emily, I love you, I do," Jonno said, "but I doubt that's the way things will happen."

"Jonno!" Laura shrieked, mortified at their laughter. They were still laughing as Jonno ushered her outside and they started the walk to the little-known side road where they'd parked Jonno's vehicle. "That was embarrassing."

"Nothing less than the truth. I can't come in a few feet of you without thinking about sex. You don't want me losing control over my feline and going feral, do you?"

Laura sniffed, knowing the man was all talk. His control might waver but he'd never hurt her, and the idea of a little close bonding sounded good to her. She'd catch up on sleep later.

Half an hour later, after a quick shower to chase away the last of the lingering chill, Laura crawled into bed beside Jonno. She melted against his warm body, cheerfully placing her icy feet on him. He laughed and rolled her onto his chest, wrapping his arms around her, holding her tight. The steady and reassuring beat of his heart comforted her, despite her weariness.

"Are you too tired?" Jonno asked.

"No." Arousal hummed through her body from just being in his proximity. While they'd been with the Mitchells she'd ignored it. Now in the privacy of Jonno's bedroom, sex jumped to the fore.

"Me neither," he whispered before closing his lips over hers. His hands stroked over her back with steady pressure, continuing downward over her butt.

Laura lifted her head and caressed his face, smoothing his tawny hair. "This bed I'm lying on is very lumpy."

"No doubt things will become worse before they get better."

Laura stared at him, her heart suddenly in her throat. If she didn't love him now, she was well on the way. Her pulse thudded in her ears in a wave of panic that came from nowhere. She couldn't love Jonno. It rated as personal suicide. Besides, she'd made herself a promise to concentrate on her career. When she'd first arrived in Middlemarch, the last thing she'd wanted was to stay permanently. No, she'd come with the object of proving herself and earning a promotion in another city, probably Auckland where her reputation wouldn't precede her, even though she preferred Dunedin.

He smiled quizzically, his mouth turning up at the ends so his lips were crooked. "What's wrong?"

"Nothing." Laura pushed aside her mounting confusion, deciding to assuage an ache of an entirely different kind. She wriggled a fraction, her hip digging into his erection, and kissed his jaw. When he bared his neck for her, she laid a trail of kisses along the underside of his jaw, becoming daring with her teeth. His soft moan of pleasure encouraged her further. Laura moved down his body, paying particular attention to his nipples. She bathed the flat disks with her tongue, delighting in his guttural groan and the way his hands tangled in her hair, silently encouraging her exploration. Smiling at the surge of power she felt, she moved across to his other nipple, giving it the same treatment.

"You're gonna kill me here. Either that or I'll lose control and take over."

Laura lifted her head to smirk at him. "So I'm doing a good job?"

"The best."

Yes, he was very male and sometimes he took over while they were in bed. Tonight he seemed to enjoy her attentions and surrendered wholeheartedly. Laura weighed the thought and decided she liked his reactions. Vulnerable but tough. And protective, she added, thinking about him backing her up with Mike. He'd allowed her to handle the situation yet made his interest clear too. Yeah, there was a lot to like when it came to Jonno.

Her tongue circled his belly button before dipping inside while one hand snaked down to grasp his erection.

"Damn, I was gonna let you control things."

"Was?"

"Yep." Jonno moved so fast she barely had time to squeak. She found herself on her back, legs splayed with his head between and tongue getting busy. A whisper of a sigh passed her lips at the delicate brush of fingers and lips over her sensitive flesh. Her heels dug into the mattress, body straining while she silently begged for more. More pressure, more pleasure, more everything. Her pussy fluttered as he breathed a stream of warm air over her clit, pressure climbing inside. She gasped, the influx of pleasure coming in blistering waves, watching his face and the intense concentration he'd focused on her. It made the protective layer around her heart crack even more.

"Jonno, I need…"

"What do you need?"

"More. I feel empty. You. I need your cock filling me, your body surrounding me."

"Plain old missionary, huh?"

"Jonno." His name came out as a wail.

"Damn, I barely touch you and you're ready for me. It's the same way with me, except all I need is a touch, a look. Laura, you're driving me crazy." He dragged his tongue over her clit and a ribbon of sensation shot down her legs. She cursed, her body tense with need while she waited for him to repeat the move, to push her into the climax she needed so much.

"I must do something about that cursing, sweet cheeks. We can't have our kids picking up bad habits. Stretch your hands above your head."

Kids? The thought should have scared her, she mused, following his terse order without hesitation.

He lifted his head, his mouth shiny with her juices. "We'll begin with a swear jar for the start. Maybe young Sylvie can take custody of it because the Middlemarch kids are fundraising to attend a camp. A dollar a swear word sounds a fair fee. Remind me to discuss the matter with Sylvie when we go to visit Ramsay and Terry."

199

"It's official police business," Laura said. "You can't go." Her mind still reeled with the idea of kids. She'd never thought beyond finding a compatible man.

"You're not wriggling out of it that easy. One word in Sylvie's ear and you'll be a poor woman. Tomasine and Emily will back me on this." His charming smile told of his smugness, and Laura didn't know whether to hit him or jump the man.

"Fine. I'll try not to swear."

"Good girl." The joyous sparkle of his hazel eyes pulled her in, mesmerizing and tugging at her sense of humor. The man was a hopeless case, or perhaps it was her. She felt powerless under his spell, attracted to him more and more each day.

Jonno moved up her body and cupped her face between his hands. His teasing faded, replaced by serious and determined. "I love you, Laura."

A soft sound of denial croaked from her. Jonno ignored it, lowering his head to seduce her with his mouth. His tongue traced the outline of her lips before slipping inside to tangle with hers. Oh yeah. Seduction big time. The panic his announcement engendered faded, replaced by deeper desire. The man held magical powers along with his shifter qualities. One word from him and she became putty, pliable and susceptible to his every whim.

Laura slipped her arms around his shoulders, glorying in the harnessed power beneath her fingers and the focused intent of him, the stroke of his tongue and messages he conveyed with his mouth. Her restraint melted away, and she knew deep down she was his.

At his silent urging she turned, rising on all fours. He pulled away, and she shivered until his warmth at her back sped her chilled doubts on the way. With his fingers, he explored and stroked her shoulders, her breasts, her bottom until her pussy burned for his possession. The scent of their heated bodies, their arousal filled her every breath. Then, when she thought she'd need to beg before he fucked her, she felt his cock push into her. He exerted a little force and filled her with a single thrust.

Laura sighed, every nerve ending and muscle quivering with pleasure. When she thought he'd move with speed, he surprised her, enticing and seducing again.

"You're wet for me," he murmured. "I like that. It makes me hot. It makes me want to fuck you."

"Yes," she hissed, pushing back against him.

"Not this time, Laura. This time I'm showing how much I love you."

She shivered, the lump in her throat preventing a reply. The L word again. How could he be so sure? How could he know they'd stay together? Things changed. People changed.

"I know you think it's too soon. You'll see." He withdrew before pushing back into her so slowly she'd swear his cock massaged every cell of her pussy. "I want to bite your shoulder. I want to feel my teeth slicing into your flesh and the mating process become complete."

Her channel contracted at the heat in his words, the clear intent and certainty. He meant everything he said, every word. Something inside Laura softened.

"For now, I'm content to wait," he whispered next to her ear. His husky voice sent a shiver speeding through her, as did his steady strokes.

Her body quivered, his seductive voice drawing her tight like a bow. She felt him kiss along her spine, felt his strokes quicken and excitement grew along with the sounds of fucking. Higher and higher he drove her, and when a single finger brushed across her swollen clit, she gasped, balanced on a precipice. Warm, strong hands grasped her hips, his cock plunging in and out of her until another stroke of his finger shoved her over the abyss into a maelstrom of dark pleasure. Bright colors flickered behind her eyelids. In the distance she heard his harsh cry, felt the buck of his hips and the splash of semen inside her.

"I love you, Laura."

The pleasure, the intimacy tore at her, ripping away the remains of the protective armor around her heart. She knew in that moment she loved him, even if she was a coward in not responding to his declaration. Laura fell asleep with a smile on her face, cocooned in his protection.

The Next Day

The phone rang in the police station and Jonno waited while Laura answered.

"Dammit, Mike. Not now." She hung up, glaring at the phone while Jonno reined back his instinct to growl and bark orders to make an official complaint. But it wasn't his place. She needed to take the step on her own. Laura wasn't interested in the man. He could see that. If the moron didn't quit with the harassment soon, Jonno would be tempted to take matters into his own hands. There wouldn't be anything official in his actions. Laura was his woman.

Almost immediately the phone rang again. She handed it to him, rolling her eyes in disgust. "That has to be Mike again. Charlie said he saw him at the Middlemarch Bed-and-Breakfast. I thought he'd given up on me. Evidently not."

"Middlemarch Police," Jonno said.

"You a cop now, Jonno? We're doing a great business taking over the police force," Isabella said with a chuckle before settling to business. "Terry is on the move. I think she's heading to the campground. She'll pass the station soon."

"Ramsay?"

"He went to Storm in a Teacup and is busy talking to Emily. When I poked my head into the café they were deep into a conversation of different styles of cuisine. Jeez, give me a good steak and I'm happy," Isabella said. "Who wants this fancy stuff?"

Jonno barked a laugh as he squinted through the window and down the road. In his peripheral vision he caught a flash of navy blue. He tapped Laura on the shoulder, pointing with his finger. She gave a clipped nod.

"She's coming this way," Jonno said. "Talk to you soon. Can we turn this off?"

Laura took the phone from him and switched it off.

"Just Terry," Jonno murmured as she sidled past the station. "Ramsay is with Emily."

"Damn, do you think Terry learned about our plan and has gone to warn them? Or do you think she intends to rejoin them and has lied to us all along?"

"We'll soon find out," Jonno said. "Let's go."

They followed on foot until the campground came into sight.

"I wonder if we can get closer without them noticing?"

"Not too close. Terry will scent us," Jonno warned as Terry ducked through a fence.

"I wish I could arrest their asses even though it'd be better to catch them in the middle of a crime." Laura waited until Terry darted past a row of tents, then followed.

Jonno trailed a determined Laura. A few minutes later, they spotted Terry with several males and crept closer in order to eavesdrop.

Jonno sympathized while surveying the campervan and the four occupants who lounged outside. They sat on deckchairs arranged around a flimsy table, drinking beer. Quite a bit of beer, judging by the pile of empty cans and drunken laughter.

A wiry male dressed in a black T-shirt with the sleeves ripped off noticed Terry first. "Where the fuck have you been?" He stood and strutted over to her, reminding Jonno of a rooster.

"Max," Terry cried out, flinging herself at the scruffy male. He curled his arms around her and ground their mouths together.

"I hope I do a better job of swapping spit," Jonno murmured.

Laura snorted. "Don't worry. You take spit-swapping to a new level. At least we've found the owner of the driver's license. It puts him at the scene of the crime."

They watched while the other teens made ribald comments. Finally the couple parted and moved away from the others. Terry talked in earnest.

Jonno cursed. "Damn, we're not close enough. I can't hear."

"No problem. We can assume those two are involved and she'll tell him everything. He'd better not be sleeping with her. She's underage, and he must know it. Let's go back and lean on Ramsay. See what he says when he learns his sister has met with suspected thieves."

"Good idea," Jonno said. "Besides, Isabella has followed and will watch them. She's better at this stuff."

"She wasn't truly an assassin."

"The rumors say yes."

"Nah, she's winding us up." Laura chewed on her bottom lip. "She's...intense at times."

"Scary is the word you want. Sometimes it's hard to know if she's teasing."

"My point," Laura said, her tone dry.

They backed away from the campervan and left the caravan park. The Middlemarch pub was doing a brisk trade and as they passed the railway station, the train departed, its mournful whistle sending a shiver along his spine.

Jonno paused, studying the passengers who had disembarked. None were out of the ordinary. A group of five all wheeled bicycles while a young couple pushed a pram down the road. Their toddler didn't sound too happy, bawling and attracting attention.

"I need to check in with Charlie at the station," she said. "See you later?"

"Sure thing. Do you want me to talk to Ramsay?"

Laura hesitated before releasing a sigh of acquiescence. "Yeah. Tag team with Emily since she's gained his trust."

"Will do." Jonno pressed a swift kiss to her lips, intending to keep things light until she responded. Damn. Desire roared through him and he sank into the kiss. She smelled of his soap, a fact he liked very much. He wondered how much longer it would take until she surrendered and admitted they were mates.

When they parted, they were both breathing harder. Laura's lips appeared swollen and his cock pressed painfully against his zipper. Instead of frustrating him, the response made him long for the coming evening. It was also an incentive to catch the thieves so he and Laura could have a few uninterrupted days together.

"Later," he said, brushing the backs of his fingers over her cheek. With a last wave, he strode toward Storm in a Teacup.

Emily and Ramsay were still deep in discussion when he arrived. Tomasine hovered, serving customers and bearing an anxious expression on her face.

Two elderly women sat at the table near the door.

"Have you heard about the ring Saber gave Emily? I haven't seen it yet but from Emily's description it's gorgeous," one said.

The gossip vine grew alive and well in Middlemarch. *Good job, Emily.* Satisfaction filled Jonno when he strode to the counter to check in with Tomasine.

"Jonno, have you seen Terry? I can't find her."

"Yeah. Isabella is watching her. Can you look after things for Emily while we have a word with Ramsay?"

"Sure." Although she obviously wanted to ask questions, she smiled at a smartly dressed female who approached the counter and took her order.

"Do Ramsay and Terry know this is a setup?" he asked in a low voice, mindful of wagging ears.

"No, we kept it from them. We discussed Saber buying the ring for Emily. That's all. Terry has been sulky and said little. Today was the first day she's showed spark." Tomasine acknowledged a customer and walked over to serve them.

Jonno strode to the table where Emily and Ramsay sat. "Emily, can we talk out the back?"

Emily seemed surprised but agreed, standing and letting him go first.

"You too, Ramsay," Jonno said.

The teenager tensed and glanced around the café. "Where's Terry?"

"That's what I want to talk to you about," Jonno said. "Out the back."

Emily and Ramsay followed him to the kitchen. Jonno scanned the work surfaces and the stack of dirty plates by the dishwasher. The scent of cinnamon and apples came from a pot simmering on the stove. No point sugarcoating this.

"Terry has gone to the campground to meet up with a group of males—late teens, early twenties," he said.

The color faded from Ramsay's face, leaving it white as the flour clinging to the board Emily had used for pastry making. "She promised me they'd finished. She promised."

"Who are they?" Emily asked. "It's time to talk and tell us the truth."

"I..." His shoulders slumped. "Okay. The truth. Terry met them in Dunedin. She ran away from the foster home we were in to go with them. They're thieves. I know they break into houses. I followed Terry and found her with them. She's close to Max, the leader. Damn, she promised me they'd finished. She said she intended to sit in the garden until Tomasine returned. I swear I thought she was still there. I should have watched her..." He trailed off, his face a picture of misery. "If they're still here in Middlemarch, it means they will rob someone's house. Tell the police."

His expression and slumped defeat made Jonno believe him, which meant everything Terry had told them was a lie.

"That's not what Terry told us," Emily said, exchanging a glance with Jonno. "She implied you were part of the gang."

Ramsay bit his lip, looking incredibly young. "No. Well, sort of..." He trailed off, subsiding into an uncomfortable silence.

"Tell us," Emily prompted.

"Don't worry," Jonno said. "It's being taken care of. Someone is watching Terry right now. Does she know about the robberies?"

"Yes, Terry has helped. I've told her it's wrong. She won't listen, and Max is such an arse." Unable to stay still a second longer, he paced. Because of his gunshot injury he held his body stiffly, listing to one side like a sinking boat. "She ran away with him. I caught up with them in Cromwell and joined them. I had to—I couldn't see any alternative if I wanted to protect Terry. No way did I want to help them."

Alarm stomped in Jonno's gut. "Does he know you're both shifters?" Hell, that could mean problems for them and for Terry if Max sold her out for a nefarious purpose. Jonno wondered if Ramsay realized the danger Max presented to him and his sister.

Ramsay stumbled back past Jonno, a strained set to his mouth. He leaned against a stainless workbench, a pained groan squeezing past his tight lips. "Terry told me Max didn't know. She wouldn't listen when I tried to tell her he's dangerous to us. Max keeps tight control of the money. Bastard stole my wallet, which is why we had to resort to stealing food. A man needs more than beer to survive."

"And especially a feline shifter," Emily said, understanding in her voice. "As long as you're with us you need not go hungry."

Ramsay squeezed his eyes shut for an instant, his throat working. Once he opened them again they glinted with unshed tears. "I appreciate everything you've done for us, but if Terry moves on with them…" His shoulders hunched into a helpless shrug. "She's my sister. I have no one else. I promised her after our parents died we'd stay together."

"Don't worry. We'll work something out, but you have to remember your sister is responsible for her own actions. You can't protect her all the time," Emily said, squeezing his arm. "She has to be accountable."

Jonno hoped like hell Emily could keep her word because from where he stood Terry was on the road to trouble.

Chapter 13

Plans for Capture

"They kept the plans from Ramsay and Terry. Tomasine confirmed it when I checked with her," Jonno said to Laura and Charlie on entering the police station. "Tomasine rang my cell just before I got here. Terry turned up. Said she went for a walk for some fresh air."

Laura snorted at that. "Interesting."

"I thought so," Jonno agreed.

"Good. We're on for tonight then," Charlie said.

"Yeah. I hope they strike this time," Laura said, her face contorted in a huge yawn. She raised her arms above her head and leaned back in her chair. "I need my sleep."

Charlie smirked and stood to place a document in the scanner. He tapped the controls and waited for the device to scan to his computer. "Tell Jonno to let you sleep."

A growl erupted from Jonno, rattling his throat. Charlie didn't even flinch, laughing at them instead. The two human cops had accepted the felines and nothing fazed them. "Some people have no respect."

"What are we going to do about Terry?" Laura asked, tapping her pen on the desktop.

"It looks as if she's lied. We can't trust her," Jonno said, after filling them in on his conversation with Ramsay.

Charlie's chair squeaked as he settled his weight. "I guess it depends on what she does next. We might use her to feed information. We assume they've cased the Mitchell homestead. It's a matter of waiting, shaking the cage and seeing what falls out."

A sense of restlessness plagued Jonno. He stalked past their two desks, doing his best to pace in the crammed police station. His upper thigh caught a stack of folders, sending them flying. Cursing, he crouched to gather the papers.

"Haven't you got work to do on the farm?" Laura asked, her eyes rolling in clear exasperation. Her chair squeaked a protest when she rose to join him. "We need to wait. That's what the police do. It's all haste with long intervals in between."

"In other words, go away and let us do our job." Charlie's mouth wreathed in a smirk while he delivered the verbal jab.

They were right. He had tasks to complete on the farm, but Jonno's gut writhed with uncharacteristic nerves. Instinct warned him of danger. The need to protect his mate simmered in him while his feline fought for release, tearing at the polite strands of civility.

Another growl rattled his throat, low and frustrated. Jonno picked up the last piece of paper and slapped it into Laura's hands. He stood with a jerky movement, inhaling while fighting another growl. "I'm going. I'll see you later tonight." Unable to resist, he pressed a quick kiss to Laura's lips and stalked from the police station. Somehow he needed to quicken the pace of his courtship and mark Laura. Patience didn't come easy to him. He snorted. The truth—this mating shit was gonna be the death of him.

"There they are," Laura murmured, her low voice carrying to Jonno. "I see two."

Jonno scanned the surrounding of the house, the deep shadows cast by the mature trees and larger bushes. "I see them. They're going through the window we left open for them."

"Good of them to wait until a fine night with an almost full moon," Charlie whispered.

"Definitely two," Isabella said, appearing from near the road. "They left their vehicle off the road, near the gate to the hill paddock."

"I say take them down," Laura said.

Leo appeared beside Isabella. "I'm with Laura. At least this way we have part of the group."

"Let's do it," Charlie said.

Adrenaline flowed through Laura as she stood and crept to the section of the house allocated to her. The others moved into position. They'd staked out the doors as well since they didn't have deadlocks. It'd be a simple matter for the thieves to leave via one of the doors rather than crawling back through the window.

She crouched in the shadows, listening for the slightest hint the thieves were heading her way. A breeze blew, rattling the leaves of a tree. She had no idea what type of tree it was—the noise reminded her of gentle breakers running to shore at the beach. A click sounded, not a loud one, although enough to raise her awareness. Heart pounding, she stared at the door and watched it open.

Showtime.

Laura stood, her hand closing over the butt of her gun.

Two figures exited the house, the one in the rear pausing to close the door.

"That was easy," one of them said.

"Good haul," the other agreed.

The gloating smugness in the males' voices prodded Laura to action. "Police," she said in a firm tone. "Put your hands up in the air where I can see them."

"We haven't done anything. This is our house," one male said.

"Think again." Isabella came up beside her. "This is the Mitchell homestead and you're guilty of breaking and entering."

Without warning, the two males sprinted in opposite directions. Laura leaped at one as he passed her. She grabbed his T-shirt. He jerked free. With a curse, she sprinted after him.

A feminine snarl told her Isabella had taken off in pursuit of the other.

Damn, the little prick ran fast. He scooped up a rock, firing it at her without breaking speed. It hit her on the shoulder. Laura swore at the solid thump of pain, slowing. Then someone—either Leo or Jonno—sprang at him with a snarl. They fell in a tangle of limbs. The thief fought but was no match in size or strength for the fully grown feline. Jonno, she saw, as she neared the two.

Breathing heavily, pulse hammering in her ears, Laura handed Jonno the cuffs. Now that she'd stopped running, her shoulder ached like hell. She moved it gingerly and decided the stone had broken no bones.

Charlie trotted over to them. "You okay?"

"Yeah," Laura said, forcing aside the throb of pain. She was fine. "Did we get the other one as well?"

"Isabella got him. He's not going anywhere. I'll get the car." Without waiting for her reply, Charlie sped off.

Isabella dragged over the other teen. Laura scanned his face, pleased when she saw they'd caught the leader. Good. That would put a crimp in the rest of the group's plans because, according to Ramsay, they were thick.

"We weren't doing anything," the leader protested.

Laura moved closer, checking his jacket packets and doing a brisk search for both concealed weapons and contraband. "Bingo," she said, pulling out a ring and a necklace. "These belong to Emily Mitchell. You're under arrest for theft and breaking and entering." A further search revealed a knife strapped to his thigh. The other youth possessed a similar weapon plus money and credit cards belonging to Emily. The added evidence of the driver's license put Max at the other robbery. Laura rattled off their rights, relieved when Charlie arrived with the car and placed the pair of sullen males into the rear of the police vehicle. Her jaw cracked in a wide yawn. The last couple of nights had taken their toll. At least they'd caught them.

Crime solved. Good job done.

After settling the two males in the holding cells, she, Charlie and Jonno stumbled from the station, ready to hit their beds.

"Sleep in tomorrow morning, Charlie," Laura said.

"What about our prisoners?"

Laura shrugged. "I'll check on them, get them a meal."

"I'm so tired I'm not going to argue," Charlie said. "Thanks."

Soon, Laura and Jonno were on their way to his house. In Jonno's bedroom, they stripped and crawled into bed.

"How's your shoulder?" Jonno asked, probing it with skilled fingers.

"It will be fine." Despite her words, Laura couldn't stop the wince of pain at his touch.

"Sorry." His lips brushed the bruised skin, a barely there skim of his mouth that sent both pleasure and longing through her.

"Jonno," she murmured, her fingers massaging his scalp and slipping through his hair.

Their lips met, unhurried and gentle. When Jonno pulled away, her breath quickened, his intense scrutiny making her wet and ready for him. So attuned to him that heat blossomed with a mere look and a kiss. Sensual energy arced between them, twists of sensation darting through her pussy.

"I love you," he whispered, taking tiny bites along her jaw and down her neck. She arched against him in silent encouragement, whimpers she couldn't contain escaping. "Spread your legs for me."

The raspy command sent a flush across her breasts. They ached for his touch and cupping one, she silently offered it to him. Smiling faintly, he lowered his head and the warmth of his mouth surrounded her tip. The suction of his mouth brought a soft cry to her lips. Heat flowed from her nipple to settle between her legs. Laura sucked in a sharp breath as he pleasured her. One hand slipped into her heat, stroking across her distended clitoris while his mouth continued to tease and suckle her breast. The ardor heightened between them.

"Jonno, I need you."

He lifted his head, his eyes dark and full of passion. "My pleasure."

With a face taut with want, he slipped between her legs, spearing her with his cock. Her eyes fluttered closed, a sigh releasing at the friction between them. They rocked together, the heat flaring until orgasm buzzed through her, boiling over into intense pleasure.

"Jonno." Laura drew his head down and kissed him. The scrape of his stubble against her cheek brought a shudder of enjoyment. She gripped his shoulders, holding on tight as he thrust his hips, large body convulsing with climax.

His arms wrapped around her, holding her so tight she could scarcely breathe. Laura wriggled, and he eased back, brushing a gentle kiss on her lips. She settled against his side to enjoy the warmth and comfort his touch brought. It was the last thing she remembered before she fell asleep.

Laura's step held a bounce despite the early hour and the lack of sleep. This capture of part of the gang of thieves appeared great on paper and a step in the right direction for possible promotion. Her mind wandered to Jonno's declaration and her good mood dissipated a fraction. He'd said he loved her.

Not once but several times.

How could he be so sure?

Although she liked spending time with him, surely he realized Middlemarch was a stop for her, not a destination. Had she mentioned it to him? She was sure she had. Maybe she'd tell him again so things were clear between them. Her conscience piped up and told her she lied to herself, that she cared more than she admitted. Laura shoved the thought aside and concentrated instead on what she needed to do during the rest of the day.

She'd checked on the prisoners, who were well albeit sulky and shouting of police persecution. She'd allowed them to ring their lawyers, had done the paperwork for a search warrant and was on her way to Storm in a Teacup to get them breakfast.

Charlie fell into step beside her.

"What are you doing here so early? I told you to sleep late."

"Too wired," he said. "My mind kept going in circles. I thought we could go to the campground once you've fed the prisoners and do a search, check for fingerprints. It occurred that some of the other crime scenes might have mystery fingerprints. If we could match them to our thieves, we might get them on other charges."

"Good thinking, Sherlock. I need a coffee first. Besides, it's possible the remaining teens at the campground have done a runner after their friends didn't return."

"No, they're still there. I drove past and checked," Charlie said with smug satisfaction. "I wonder if they'll consent to a search without a warrant."

"Probably not, which is why I've done the paperwork and sent it off to Dunedin. It could take a day or two though." Laura pushed open the front door to the café. Even at this early hour three bicycles stood in the cycle stand while their owners ate breakfast. The bell tinkled their arrival.

"You're early after the excitement last night," Emily said.

"We need two breakfasts to go for our guests at the police station," Laura said. "What do you send over?"

"A cooked breakfast. Anything for you and Charlie?"

"Latte for me, thanks," Charlie said.

"Same for me plus a blueberry muffin to go."

Twenty minutes later and feeling awake after the coffee, Charlie and Laura returned to the station.

Isabella met them outside. "Reporting for duty."

"Oh we—"

"Yes, you do. At the least you need someone to keep an eye on your prisoners."

"Thanks," Charlie said. "We appreciate the help. The guys from Mosgiel are meant to collect them today, hopefully this morning. They couldn't give us an exact time. Come on, Laura. Let's hustle and get to the campground."

"I wish we had the warrant," Laura said. "It's frustrating knowing they'll leave once we show interest."

Charlie thumped his fingers against the doorjamb, his body coiled ready to spring. "Maybe they'll stay because we have their leader."

"Solidarity amongst the brothers," Isabella said. "Stranger things have happened."

Laura snorted. "We don't want strange." She cast a quick glance at Isabella. "There's enough weird in Middlemarch without adding to it."

Isabella's chuckle of amusement followed them out the door. Laura figured breaking a few more rules and leaving Isabella in charge wouldn't matter. The only locals who knew the full situation were shifters. Not likely that they'd tell. Charlie drove to the campground, to make the visit appear more official, and Laura thought of the coming confrontation, hoping it'd go well.

"Good, they're still there." Charlie turned the police car into the campground and drove along the access road to the campervan. He parked, and they both studied the area.

"I'll do the talking," Laura said. "Don't get too close to them. I'm thinking they'll have concealed knives like the two we caught last night." Laura climbed out of the police car, adrenaline pumping through her as it always did when she walked into a dangerous situation.

"Whatcha lookin' at, lady?"

The leather jacket should have made the kid appear tough. It didn't. Topped with the pale face and scowl, his attention skittering and never stopping, he seemed young and scared. All the bravado in the world couldn't cancel out the silent language his body screamed. Good. He looked worried and nervous. Laura scanned his friend before turning her attention back to the first belligerent male.

"We want to search your campervan." Laura paused, staring at the male until he lowered his gaze.

"Why?" the second male asked, his tapping foot and fidgeting sure signs of uneasiness.

Confidence built in Laura. They'd confiscated their vehicle—the one the thieves had left parked on the roadside, near the Mitchells' land. They had to have their stash hidden somewhere because there was nowhere to sell or dispose of the stolen goods here. They'd require a large town or city to move stolen merchandise. Of course they might have driven to Dunedin or Queenstown between burglaries. Laura didn't think so. Some of the dates were too close together. These kids had planned the robberies, staked out properties to hit.

"Because we believe you and your friends committed several robberies in the area," Laura said, fixing the male with an intent stare.

"We ain't done nothin'." Leather Jacket refused to look her in the face.

"Don't ya need a warrant?" the other asked.

Laura turned her attention on him, taking in the tattoo snaking down his arm below the sleeve of his faded yellow T-shirt. "Not if you give us permission to do a search."

"We don't give no permission." A tinge of triumph crept into Leather Jacket's voice, as if he felt more confident. He smoothed his jacket, reminding Laura of a preening blackbird.

Laura pulled out a notebook and stalked away from the two males. She rounded the campervan, jotting the name of the rental company plus the registration number. These vehicles were expensive to hire. There must be good money in the breaking-and-entering business.

"What are you doing?" Leather Jacket demanded.

Not so much bravado now. She should have felt like a bully but enjoyed it too much. "Noting a few details. We'll be back with the search warrant." The kid didn't need to know she'd recorded the details earlier and included the registration numbers of both the campervan and the car in the warrant. "Where are your friends?"

"Out," Tattoo said.

"None of ya business," Leather Jacket snapped, almost at the same time. They glared at each other, uneasiness passing between them despite the bravado they tried to project.

"When they turn up, tell them we want to see them." Laura jerked her head at Charlie and they headed back to their car. Neither spoke until Charlie pulled out of the camping ground.

"Why didn't you tell them we had their friends at the station?"

Laura smiled with little humor. "I figured I'd give them a reason to hang around. They didn't seem concerned at their friends' absence. Not yet. Let them stew."

"Good thinking. How long do you think the warrant will take?"

"A day, they told me. We should get rid of our prisoners this morning."

"It would be easier all round," Charlie agreed.

Back at the station, Isabella reported no problems. Laura rang Mosgiel again to receive an update of when they could expect the pick up for their prisoners and learned they were on their way. The paperwork involved made her want to tear out her hair. She settled down to attack it, pausing to answer a phone summons.

"You fuckin' bitch!" a woman screamed.

Laura winced and moved the phone away from her ear. "Can I help you, ma'am?"

"Whore."

Laura glanced at Charlie then Isabella. The other woman stilled, her attention caught by the viciousness layered into the speaker's voice. Shaking her head, Laura hung up and concentrated on her paperwork again. Her heart beat faster than normal, her mind on the phone call. The woman's voice sounded familiar. Given time, she'd remember where she'd heard it before. She continued to fill out the form she was working on until she realized her concentration had gone. Her mind kept going back to the plain ferocity in the woman's voice.

"Do you think that phone call was for me?" she asked, giving up the pretense of work.

"She didn't mention your name," Charlie pointed out.

Isabella shrugged. "A wrong number."

The phone rang in that instant and they stared at it for three rings.

"I'll answer it," Charlie said in a firm voice.

Laura indicated he should with a wave of her hand, having no intention of answering it herself.

Charlie picked up the phone, silencing the loud rings. He listened. "Hi, Tomasine. She's gone again? Okay. We'll watch out for her. Is Ramsay still there? Yeah. We'll call you as soon as we locate her."

"Terry?" Isabella asked.

"Yeah, she's disappeared." Charlie stood.

"It'd be better if I went," Isabella said. "I can track better than either of you."

"A feline thing?" Charlie asked. Laura noticed he exhibited the same fascination as she regarding the Middlemarch shifters.

"I'm not feline," Isabella said. "If you stick around long enough, one day I might tell you."

Before Laura could ask questions, Isabella disappeared out the door, her body moving with sinuous grace. "What do you suppose she meant by that? It sounds as if there are other supernatural creatures around the place."

Charlie's wide shoulders rose and fell in a shrug. "No idea. I'm still getting used to the idea that some of them turn into cats. Although I'm tempted to tell someone, I don't want to end up inside a padded cell."

"I should check the campground to see if Terry heads over there." Laura stood, pausing as a thought occurred. "Did Tomasine say if Terry knows we arrested her boyfriend?"

"Good point. If Terry knows, she might head here to the station. I'll ring Tomasine and check." Two minutes later Charlie turned to Laura. "She knows. She overheard Tomasine and Felix talking and screamed at them. I'd say we've solved the puzzle of your mystery caller."

The front door opened and two uniformed officers strode inside. "We've come to pick up the prisoners."

"Good," Laura said.

By the time they'd loaded the two men and exchanged the paperwork it was almost two o'clock. Laura's stomach growled.

"How about we switch the phones over to mobile and go to the café for a late lunch?"

Charlie leaned back in his chair until it seemed in danger of toppling. "Works for me."

"I thought I'd die of boredom when I learned of the Middlemarch transfer," Laura said as she and Charlie left the station. "It's surprising how much I'm enjoying it."

"And it's nothing to do with the locals," Charlie said, sending her a sideways glance.

Laura considered Jonno, the Mitchells, and nodded. "Maybe."

"Are things serious between you and Jonno?"

"What are you? My girlfriend?"

Charlie laughed. "I'd like to think I was a friend. I'm offended you think I'm a girl."

They paused for a car to pass before crossing the road to the café.

"You arrested Max!"

The feminine shriek rang down the street, halting both Laura and Charlie mid-stride. Laura turned and seconds later, Terry flew at her, fists swinging. The first punch grazed her chin, the second connected, whipping back her head. Before Laura could move, Terry sprang, feline genes giving her a distinct advantage. Damn, she was quick. Laura rolled, thankful when Charlie grabbed Terry and hurried footsteps heralded Isabella's arrival. Together they pulled Terry off Laura before the teenager slugged her with another punch.

226

With unsteady legs, Laura climbed to her feet and surveyed the blood trickling from the gravel rash on her arm and elbow. Her face ached, her bottom lip feeling tender. Gingerly she probed her inner lip with her tongue and tasted blood.

"You okay?" Isabella held Terry with ease, her strength no match for the younger girl.

"She arrested Max. He hadn't done anything," Terry screeched, her face scarlet, dark hair flying wildly while she fought for freedom.

"I'm fine," Laura said. Not quite the truth. She'd have a few aches and pains tomorrow.

"I'll take Terry back to my place," Isabella said.

"Do you need a hand?" Charlie asked.

"Nah, I'll be fine." She marched Terry off, making short work of the teenager's struggles.

"I'm starting to believe Isabella was an assassin," Laura muttered. "Glad we're on the same side."

"An assassin?" Charlie's head snapped around so fast it was a wonder he didn't get whiplash.

"Another secret." Laura wrinkled her nose. "I'm sure they're kidding me. Like I said, we're on the same side so we should be okay."

"I'm liking this job more and more," Charlie said, his blue eyes glinting with curiosity while he stared after Isabella.

"It hasn't been dull, that's for sure. Still up for lunch?"

"Yeah. Looks as if Jonno is joining us."

Laura turned toward him, both pleasure and excitement filling her. The grin on Jonno's face brought warmth and the moment in which she knew perhaps she felt something other than lust for him. She wasn't certain how to define the feeling, just knew it was there inside her—a glowing ember. Her hand lifted in a wave of welcome.

Behind Jonno a figure appeared. A shot fired, the sound loud and explosive like a car backfiring. Fire hit Laura in the chest. It stole her breath, her limbs jellifying as she gasped for air. Sound echoed inside her head, vision blurred and she felt herself crumple. The ground rose to meet her, hard and unforgiving. Her head thumped against the bitumen and the world went dark.

"No!" Jonno shouted, sprinting toward Laura. Fear grabbed him by the throat. Another shot rang out, but he didn't stop until he reached her.

"Police," Charlie yelled. "Put down your weapon. Now."

A woman screamed, the notes high and carrying hysteria. A child wailed. The revving of an engine and the shriek of tires, followed by an indignant shout from the postmistress. Jonno heard the pounding of feet and didn't remove his attention from the still form of his mate.

"Blast. She's getting away." Charlie grabbed a notebook from his pocket while reading the number plate aloud. Charlie continued to mutter the combination of letters and numbers while he scrawled it on paper.

"Laura. Laura?" Jonno knelt beside her in the middle of the road. She didn't move, her stillness adding to his growing terror. "Laura." He checked her pulse. Faint. A smear of blood came away on his hand as he smoothed it over her hair. She must have hit it when she fell. Gentle fingers probed her head and found a slight bump. His fingers were bloody when he raised them. He turned her onto her back. A shocked gasp escaped. Damn. She was bleeding from a wound on her chest.

Charlie hurried to his side, crouching beside them. "Is she all right? Aw, shit. She's bleeding bad."

"Ring Gavin." Jonno unfastened her shirt, revealing the gunshot wound in her chest. Blood soaked into both her shirt and the white bra she wore. Jonno ripped off his shirt and tore it into pieces, wadding a large scrap of fabric and pressing it against the wound. "Now."

"But he's a vet," Charlie protested. One look at Jonno's face stilled further protest "What's his number?"

Jonno fumbled for his cell and tossed it to Charlie. "It's on speed dial. Number three. Gavin's the closest thing to a doctor we have. We'll go to Gavin's surgery." Jonno scooped up Laura and hurried along the road toward the house where Gavin lived and had a surgery for both animals and felines. "You're going to be okay. You will not leave me." Harsh breaths seared his lungs and burned his throat. His heart raced. "Laura." He could scarcely force her name past the thickness barricading his throat.

Charlie's voice, the tone low and urgent, faded into the background.

"Is she all right?" Saber ran across the road from the direction of the café and fell into step beside him, his face stern and mouth grim. "Gavin on his way?"

"Yeah, Charlie's ringing him now. God, Saber. What am I going to do?"

Saber opened the door to the surgery and Jonno maneuvered past. Jonno set Laura on a pristine gurney and checked her breathing again. She didn't seem any better. He lifted the wad of material and saw the bleeding had slowed. Aw, fuck. Maybe not. Moving her hadn't been a good thing.

Charlie rushed into the surgery. "Gavin's just arrived. Luckily, he was at the Radisson place down the road." He strode over to a phone sitting atop a neat desk and picked it up. Jonno was vaguely aware of Charlie detailing the make, color and registration number of the car plus the circumstances.

Gavin strode into the surgery and hurried to Laura's side. Without a word he set his bag on the floor and nudged Jonno aside. A growl erupted from deep in Jonno's throat. *Mine.*

"Knock it off," Gavin snapped.

Saber curled his hand around Jonno's upper arm. "Steady. Gavin will help."

Jonno growled again, his mind knowing it was the truth. Rational thinking didn't appease the feline. The hair at the back of his neck lifted as he bristled again.

"Jonno." This time Saber's tone left nothing in doubt. As an older male and council member, he expected obedience. Grudgingly, Jonno acceded and moved back to give Gavin room. However, he couldn't restrain yet another rumble of protest when Gavin used a pair of scissors to hack away Laura's shirt and bra to reveal her chest.

Saber's hand tightened on his arm to the point of pain. Instead of objecting, he used the pain to focus. Laura. He...she...they needed Gavin to help her.

"Charlie, she's gonna need a hospital. See if the rescue helicopter is available. We don't have time to wait for an ambulance." Terse. To the point. Gavin's words scared the hell out of Jonno. Fear gripped him, and when Saber's hand tightened, he realized his legs shook and he leaned on the other man.

Charlie spoke, his tone urgent and panicked. The phone crashed down. "They can't come because they're on another call. Another hour at least."

"Fuck," Gavin said. "Right, this is what we're gonna do. I need to get the bullet out. I can see it, so it shouldn't be too bad. Ring for the ambulance. Tell them it's urgent," he fired at Charlie.

Jonno stood, numb and shivering.

"What about the bleeding?" Saber asked.

"That's the problem," Gavin said, his expression grim.

The knot in Jonno's throat threatened to choke him. "Help her."

Gavin shot him a sympathetic glance. "I'll try."

Jonno nodded, reading the determination laced with compassion on the man's face. Gavin didn't think Laura would survive. The idea brought a knifing sensation to his gut, the pain so intense he doubled over. For the first time since childhood, emotion found an outlet in stinging tears.

She couldn't die. She couldn't leave him.

He refused to let her off this easily. She hadn't told him she loved him yet. He knew she did, but Jonno wanted the words to treasure. He wanted his mate alive and at his side. Arguing. Loving. Laughing.

He sucked in a deep breath. "What can I do to help?"

Laura groaned, the pained sound sending renewed fear skittering through him. Charlie arrived with boiling water and a stainless bowl, setting it beside Gavin. The man worked with speed, yanking supplies from his bag and the cupboards. A disinfectant scent filled the air.

"I could give her a mild painkiller, though I don't think I should. It will raise questions," Gavin said.

Jonno protested and Saber's grip tightened. His jaw worked while he fought the urge to slug Saber with his fists. This was Laura. His mate. No, she wasn't feline. It didn't matter. *Laura was his mate*. "She'll die," he gritted out.

"I know," Saber said, his voice heavy with regret. "We have to be careful. Gavin will do as much as he can before the ambulance arrives. The last thing we want is to lose Gavin's services because officials decide he's overstepped in his capacity as a vet."

Yeah. He knew Saber had to act for the best for the shifters. It didn't make it any easier to accept. Damn, he felt so helpless.

Shrugging away from Saber, he rounded the gurney and stood by Laura's head, smoothing her hair from her face and away from her shoulder.

Gavin picked up a stainless implement from a sterilizer machine that reminded him of a large pair of tweezers. He dug around in the wound, grunting once he found the bullet.

"She's waking up," Jonno said.

Laura groaned, her eyes flickering. Her limbs thrashed.

"Hold her," Gavin ordered, her voice terse.

Saber took one arm and Jonno took the other. Charlie moved to her legs.

"Steady, Laura," Jonno whispered.

Saber shot him a look of encouragement. The silent approval lent Jonno strength, grounded him despite the fear pulsing through him.

Gavin probed the wound again. Laura cried out, the sound tearing at Jonno's heart. He continued to hold her tight to prevent her moving or lashing out at Gavin. She moaned.

"Jesus," Charlie said.

"Almost got it," Gavin said.

Laura let out a pained cry. Jonno swallowed.

"Got it." Satisfaction filled Gavin's voice, punctuated by the clink of the bullet when it hit the interior of a stainless bowl. "Keep holding her for a sec. I have a battlefield wound dressing I can use. It should slow the bleeding and will help fight infection."

"She's lost consciousness again," Saber said.

"Probably for the best," Charlie said.

Gavin bustled around, the scent of alcohol filling the surgery. He ripped open a package, his hands steady and each move competent as he poured a gel-type substance into the wound. Jonno envied the man's composed manner when his knees threatened to buckle.

"Done," Gavin said after a few minutes. "Let me get a cloth to clean off the blood."

Jonno stilled the instinctive protest, gritting his jaw while another man tended his mate, touching her in an intimate manner. Gavin stopped without warning, his head jerking up to stare at Jonno.

"She's not marked."

Chapter 14

Saving His Mate

J onno growled under his breath, not holding back in communicating his fury. Every muscle in his body tightened while he fought to remain civil. The last thing he wanted was to run afoul of Saber, so he tried to control the bubbling rage inside.

"Back off," he snarled, moving his body between Laura and Gavin. Tension vibrated through him and another low-pitched growl filled the surgery.

The hostility in the surgery ramped up while Jonno and Gavin faced off.

Jonno prowled closer until their faces almost touched. Worry for Laura and sheer panic made his heart crash against his ribs. At the back of his mind he knew he was overreacting yet he couldn't rein the feline back.

"Keep away from my mate."

Gavin remained silent. Watchful, he didn't give an inch.

Saber darted between the two males, forcing Jonno to step back.

"Dammit, I'm not interested in Laura for a mate." Gavin backed away from Jonno and Saber until he stood next to Charlie. He raised his hands, still moving with caution. "I have my mate, my own problems, dammit. I want to help Laura. Okay?" He grabbed a thin blanket from a cupboard along the far wall and walked over to the gurney to spread it over her.

"What do you mean then?" Jonno's voice held clear challenge. His limbs shook. A sharp pain in his palm drew his attention, and he saw he'd done a partial change. Fighting for control, he dragged in a deep breath. The combined scents of antiseptic, blood and sweat brought a frown, a surge of nausea. He fought it, knowing the smell would haunt him for the rest of his days. Closing his eyes, he dug deep for control. He opened them again to glare at Gavin. "What the fuck do you mean?"

"The enzymes exchanged during the marking process should help her heal better," Gavin said. "They take time to work, but if she makes it through the next few hours, they'll speed her recovery."

His words were a kick in the gut. Laura might be his mate, but he hadn't wanted to rush her. Everything had happened so fast between them. Love. It was there on his side—without a shred of doubt. Laura...

"Are you saying I should mark her now?" Jonno glanced from Saber to Gavin and back. Neither man said a word.

"Why can't you mark her, if it might save her life?" Charlie asked. "What's the big deal?"

"Because Laura hasn't agreed. If I mark her, she'll be tied to me," Jonno said. "For life."

"She loves you," Charlie said.

"Has she told you?" Jonno winced at the need in him, the eagerness for confirmation. Charlie took so long answering he took two steps toward the cop, ready to throttle him. Gavin stepped between them and growled. Astonished, Jonno came to an abrupt halt.

Charlie peered from behind Gavin. "What's with the growling?"

"Nothing," Gavin said, brushing it aside.

Gavin and Charlie? Jonno shoved the revelation away to concentrate on his mate. "If I mark her, you think it will help?"

Gavin shrugged. "Yeah. How long before the ambulance arrives? Another hour?"

"Less," Charlie said. "They had to come from Dunedin. There wasn't a closer one."

"What do you think?" Jonno asked Saber, turning to his friends' brother for advice.

"If it were me, I'd do it," Saber said.

"Okay." Jonno sure as hell didn't want her to die. "I'll do it." He walked over to the gurney and stared at her colorless face. She seemed so still. Defenseless. He couldn't bear it if she died. Part of him would die with her.

"One thing." Gavin's hand closed on his shoulder. "Normally the marking process takes place while a couple makes love. From what I've heard that counteracts the pain of the bite." He glanced at Saber for confirmation. Saber nodded. "This marking will be painful for her."

Jonno swallowed, his hands closing to fists at his side. He ignored the sharp bite of nails against his palm. "How much pain?"

"From my research, I've heard it's bad. On a level with the gunshot wound."

Jonno stroked a finger over her smooth cheek. His mouth twisted when he looked back to the others. "Not much choice. Either I risk her dying or have her hate my guts because I've marked her. Painfully."

"Jonno? What happened?" Laura's voice sounded weak and thready.

"Laura?" Jonno bent over her and couldn't resist pressing a kiss to her lips. "You're awake. How do you feel?"

"Like a pile of shit after it's run over by a truck. Hurts. I don't remember..."

Gavin spoke from behind him. "Jonno, can I take a look at Laura?"

"Yeah." Jonno moved away to let Gavin check on Laura. This time he didn't act as territorial, not with the reaction Gavin had shown when he'd stepped too close to Charlie.

After a quick check, Gavin stepped back. "She needs blood, antibiotics and stitching. I've done as much as I can," he said. "She's weak." He glanced at his watch. "Damn."

"Jonno?" Saber's voice held a question.

Jonno ran his fingers through Laura's hair, and knew there was only one solution. He'd do it. If she recovered, it'd be worth it. Yes, he'd be bound to her for life, but that was what he wanted anyway. "Won't marking leave a noticeable wound? Won't it raise more questions?"

"We'll plead ignorance and say it was there beforehand," Gavin said.

A frown creased Jonno's forehead, apprehension bubbling through him. Hopefully Laura would feel the same way, if the bloody ambulance arrived in time. And if she didn't...well, he'd face that challenge once it happened.

"I love you, Laura." Jonno bent his head and kissed her lips, foreboding coloring his emotions. Anxiety filled him, spreading through his body and finding an outlet in a tremor. He trailed kisses from her mouth and across her jaw, disquiet growing proportionately the nearer he came to the marking site. Hurting her, causing her more pain didn't sit well. Marking her without permission didn't feel right either. He wanted the words. He wanted to know she returned his love.

A whimper escaped Laura. Fire burned her chest, stealing her breath. She heard the murmur of voices. None of the words made much sense. Jonno kissed her. She knew it was him because she recognized his musky scent. Damn, he didn't want to have sex now, because she felt like crap.

She tried to move, and a dagger sliced her chest. Jonno's lips brushed her throat. Heat filled her, perspiration coating her skin. She shivered, nausea dancing through the pit of her stomach. Fuck, she thought she might puke. Laura groaned.

"Go away." She pushed weakly, but Jonno grasped her shoulder and smoothed her hair aside. He ran his mouth back and forth over the fleshy part where shoulder and neck met. The nausea rose. She swallowed hard, bile filling her throat. It hurt. Everything hurt. Laura pushed against Jonno, trying to get him to move. "Jon—"

He struck. Teeth sliced through her flesh, fiery pain searing from her throat to join the heavy weight throbbing in her chest.

She screamed, her body arching upward. A twin sensation ripped through her as she moved, sapping the air in her lungs. A pained croak was all that emerged. She shuddered, blackness stealing through her mind. Jonno. He'd done this. Through blurry eyes she stared at him.

Why?

When he moved, she flinched, cringing away despite the searing pain caused by the move.

"Sorry, Laura. I'm so sorry." Jonno dipped his head again, angst clouding his face. He rasped his tongue across the bite, each lick sending another jolt of pain streaming down her shoulder and chest.

A high-pitched scream deafened her, ripping through her mind with sharp daggers. She moaned, frightened to move. Laura wished it would stop.

"That's enough, Jonno," Gavin murmured. "Let me take a look."

"It's not healing like Emily's mark," Saber said with concern.

"Damn, there's so much blood," Charlie said.

Laura's stomach lurched, and she threw up, vomiting all over Gavin, the gurney and her clothes.

Agony seared the length of her body, along with embarrassment at being sick. She closed her eyes, shutting out the condemnation she was sure she'd see. Instead, gentle hands cleaned her, voices murmuring.

It hurt.

Everywhere hurt so bad.

Sickness roiled in Jonno's stomach while his cock filled, pressing against his fly. He stirred uncomfortably and hoped none of the others noticed. The metallic flavor of blood filled his mouth and no amount of swallowing shifted it. The idea of fresh air came to him, but he refused to leave Laura's side.

He needed her.

The connection between them seemed much stronger now, and he ached with need. Sick pervert. He glared at his groin, the twitch in his trousers bringing both self-hatred and derision.

What the fuck sort of man was he? His mate lay in agony and all he could think of was sex.

Gavin walked over to him. "The bleeding's slowed. I think the field dressing has helped. It should help mask any anomalies the medical staff might find in her blood. They'll assume it's the components of the field dressing."

From where he stood, Jonno could see the mark. It didn't resemble any mating mark he'd ever seen. This one appeared like a livid bruise with a clear and defined set of teeth prints. No doubt it would turn a vivid purple and dwindle to yellow in time. A long reminder of a brutal act.

Jonno's breath eased out in a hiss of self-loathing. "What are you going to tell the ambulance men? They'll ask."

"I can play dumb," Gavin said, compassion in both his face and manner. "You did what you had to. I would've done the same."

A siren sounded in the distance.

"Damn, they made good time," Charlie said. "I'll stand outside to wait for them."

"I'll go to the hospital with them," Jonno said.

Saber clapped him over the shoulder. "I'll follow so you have a way of getting home."

Jonno nodded, swallowing, and walked over to the gurney. Laura's eyes were open, and they stared at each other.

"Laura," he whispered, relief flowing through him.

"Get away from me," she whispered.

Jonno froze, his hand hovering above her head. Slowly, his hand returned to his side.

"Get away from me." This time the words were more forceful.

In shock, he stared at her, not moving.

"Get away! Don't touch me," she screamed. "Away. Get him away." Hysteria throbbed in her voice and she thrashed around, a heartrending screech echoing around the surgery.

"Move back, out of her range of sight," Gavin ordered.

Saber gripped his arm and Jonno stumbled to the edge of the surgery, tears shrouding his vision. Laura's sobs made him feel terrible. Guilty. His mate hated him, and he could hardly blame her.

"I don't want to see him. He's not a man," Laura said to the nurse. She caught the roll of the nurse's eyes before the young woman smiled.

"I'll tell him, but wouldn't it be better to see the man and tell him yourself? He won't believe any of us. He keeps getting in the way, littering the corridor."

Laura's stomach roiled, and a tremor racked her body. She risked a glance at the door and noticed a shadow. Her throat tightened. The man was a savage, an animal. "I'm too tired for visitors." It wasn't a lie. Nightmares filled the night. Spotted leopards with bright red eyes... Laura swallowed and sent the nurse a beseeching glance.

A head peeped around the door. "Laura. You're looking much better."

"Emily." Caution sounded in her voice.

"I've brought Jonno with me. I know he wanted to see you," Emily said, her cheerful manner hiding none of the determination glinting in her eyes. She reached around the corner of the door and tugged the man into the room.

Laura let out a frightened squeak that had the nurse rushing to her side. "I can't have you upsetting her."

"Of course not," Emily said.

Laura let out a strained sigh once Jonno disappeared.

"How much longer will it be before she's released from the hospital?" Emily asked.

The nurse smiled. "All going well, the doctors say she can go home tomorrow morning. She's healed well."

Laura sobered. She had nowhere to go, apart from the police house in Middlemarch.

"Good. I'll be here to pick you up in the morning," Emily stated. "You're staying with me."

"What about the café?"

"That's what I have sisters-in-law for." Emily patted Laura's hand, her head turning when she saw Charlie. "I'll leave you to visit with Charlie. Tomorrow," she said.

Laura tensed, waiting for Emily to leave and hoping that she took Jonno with her. After a minute, she relaxed, something in her sensing Jonno had left. Contrarily, as had happened every day for the last two weeks, the minute he left she had an urge to see him, touch him. It was difficult to reconcile her fear with the strange longing. The doctors had commented on the ugly bruise at the base of her neck. She fingered it while Charlie commandeered a chair from the neighboring bed. Laura stilled her fingers, her face coloring on noticing Charlie's close attention.

"Is that still bothering you?"

Laura considered her answer. It didn't exactly ache. No, it itched and throbbed at unexpected times. "It's nothing—just a bruise."

"Hell, no! It's more than a bruise. It was the darnedest thing. Gavin explained it to me." He scrutinized her closely. "Do you remember Gavin? The vet." Charlie glanced over his shoulder and leaned closer to whisper. "The feline doctor. He removed the bullet and suggested that Jonno mark you in the feline way. Jonno didn't want to do it, but everyone thinks the mark has helped to speed your recovery. The doctors are saying it's your willpower, but we know better. Jonno saved your life." Charlie hesitated and shook his head. "I don't know why you're treating him like shit. If it wasn't for Jonno, you'd have died. You know they had to pump a hell of a lot of blood into you, right?"

Guilt rained down on her. She avoided Charlie's gaze, studying her clasped fingers instead. "I remember little."

"You're putting Jonno through hell," Charlie said. "The man loves you, and you're treating him like a contagious disease."

Fear gripped her, tightening around her lungs and restricting her breathing. Laura panted, trying to force air into her body and lessen the panic. "I...I didn't know."

"Yeah, I know you've been out of it for a while," Charlie said. "Hey, good news. We got the woman who shot you."

"Who was it?" Laura asked, her attention diverted. "I remember the sun shining right in my eyes. I didn't see who shot me."

"You know your ex-boyfriend Mike?"

"Mike shot me? I thought I saw a woman."

Charlie shook his head. "No, Mike's wife shot you. He'd told her he intended to leave her. For you."

Laura felt her mouth open. "But we finished ages ago. Once I heard he had a wife I wasn't interested." She leaned back on her pillows, wariness hitting without warning. "I didn't want him."

"I know that. You and Jonno hit it off straightaway. I had some of the top brass arrive in Middlemarch to question me. They wanted to know if you were still having an affair with Mike. I told them he kept ringing the station and bothering you. I told them you weren't interested and was going out with someone else."

"Hell," Laura muttered. "Do I still have a job?"

"You do. I suggested they talk to Jonno and Saber. Isabella spoke up for you and said Mike rang while she was at the station. He received a reprimand and the department head ordered him to stay away from both you and Middlemarch."

"And his wife?"

"Charged with attempted murder and unauthorized use of a firearm."

Laura nodded, stilling once she realized her fingers had crept up to massage the bruised area of her neck. She stopped the instant she saw Charlie watching.

"I'll tell Jonno you'll talk to him once you arrive back in Middlemarch," Charlie said, his tone daring her to argue. "Emily said you were to stay with them until you were better and your strength returned."

The familiar fear circled through her mind again. Cats with sharp teeth. Slashing claws. Searing agony. Laura shivered, clutched the blankets and held tight. This was Charlie. No cats here. "Jonno saved my life?"

"Yeah. Gavin said it stressed him, made him out-of-his-mind worried."

"I should talk to him," she said almost to herself.

"That would be good. He might calm after you speak to him. He's out of control. Isabella is ready to deck him. She threatened to get out her assassin rifle. Even Emily mentioned avoiding Jonno, and she likes everyone."

"You like living at Middlemarch," Laura said, studying the relaxed attitude, the grin that had started in his eyes and moved across his face like a gentle wave to finish in a wide stretch of his mouth.

"Yeah." The smile faded to serious. "I enjoy working with you, the people, the friends we've both made. I enjoy the autonomy of working in a country station."

"That's great." The enthusiasm in his voice echoed in her heart. Everything he said resonated with her. Caution crept inside when her thoughts drifted to Jonno. Caution and longing. She didn't know how to reconcile the two. Charlie was right. She needed to face the boogeyman head-on or she'd never have peace, not during waking hours or in her dreams. Her cheeks heated as she recalled the dream she'd had early during the morning hours...

Jonno and her, naked bodies sliding together. Slow and languid they'd kissed, lips brushing, exploring. Their tongues touched and swirled in a dance of passion. The tips of her breasts tightened, abrading against his chest. The friction created echoes in her pussy, a decadent warming.

"Hmm, I love to touch you." Jonno slipped a hand between their bodies and twisted one tight nipple.

Laura groaned, wanting more. Needing more. His lips lingered against the warmth of her neck. She clutched his shoulders, luxuriating in his body, packed with muscle. It made her feel feminine. Sexy. And the way he touched her made her feel loved. He kissed his way down her body, pausing to lick her mark. Sweet pleasure arced straight to her pussy. She shuddered, and he repeated the move, nibbling with his teeth.

"Jonno," she whispered. "That feels so good."

"There's more where that came from." The husky promise speared straight to her core and heat blossomed, plumping her folds for his cock. "I need your cock. Now," she demanded, wanting the pleasure of the first stroke parting moist tissues.

"Take what you need," he offered. "Use my body for your pleasure."

Laura laughed. "I'm under you. How can I control anything with you looming over me?"

"Simple," he said, and rolled, grinning at her when she squeaked. "There you go. Ready to rock 'n' roll." He placed his hands behind his head. "What are you waiting for?" The gleam in his eyes challenged her, made her want him to beg, so she set about seducing him, pushing him as he tested her.

She ran her hands across his chest, savoring the faint sprinkling of hair beneath her fingertips. His flat nipples tightened when she touched them, and as she stroked her fingers along his collarbone, his entire body shuddered.

This teasing was a double-edged sword. Even though she wanted to take her time and push him, she didn't think she'd last. Her attention drifted to his lips. A generous mouth, it curved in laughter—something she liked in a man. A sense of humor. The touches of humor were clear in the faint crinkle around his eyes. Oh, he was smiling now, knowing he'd claimed her attention.

Laura clambered over his body until she straddled him and leaned forward. She inhaled, dragging his scent of soap and man into her lungs. She fit her lips to his, a mere brush, to taste him before settling in to explore. With her tongue she traced the shape of his lips. He seemed content to let her lead, although he wasn't submissive. His mouth moved beneath hers, a silent invitation to go deeper. Helpless to fight the temptation, she slipped her tongue past his lips, exploring the contrasting hardness of his teeth and the softness of his inner mouth. Heat blossomed in her pussy, the increasing eager pressure of their mouths making her wet. Needy.

The urge to breathe had her lifting her head. The urge to continue touching and exploring set her lips blazing a trail of kisses across his jaw to his ear. She teased the rim of his ear with her tongue, nipping his lobe before nibbling at his neck.

"Damn, Laura. Bite me. Please, Laura. Bite me."

Shocked, Laura glanced up at him, noting the slight glazing of his eyes, the firm and starkly male lips. She bent her head again and grazed her teeth across the fleshy part between shoulder and neck. A choked and breathless sound escaped him.

"Laura." Her name sounded like a growl. "Take me inside you. Ride me." His taut face glowed with desire, the flush of passion blooming on his lean cheeks.

The pulsating walls of her sex agreed with him. She needed his cock and the coiled power of him. As if to encourage her, Jonno lifted his head and reached for her breast. Not a gentle seduction. His mouth surrounded her nipple and heat flowed with each draw of his lips. Laura gasped, her heart beating in uneven thumps as she felt the hot, tight suction of his mouth and the sharp vibration in her core. The gasp turned into whimpers she couldn't contain. Desperation filled her along with savage need. She pulled away from Jonno and guided his cock to her entrance, sliding down on his shaft with exquisite slowness.

"Damn, that's good," Jonno whispered. She could tell he wanted to take over. The clenched jaw and almost-anguished expression on his face gave it away.

"Yes," Laura agreed. It was excellent, and she couldn't go slow any longer. She forced her body downward, his cock slipping into her wet flesh. Fully seated, she paused, feeling the pulse of his cock deep inside her body. She studied his face before she moved, changing the angle until she found the perfect one. With her fingers she stroked across her swollen clit, enhancing her pleasure. A twist of sensation shot through her lower body and she groaned, increasing her pace, wanting more of the same. She watched him the whole time, judging his needs and her own. Her gaze strayed to his neck, his words hammering through her mind.

Bite me. *Bite me*.

Some urge deep inside made her move closer. Her teeth nibbled on the spot. Back and forth. Back and forth. She used more pressure, and he groaned, a dark sound full of passion. Encouragement. His shaft pulsed. Laura rubbed her clit, a choked and breathless murmur emerging against his shoulder. Sensations jumped through her, one on top of another, her finger moving faster over her swollen nub.

Jonno thrust, pushing pleasure through her in waves. "Bite me now." His order lashed between them, and she obeyed, biting hard. Then she was flying, hurtling into pleasure so good it was almost painful. Jonno's large body shuddered beneath hers, the spasm of his cock spurting his seed deep into her pussy.

When they moved, Laura realized she still gripped his flesh with her teeth. She tasted blood, earthy and metallic in her mouth, saw the circle her teeth had left on his neck, the vicious wound she'd left...

Laura had woken, her heart pounding, and realized her fingers stroked the wound at her neck. It had taken a long time before she drifted off to sleep again—a long time where she had nothing to do but think.

"She's here," Jonno said.

"Thank god for that," Saber said. "Your pacing is wearing tracks in the floor. Emily and I will be in our bedroom."

"What if Laura freaks out?"

Saber's eyes narrowed. "We'll hear her. We'd prefer no interruptions. I'll intercept Emily." He disappeared from the kitchen, leaving Jonno sitting at the table nursing a coffee. His hand shook so much liquid splashed over the side, splattering across the blue tablecloth. He set the cup on the table.

The soft murmur of voices had him staring at the doorway. Footsteps sounded and Laura appeared in the doorway. She hesitated on seeing him but didn't scream. He took heart from that.

He stood. "Take a seat. Would you like a cup of coffee?"

"Yes, please." She hovered, looking as if she might make a run for it.

"Sit," he said. "I don't bite." *Fuck. Way to go, Jonno.*

"You bit me."

Confrontation. Well, that was unexpected. His heart slammed against his rib cage when her fingers smoothed across her blouse, near her collar. She sensed the ties between them even as she denied them.

"I didn't want to do it that way." His voice cracked with pained emotion, the heaviness in his heart something he had to live with every day while she'd refused to speak with him. "I wanted to wait until you were sure of me, as sure as I am of you." He ran his hand through his hair, his agitation demanding movement, yet he didn't want to scare her with obsessive pacing. "I knew you might end up hating me. But I couldn't let you die. I couldn't."

Laura settled into a chair, her face softening into something he thought might be understanding. Jonno hoped it was understanding. Forgiveness.

"Charlie explained things, and my memory has returned. When I was first in hospital there were huge gaps."

Some of the tension in Jonno seeped away. This time she hadn't screamed. He'd take that as a positive. "You realize we're tied together now, that we're mates?"

"I feel it," she said in a low voice, although she refused to look at him. "The connection between us."

Relief came in a wave. "Good. That's good." Jonno wanted to touch her, to kiss her, knew it was too soon. He wanted her to at least look at him, much preferable to this wariness that made him feel like a wild animal. Instead he poured her coffee, adding milk and making it how she liked it. He passed the cup across the table and forced himself to return to his seat. Words trembled on the tip of his tongue, the need to ask what she wanted to do next. Fear kept him silent.

Laura picked up her coffee and took a sip. "I dreamed about you yesterday."

"Yeah?" Jonno cocked his head, wanting to know details, afraid to push. He'd scared her enough. This time he snared her gaze before she glanced at her coffee cup.

"Yeah."

The slight reddening of her cheeks gave him hope. A sexy dream. Even better. "Oh?"

Gavin had told him he needed to go slow. Heck, Emily and Saber had reiterated Gavin's suggestions. While he'd agreed, it wasn't easy battling his natural inclinations, the need pulsing through the feline.

"I bit you." The stark words echoed between them in the silence in the kitchen. Only the tick of the wall clock intruded.

And? Was that it? Surely there was more, otherwise why would she mention it?

"I woke up with the taste of blood in my mouth." She risked another glance at him, this time observing him for longer, her look a subtle caress. Jonno felt the jerk of his cock and picked up his coffee cup. Cold liquid. He took a sip anyway.

"And even though it frightened me, I realized my fingers stroked the wound on my neck. Touching myself there comforted me. The strangest thing."

Jonno managed a nod. He wasn't sure where this was going but realized the delicacy of the situation. He sipped his coffee again.

"Charlie said that even though we hadn't known each other long, we were good together. He thought it was serious."

"It is from my side," Jonno said, needing to push the words past the lump in his throat. Maybe there was hope and this could work out between them.

This time Laura shrugged, her face inscrutable and making him wish he could read her mind. Her breasts rose and fell as she inhaled. The silence grew along with his dissatisfaction. He loved Laura. He wanted her in his life, couldn't imagine anyone else, even if he hadn't marked her. They belonged together. Frustration grew, finding an outlet in clenched fists.

"We should take things one day at a time," she said. "I need time."

Jonno bit back a curse, wanting to yell and tell Laura time wouldn't make a blasted bit of difference with him. Instead he took a deep breath and fought for calm. "If that's what you want." He was proud of his even tone when inside panic rioted.

"Thanks. I appreciate it." She reached over and patted his hand.

The touch, an innocent one, designed to express thanks and gratitude. For Jonno it held complexities. He caught his breath, heart hammering at the warmth that pulsed from the brief touch. She licked her lips, a slow stroke of tongue over the bottom curve and a quick dart over the top, leaving them glossy.

Jonno closed the distance between them before he knew he'd moved. Her quick intake of breath sounded loud, although to his relief, not panicked. Taking heart, he went with the impulse and pressed his mouth to hers, coaxing rather than taking. Her lips were warm and moist, the innocent touch doing more damage to his restraint than a passionate ravishment of mouths. Despite every particle in his body protesting the move, he lifted his head to gaze deep into her eyes. To his relief he didn't see panic. Instead he saw thoughtful curiosity and a spark of awareness, but that might have been wishful thinking on his part.

Enough, he told himself. He had to move slowly. Full of regret, he pulled farther away, but Laura stopped him with her hands on his shoulders.

"I liked that. It made me happy."

"Because I love you," he said, restraining a flinch. A guy could only give so many declarations of love before he gave up looking for the requisite response.

"I said before I feel the tug of belonging. My...mark?" She continued on seeing his nod of confirmation. "It throbs. Will it always be like that?"

"I don't know." Jonno went with honesty. "Gavin says the reaction varies depending on the individuals."

She cocked her head to the right, her hair falling over one eye. She swept it back with an impatient move and reminded him of an inquisitive bird. "How does it feel to you?"

"If we're not in the same room, there is a part of me missing. When I can see you I'm happy and whole." Fuck, bring out the violins. That had sounded so corny, and yet it was true. That was how he felt when it came to Laura.

Laura didn't laugh, which gave him hope. "It frightens me."
"What?"

"The intensity. The sense of feeling out of control."

"Sweetheart, I know. Do you think I didn't have a few worries? It will be okay. We'll take things as slow as you want."

Her bright smile and the relief on her face rewarded him for his promise of patience. He just hoped he could wait for as long as she needed.

Chapter 15

Impatience Simmers

*O*ne Week Later

    After the sexy dream, her nightmares of the bite, the pain and horror of it, had faded. She'd thought long and hard about her behavior after Jonno had marked her. Yes, the bite had bloody hurt, but it hadn't just been the pain that had prompted her reaction to Jonno. Shock and the treatment she'd received from Mike had added another layer, and in her traumatized state, her mind had combined it together and she'd lashed out at Jonno. She no longer blamed him, although she hadn't told him. The song said it all—sorry is the hardest word.

As the days passed, Laura waited for Jonno to make his move. It hadn't happened. Each day he visited her at the Mitchell homestead to spend time with her, treating her like a sister.

"Is Jonno staying for dinner?" Emily asked, interrupting her reverie.

"I don't know. I guess." Laura stabbed the potatoes with a fork, testing to see if they were cooked yet.

"I've invited Charlie. It's no trouble catering for two extras."

Laura nodded and continued with dinner preparations. "Gavin said I should be able to return to work next week."

"Not what he told me," Emily said, refuting her claim. "He said you could go into the station for a few hours and that you should take things easy."

Laura's bottom lip pouted before she realized she'd done it.

"I second that," Jonno said, prowling into the kitchen. He brushed a gentle kiss on Laura's cheek and stepped away before she could return the caress. The lack of a more intimate touch frustrated her. Since the first dream, she'd had others and now they were spilling over into daydreams.

"He told me the same thing," Charlie confirmed, coming in behind Jonno. "And told me I was in charge."

Laura snorted. "As if." Her chin jutted upward. "I'm going home tomorrow. Gavin said I could. He said I've healed remarkably quick." And she felt ready to get back to her routine.

"I'm mortally offended," Emily said. "What's wrong with here?"

"Will you be okay on your own?" Jonno asked.

"You'll be there," Laura said.

"You're coming home with me?"

Nothing in his expression told her if he wanted her. Too bad. It was what she wanted. "Yes."

"Thank god," he said, grabbing her and wrapping his arms around her. His mouth met hers, urgent and full of hunger, everything she'd craved during the past week. It was like arriving home and she gave herself freely, falling into the kiss and melting into his hard chest.

"That's enough of that," Charlie said. "This is a kitchen."

"Huh," Emily said.

"I second that," Saber said, coming to a halt beside his mate. "The kitchen is for more than cooking."

Jonno lifted his head and laughed. "Thanks for the info, but I don't think you should give us ideas. We wouldn't want to offend anyone."

Laura cuddled up to him, every instinct telling her this was right between them, despite the newness.

"Dinner is almost ready," Emily said. "Saber, why don't you pour everyone a glass of wine while Laura and I bring over the food?"

The men took seats, and after placing several serving plates of food onto the table, Emily and Laura joined them.

"How are Ramsay and Terry?" Laura asked.

Charlie frowned. "Didn't you tell her?"

"Tell me what? Are they okay?" Laura asked.

Emily answered. "Terry ran away while you were in hospital. We're hoping she'll come to her senses and return to be with Ramsay."

"So Ramsay is still here?"

Emily snickered as she picked up her glass of wine. "Yes, he's still staying with Felix and Tomasine. Sylvie loves him. She says she will marry him when she grows up."

"Ramsay is a good kid," Saber said. "We've asked him to stay with us in Middlemarch."

"And is he?" Jonno asked.

"I hope so," Emily said. "He's a natural cook. The café is becoming so busy now I'd love the extra help. I thought London Allbright, Gerard's mate, would be a handy backstop, but she has set up business as a virtual assistant and doesn't have as much free time. You haven't met Gerard and Henry, have you?"

"No, not yet. How's Ramsay taking it?" Laura asked.

"He's furious at Terry. Evidently he's spent the last six months running around after Terry, keeping her out of trouble. He's tired of it," Saber said. "He feels guilt as well, but he's realized he can't take responsibility for her actions."

Laura accepted a piece of bread from Emily. "Surely he doesn't want her to land in trouble?"

"No, I think he's hoping she'll come to her senses on her own," Charlie said. "There was a sighting in Mosgiel. Isabella's keeping an eye on her from a distance. She won't come to any harm."

"And the guys at the campground?" Laura asked.

"They left the day after your shooting, in the middle of the night. Isabella has seen them in Mosgiel. She's watching them too." Charlie helped himself to roast lamb before passing the serving platter to Saber. "At least we captured part of the gang—the brains behind the operation."

"What about the missing jewels?" Emily asked. "I recovered my beautiful faux jewels. But the other victims?"

"We found a few items hidden in their campervan. We're hoping they'll do a deal with us, and we'll be able to recover more of the goods." Charlie said. "This roast is good, Emily. Thanks for inviting me."

Emily smiled. "You're welcome. One more isn't a problem. And, we're having a big party to celebrate Saber's birthday. You're invited."

Saber glowered at Emily. Laura saw her new friend merely smirked and winked at her husband. They had a good marriage, which gave her hope. Not all men were the same as Mike. She glanced along the table to Jonno and found him looking at her. For a drawn-out moment they stared at each other, the heat between them palpable. Her cheeks glowed, and she swallowed a mouthful of peas before she did something stupid like choking.

"Enough of that, you two," Charlie said. "I'm trying to eat my dinner."

"I could find a date for you," Emily said. "I'd enjoy trying to matchmake."

Laura laughed at Charlie's horrified refusal. "Maybe there's already someone he's interested in dating?"

"Let the man eat his dinner in peace," Saber said.

"Huh! You're allowed to act the matchmaker and I'm not?" Emily waved her knife around to illustrate her point.

The corners of Saber's eyes crinkled despite not cracking a grin. "That was different. My brothers were out of control. Thank goodness there's only the twins left."

"Are Sly and Joe coming to the party?" Jonno asked.

"They said they'd be here," Emily said. "It will be great having the family together. I'll get back to you with the details."

Laura nodded and thought of family with envy. Her family wasn't as close, and they hadn't supported her while the debacle with Mike had occurred. Some of the residents of Middlemarch might be shapeshifters, but they could teach most people a thing or two regarding relationships and families. Which reminded her...

"Charlie and I want to know if vampires are real," she said with a glance at Charlie.

"Ooh, good question," Emily said, brows rising while she studied Saber. "Do tell."

"I've never met one in person," Saber said. "I believe a few live in Auckland."

"Really?" Charlie asked. "They drink blood?"

"From what I understand," Saber said. "Although you shouldn't believe everything you hear."

After a moment's startled silence, they bombarded Saber and Jonno with questions. The easy conversation and good-natured sniping between them made Laura realize she had a family here in Middlemarch—if she wanted. It took little thought. Despite her initial fears, life in Middlemarch had grown on her, and Jonno had played a huge part in that.

"Emily, I think I might go home with Jonno tonight," Laura announced.

"Do we have to discuss sex?" Charlie complained.

"I didn't hear the word mentioned," Saber said. "Although it works for me."

Emily distributed dessert for everyone. "As long as you're thinking about me rather than anyone else in the room."

Laura felt the surge of passion between them almost as distinct as the physical touch of her hand clasped in Jonno's. Thankfully, the rest of the meal passed swiftly and she and Jonno escaped soon.

Jonno followed her to her bedroom to collect her bag. "Are you sure?"

"Very," Laura answered. "I want this. I want you. It took me a while to work it all out—the past rearing its ugly head—but I know what I want now. You."

"Thank you," Jonno said, his voice husky and throbbing with emotion. "Are you ready to leave?"

"Aren't you going to kiss me?" A note of teasing sprang forth and she arched her brows in playful emphasis.

"If I touch you now, I won't be able to stop."

"Oh."

"Is that all you're going to say?"

"There's nothing left to say. I'm ready for action now." Arousal slipped through her body, elevating her breathing. No doubt—Jonno pushed her buttons.

Jonno slanted her a look, his eyes glowing in the dim lit room. "I can think of a few words that still need saying."

A chuckle slipped out. "In my own time," Laura said, knowing what Jonno referred to. Love. Yeah. She thought she could say the words. Soon.

Jonno took her bag from her, and the mere touch of his hand sent a warming shiver through her limbs. He guided her along the passage, his hand at her back. Every sense worked overtime, converging to heighten her desire. His touch. His scent. She couldn't wait to taste him—his mouth, his cock, and she even wanted to sink her teeth into his shoulder.

"Thanks, Emily." Laura hugged her friend, and even ignored the faint rumble of protest coming from Jonno to give Saber a quick kiss on the cheek.

The trip to Jonno's house took place in taut silence, as if they both realized the commitment they were making.

A couple. A mated pair.

Laura wondered at her lack of fear, but this felt right. She loved him.

Jonno pulled up outside his house. "Let me get the outside light so you don't fall." He grabbed her bag and hurried to the front door while Laura climbed out of the car. She didn't need the cosseting, even though it made her feel treasured.

"I told you to wait."

"Are you going alpha on me?"

"If that's what it takes. Gavin said you've healed well, better than a normal person. We still have to take it easy though."

265

"Hmm," Laura said. "We'll see."

Jonno scooped her off her feet and carried her to the bedroom. After placing her in the center of his bed, he followed her, caging her within his arms. She grinned up at him with impish humor. Laughter. It was a good thing to have in her life.

"I'm going to kiss you." He switched on one bedside lamp, allowing her to see more, although she'd noticed her vision seemed enhanced after the marking. Something else to discuss with Gavin when she saw him next.

"Good plan," Laura said with approval. "But you should take off your clothes first."

"I'll take off one item of clothing for each kiss you give me."

"A good incentive," she purred. Seconds later, she drew his head down and started on her seduction. She'd had a week to plan this and knew exactly what to do. She nibbled at the corner of his mouth and, with delicate precision, licked his bottom lip until he groaned. Immediately she took advantage, pushing her tongue into his mouth in a slow move designed to make him think of sex. In and out. In and out. Her blood seemed to thicken and her heartbeat raced, the kiss having a ricochet effect.

Her hands threaded through his thick hair, drawing him closer while she varied the pressure of her mouth and the strokes of her tongue. When she pulled back they were both breathing hard.

"Damn, I've missed that." Jonno glided one hand across her face, cupping her cheek with a gentleness she'd come to associate with the feline male.

"Me too."

Jonno moved away and ripped off his shirt. Laura was amazed the buttons didn't fly across the room in his haste. He never took his gaze off her, his eyes glowing in the way she associated with felines. He slipped off her shoes and knee-high stockings then massaged her feet.

"That's cheating," she said even as she enjoyed his deft touch and relaxed.

"I like to touch." Jonno removed his own shoes and socks. He stood and peeled off his jeans and underwear, finally standing before her naked. "Your kiss was worth several items of clothing."

"Smooth."

"Impatient," he corrected. "I want to make love to my mate."

"Yes," Laura whispered. When she went to push to her feet, Jonno stayed her and divested her of clothing.

"Beautiful. I can't believe I'm lucky enough to have such a beautiful mate." His face glowed with truth, and Laura basked in the heat arcing between them. He caged her in his arms again, exploring her body with his fingers and mouth until she tingled all over. Magic. Pure magic. He fingered one nipple, tugging until blood rushed to the taut peak. The scrape of his stubble against her breast increased the pleasure until she writhed beneath him, desperate for him to fill her aching flesh and drive them both to climax.

Instead he seemed intent on driving them both higher. Laura ran her hands over his muscular back, savoring the intensity, the swishes of his tongue as he moved down her body. He nipped at the soft flesh of her inner thighs, licking the sting with his tongue while murmuring encouragement. Laura parted her legs farther. Her hips jerked as his moist breath misted along her slit. She shivered, feeling the bead of moisture and smelling the tang of arousal. Cupping his hands under her ass, he lifted her to his mouth, using his talents to arouse her further. Raw need battled with shivers of excitement.

"Please," she murmured. "Please."

Jonno obliged, raking his tongue across her clit, teasing it with his lips and even using his teeth. Jolts of excitement shot through her. She arched into his mouth in silent encouragement, rocking against him. A rough growl vibrated in his chest, and he pumped a finger into her pussy.

Laura gasped, pleasure hazing her mind. Close. So close. "Jonno, do something."

"With pleasure."

Jonno pounced, making her laugh. One second he was tonguing her clit, the next he pushed inside her, exquisitely filling her with a hard stroke. She sighed and wrapped her arms around him, burying her face in his neck and breathing in his musky scent. He stroked his tongue into her mouth, the timing echoed in the thrusts of his cock. Laura eagerly returned his kiss, melting into his body, letting the desire take her.

Jonno lifted his head, a slow smile crawling across his face. "You're beautiful. I can't believe you're here."

"Were you worried?"

"A little. You're scary when you scream."

Laura pressed a kiss to his chin, and in a burst of mischief, bit his bottom lip. "Perhaps you should make me scream in a good way to counteract the bad memories."

Jonno grinned, placed a kiss on each eyelid before nuzzling her neck. "Sounds like a plan." He resumed his thrusts, each one even and deep, giving her perfect stimulation. The wet rasp of his tongue against her neck made her groan. Damn, he excelled at this. He made her feel so good. Then his lips brushed across the mark he'd made almost two weeks earlier. She flinched, and he stilled, lifting his head.

"Did that hurt? The bruising isn't too bad now."

"No. No, it didn't hurt." Laura analyzed the sensations and realized that while it hadn't hurt, it was sensitive. "Do it again."

"Are you sure?"

"Yeah." Laura turned her head, giving him easy access, and waited.

Jonno hesitated, retreating and surging into her wet pussy before dragging his tongue across her mark. At the same time he pulled back and thrust again before rasping his tongue over the mark. It was like an electric current shooting from her clit and mark together, bursting into a starburst when they met. Her pussy clenched around his cock and instinctively she nuzzled his neck, biting on the fleshy part.

His large body shuddered when her teeth sank into his neck. He groaned, his hips jerking, muscles contracting beneath her fingers. Laura licked across his neck and his hips jerked, the wet sound of arousal filling the room. She kissed him again and his cock jerked with explosive contractions, a raw and guttural groan coming from deep in his chest.

Jonno lifted his head to stare at her, and she smiled.

"I love you," she whispered, holding his gaze.

"And I love you," he said, sincerity throbbing in his voice. "So much. How did I ever get so lucky?"

"That works both ways." Laura smoothed back his hair and her smile widened. "I didn't make you scream."

"It was a close-run thing," he said, his tone wry. "I've never come so hard in my life."

"Maybe next time."

"Perhaps."

"I'll look upon it as a challenge," Laura said.

"You'll marry me?"

"Are you asking?"

Jonno cupped her face, staring deep into her eyes. "There's no one else I want to be with. We belong together."

Laura nodded, liking how that sounded. A life with Jonno and children... "Can we have children?"

"How about a year or two together first?"

A grin burst to life in Laura. "Sounds good. It's gonna be fun doing all that practice."

"I like the way you think."

"That's a yes then. Marriage and kids." A life together. A future. Warmth and belonging filled Laura, and that was when she knew she'd come home.

Chapter 16

Bonus Chapter

Storm in a Teacup, Middlemarch, New Zealand

"Ah, there you are, Saber." Agnes Paisley, one of his fellow Feline council members hailed him from across the café. Her cohort, Valerie McClintock, sat with her, enjoying a late lunch.

Saber shot a quick glance at Emily, his mate, and knew, just knew she'd set this meeting into motion. Yeah, he'd glimpsed the wicked smile, quickly wiped clean, as she'd heard Agnes summon him. He quirked a brow at Emily and a laugh bubbled out of her.

Right. That did it. The instant they had some alone time he'd spank her bottom and enjoy doing it. Then, he'd make love to his sexy mate. He'd enjoy that too. But even more, he couldn't wait to present Emily with the travel itinerary he'd worked out for their upcoming holiday. The surprise one that he and Emily had discussed but not booked until now.

Cheered by that thought and the romantic encounter in his future, he winked at Emily. He briefly savored the narrowing of her eyes, before he sauntered over to Agnes and Valerie.

Valerie peered at him over the top of her glasses before she shoved them back into place. "You've been working with cattle. I can smell them on you."

"I am a farmer." Saber glanced at Agnes, then shifted his attention back to Valerie, barely resisting the urge to shuffle his feet. Valerie was a retired schoolteacher, and she'd taught him for two years at primary school. His knuckles throbbed in remembrance of a ruler slap. In hindsight, he'd deserved the chastisement, but Janie Marshall's long plait had been right in front of him. Hard not to play a prank with that sort of temptation.

"Emily said you wanted to ask us something. Spit it out, lad," Agnes said in her querulous voice.

"Saber, I thought you might like a coffee and a sandwich," Emily said from behind him. With a bright smile and dancing mischief in her eyes, she set them on the table.

Saber glared at her, and Emily clapped a hand over her mouth, but not in time to halt her gurgle of laughter. He risked a glance at Agnes and Valerie. *All* the women were laughing at his expense.

He jerked out one of the spare chairs and dropped onto it. "Thanks, Emily."

Her laughter dispersed and she came closer. His hand darted out and he tugged her onto his knee, kissing her to hold back her surprised screech. As always, contact with his mate soothed him. He softened the kiss, briefly enjoying the softness of her before pulling back.

Someone whistled and others, led by Jonno and Charlie who were sitting at a nearby table, clapped and cheered. Emily's cheeks flushed and she tried to scramble off his knee.

"Payback," he whispered in her ear before releasing her.

Emily scuttled away, and Saber sucked in a quick breath. He *had* been procrastinating about this conversation.

"I don't suppose you know who took those photos of us trying out the zombie run obstacles?" Agnes asked.

"We asked London Allbright. She said she didn't know who took the photos, but even if she did, she wouldn't tell us," Valerie said with a sniff. "Something about protecting her sources."

Saber took a sip of his coffee.

"At least your butt didn't look as big as mine," Agnes muttered.

Coffee spewed from Saber's mouth, and he seized a napkin to dab at the brown, milky marks on the table.

"It's not funny," Agnes scolded, but there was no heat in the words.

"Would you like my opinion?" Saber asked.

"Out with it, lad," Valerie said.

"The younger people who have mentioned the newsletter London made for the council have sounded positive. I think they admire everyone on the council for trying the obstacles.

Not one person has had a bad word to say to me. They like the newsletter. The photos make us seem more approachable to the younger ones." He refrained from mentioning felines since several of the tables around them were full of humans.

"I have to admit my grandchildren haven't teased me," Agnes said.

"Emily says women are hard on themselves. They make small faults appear big when no one else notices their big nose or freckles or rear end."

"Your Donald likes your shape, Agnes," Valerie said with a nod.

Agnes nodded with a faint smile. "That's true."

Saber stuck his fingers in his ears. "I don't want to hear that!"

Valerie reached over and yanked at his right arm. "Don't be silly, Saber. You're old enough to know about the birds and bees by now."

"Have you finished talking about S. E. X?"

The women yanked at one arm each, returning his hearing to normal.

"You're shouting," Valerie said. "Everyone heard."

Saber glanced around and saw they were the center of interest. He heard a giggle—one he'd recognize anywhere. His mischievous mate. "Sorry," he said, lowering his tone.

"What did you want to discuss with us?" Agnes asked.

Saber sucked in a breath to aid his bravery and started. "Remember the last meeting where one of the suggestions was a wet T-shirt contest?"

Agnes's brows drew together.

"Yes," Valerie said crisply.

"After you left Ben suggested we take this idea and adapt it for use at a picnic." Saber held up his hand when both women opened their mouths. "No, please listen. Ben suggested we make a selection of fake bras with weird shapes and the council members have a parade. His idea is to make it funny and humorous and allocate one as a lucky bra. Have everyone at the picnic line up in front of their favorite volunteer and give a small mystery prize for everyone who chooses the right line. A voucher for a muffin at the café or a free sausage at the sausage sizzle. Something like that. Think about it, Agnes. Your grandson Brian was one of those who suggested the wet T-shirt contest. They won't expect anything like this, and it will show we have a sense of humor."

"What about the children?" Valerie asked.

"Sid suggested we have an organized event for the children at the same time."

Agnes sipped her coffee and set her cup down with a clunk. "My grandson wanted to embarrass me with that suggestion."

Saber grinned. "Of course he did, but if you participate, you'll be turning the tables on him." A wicked thought occurred. "We could get London Allbright to snap a photo of you in your costume with Brian at your side since he made the suggestion."

Agnes and Valerie exchanged a glance then turned back to him.

"We'll do it," Valerie said. "Agnes, we'll talk to Isabella Mitchell. She's the one who runs that popular clothing stall. We can keep our designs private until the day?"

"Of course you can," Saber said.

"And will Brian attend the council meeting with those who have the chosen ideas?" Agnes asked.

"Yes." Saber thought for a moment. "Maybe London could take photos of that too."

Agnes and Valerie exchanged evil grins and nodded their agreement.

"The newsletter is very popular—with humans too. London was right when she told us it would be better to design the newsletter for every resident. The *Middlemarch council* looks good in print and all the felines know she's referring to the Feline council. She told me she had to print another fifty copies," Agnes said. "I'm very pleased with the way things are going in the town."

"The new cops are fitting in well," Saber said as he waved goodbye to Jonno and Charlie.

"I heard they caught the gang of thieves and even managed to get back some of the jewels." Valerie ate the last of her sandwich. "If this was Ben's idea, why didn't he mention it to Agnes and I when we were at his place for dinner last night?"

"They delegated me," Saber said dryly. "I get all the *plum* jobs."

Agnes snorted. "They thought we'd disapprove."

"Something like that," Saber agreed.

"Huh!" Valerie wiped her mouth with a napkin. "And they call us old women."

"So you're fine with the idea?" Saber asked.

"I think it will be fun," Agnes said. "And I believe you're right. It will make the community see us as more approachable. We want residents of all ages to come to us if they have problems or suggestions."

"I agree." Valerie stood. "I'm off to pick up the grandchildren from school."

Agnes stood too, and stooped to kiss Saber's cheek. "You're a good lad. We'll see you at the next meeting."

Saber wanted to wipe his cheek. He didn't. Instead, he ignored the stares and whispered comments to pick up his ham sandwich. His mind drifted to his upcoming holiday. Although he disliked flying, he'd booked flights to Auckland. After a couple of nights in the city he and Emily would drive south and spend time in Rotorua and Taupo. He'd organized Tomasine to help in the café and Felix to take care of the farm. London Allbright had promised she'd step in for Emily on the cooking side for the month they'd be away. He couldn't wait to tell Emily about his holiday surprise. Of course, the celebration sex would be good too. And the spanking. He wouldn't forget the spanking...

Special Feline Shapeshifter Council Meeting.

Sid Blackburn's house, Middlemarch

Present: Sid Blackburn, Kenneth Nesbitt, Agnes Paisley, Valerie McClintock, Benjamin Urquart

"Where is Saber?" Kenneth pulled out his handkerchief and mopped his forehead.

"We left him at the café," Valerie said. "Don't worry. He won't turn up unexpectedly."

"Emily asked if we could keep him busy so she can organize his birthday party," Agnes said. "You all seem good at delegation. Any ideas?"

"What are you talking about?" Ben asked.

His look of innocence didn't fool Valerie. She reached over to poke him in the belly. "The wet T-shirt contest."

"Oh," he said, his eyes twinkling.

"Are you going to do it?" Kenneth reached for another beer.

"Your wife told me Gavin said you shouldn't drink," Valerie said. "He said you're a heart attack waiting to happen. And yes, we think the contest will be fun."

Kenneth sniffed. "I'm a feline. We don't have heart attacks."

"You couldn't get over the obstacles," Agnes stated firmly and moved the can of beer from his reach.

"Stop ganging up on him," Sid said. "I have an idea. There is a sheep sale in the McKenzie around Saber's birthday. I want to look at the Merino sheep. I'll ask Saber if he'd mind going with me. The lad has a good eye for stock."

"Why do you want Merino sheep?" Kenneth asked.

"Want to increase my wool production," Sid said. "I know they don't do as well on the flat and suffer more foot rot, but a good two-thirds of my farm is hill country. I think Merino might work for me."

"All right," Valerie said. "Ring him now. If he doesn't want to go, then we'll know to think of another idea."

Sid rang Saber and hung up a few minutes later. "Done. We'll be back about five, which will give Emily time to organize things and be ready when Saber gets home."

Ben scratched his head, looking puzzled. "I thought Saber knew about the party?"

"He does," Agnes said. "But it's going to be a bit bigger than he expects and hold a few surprises."

"What about a present?" Ben asked.

"All sorted," Valerie said. "Felix said Saber has organized a surprise holiday for Emily. We're all—the Feline council—putting in to buy them a two-night package at The Chateau in Tongariro. A voucher that they can use during their holiday."

Ben whistled. "That sounds pricy."

Valerie let out a cackle. "It is pricy, but since you lot made Saber do your dirty work, you can fork over your money. He works hard for this community and deserves a little relaxation with Emily."

"Emily works hard too," Kenneth said. "I think that's a wonderful idea."

"We're all agreed?" Valerie glanced around the circle of faces, friends she'd known since her family moved to Middlemarch when she was five. At their nods, she grinned and rubbed her hands together. "Agnes and I were talking on the drive here. How do you feel about a small wager? Agnes and I bet we'll get more votes in the bra contest than you three old coots. What do you say? Are you willing to put your money where your mouths are?"

"You're on," Ben said, thrusting out his hand. "Ten dollars?"

"If either Agnes or I win, you can shout us afternoon tea at Storm in a Teacup. A proper afternoon tea with scones and cucumber sandwiches."

"And cream cakes," Agnes added.

Kenneth thrust out his hand to seal the deal.

Sid frowned. "You're taking this well."

"Boys, you started this," Valerie said. "Agnes and I are merely upping the stakes. Afternoon tea?"

Ben patted his stomach. "I could do with afternoon tea. Emily makes a good scone. It's a bet."

"Sid? Kenneth?" Agnes prompted.

"Very well," Sid said. "Afternoon tea, it is."

"Deal," Kenneth said. "No trolling for votes beforehand. Agreed?"

Valerie shared a glance with Agnes. "Agreed. And you'll all contribute to Saber's stay at The Chateau?"

"Yes," Sid said.

Kenneth nodded.

"I'm in," Ben agreed.

"Excellent." Valerie stood. "I think that's everything until the next meeting. Are you ready, Agnes?"

Agnes glanced at her wristwatch. "I promised my granddaughter Suzie I'd help her make cupcakes."

"See you later, boys." Valerie lifted one hand in a wave and walked outside to her car. She waited until Agnes settled in the passenger seat and started the vehicle.

"Those boys don't have a chance," Agnes said.

"Nope." Valerie grinned at Agnes before she backed from the drive. "We have Isabella Mitchell on our side. A secret weapon. We can't lose."

They exchanged smug grins and headed for home. Life, Valerie thought, was still lots of fun—especially when they got one over on their long-time friends.

About Author

USA Today bestselling author Shelley Munro lives in Auckland, the City of Sails, with her husband and a cheeky Jack Russell/mystery breed dog.

Typical New Zealanders, Shelley and her husband left home for their big OE soon after they married (translation of New Zealand speak - big overseas experience). A twelve-month-long adventure lengthened to six years of roaming the world. Enduring memories include being almost sat on by a mountain gorilla in Rwanda, lazing on white sandy beaches in India, whale watching in Alaska, searching for leprechauns in Ireland, and dealing with ghosts in an English pub.

While travel is still a big attraction, these days Shelley is most likely found in front of her computer following another love - that of writing stories of contemporary and paranormal romance and adventure. Other interests include watching rugby (strictly for research purposes), cycling, playing croquet and the ukelele, and curling up with an enjoyable book.

Visit Shelley at her Website
www.shelleymunro.com

Join Shelley's Newsletter www.shelleymunro.com/newsletter

Visit Shelley's Facebook page
www.facebook.com/ShelleyMunroAuthor

Follow Shelley at Bookbub
www.bookbub.com/authors/shelley-munro

Also By Shelley

Paranormal

Middlemarch Shifters
My Scarlet Woman

My Younger Lover

My Peeping Tom

My Assassin

My Estranged Lover

My Feline Protector

My Determined Suitor

My Cat Burglar

My Stray Cat

My Second Chance

My Plan B

My Cat Nap

My Romantic Tangle

My Blue Lady

My Twin Trouble

My Precious Gift

Middlemarch Gathering

My Highland Mate

My Highland Fling

Middlemarch Capture

Snared by Saber

Favored by Felix

Lost with Leo

Spellbound with Sly

Journey with Joe

Star-Crossed with Scarlett